PENGUIN MODERN CLASSICS

Steppenwolf

Hermann Hesse was born in southern Germany in 1877. Hesse concentrated on writing poetry as a young man, but his first successful book was a novel, *Peter Camenzind* (1904). During the war, Hesse was actively involved in relief efforts. Depression, criticism for his pacifist views, and a series of personal crises led Hesse to undergo psychoanalysis with J. B. Lang. Out of these years came *Demian* (1919), a novel whose main character is torn between the orderliness of bourgeois existence and the turbulent and enticing world of sensual experience. This dichotomy is prominent in Hesse's subsequent novels, including *Siddhartha* (1922), *Steppenwolf* (1927), and *Narcissus and Goldmund* (1930). Hesse worked on his magnum opus, *The Glass Bead Game* (1943), for twelve years. This novel was specifically cited when he was awarded the Nobel Prize for Literature in 1946. Hesse died at his home in Switzerland in 1962.

David Horrocks (1943–2011) was Lecturer in German at Keele University from 1967 until his early retirement in 2000. His research and teaching focused on literature of the First World War, German Modernism, West German post-1945 literature and recent writing by Turkish-German authors. Previous literary translation work includes a story by the Austrian writer Thomas Bernhard for Penguin Parallel Texts (*German Short Stories*, ed. D. Constantine, 1976), poetry by Olga Sedakova (with Valentina Polukhina, in Sedakova's *The Silk of Time*, 1994) and work by Turkish-German author Emine Sevgi Özdamar (in *Turkish Culture in German Society Today*, ed. D. Horrocks and E. Kolinsky, 1996). He also contributed articles on Hermann Hesse and Günter Grass to the *Encyclopaedia of Literary Translation into English* (ed. O. Casse, 2000).

HERMANN HESSE

Steppenwolf

Translated from the German and with an Afterword by David Horrocks

PENGUIN BOOKS

PENGUIN CLASSICS

Published by the Penguin Group
Penguin Books Ltd, 80 Strand, London WC2R ORL, England
Penguin Group (USA), Inc., 375 Hudson Street, New York, New York 10014, USA
Penguin Group (Canada), 90 Eglinton Avenue East, Suite 700, Toronto, Ontario, Canada M4P 2Y3
(a division of Pearson Penguin Canada Inc.)
Penguin Ireland, 25 St Stephen's Green, Dublin 2, Ireland (a division of Penguin Books Ltd)
Penguin Group (Australia), 250 Camberwell Road, Camberwell, Victoria 3124, Australia
(a division of Pearson Australia Group Pty Ltd)
Penguin Books India Pvt Ltd, 11 Community Centre, Panchsheel Park, New Delhi – 110 017, India
Penguin Group (NZ), 67 Apollo Drive, Rosedale, Auckland 0632, New Zealand
(a division of Pearson New Zealand Ltd)
Penguin Books (South Africa) (Pty) Ltd, 24 Sturdee Avenue, Rosebank, Johannesburg 2196, South Africa

Penguin Books Ltd, Registered Offices: 80 Strand, London WC2R ORL, England

www.penguin.com

Der Steppenwolf first published in Germany by S. Fischer Verlag A.G. 1927
This translation first published by Penguin Classics 2012

011

Set in Dante MT Std 11.25/14 pt
Typeset by Palimpsest Book Production Limited, Falkirk, Stirlingshire

Printed in Great Britain by Clays Ltd, St Ives plc

978–0–141–19209–3

MIX
Paper from
responsible sources
FSC
www.fsc.org   FSC™ C018179

Penguin Books is committed to a sustainable
future for our business, our readers and our planet.
This book is made from Forest Stewardship
Council™ certified paper.

Contents

Translator's Note

Basil Creighton's 1929 translation of *Steppenwolf* has seen long service but, despite being revised by Walter Sorell in 1963, is seriously flawed. In addition to lots of errors in vocabulary, syntax and tenses, it is marred by a number of significant omissions. It is also a heavily gendered version, often opting for 'man' to render the frequently occurring German word 'Mensch' which, though grammatically masculine, is not a marker of sexual gender, simply meaning 'human being'. I have tried to remedy these faults and also to adopt a style better suited to a novel of the 1920s, avoiding anachronisms like 'poltroon' and old-fashioned inversions after direct speech such as 'said I'. Hesse's German has not dated that much, especially when he is writing direct speech, and I have endeavoured to reflect this by introducing a more colloquial tone than that of the earlier translation when rendering the characters' conversations. Any remaining errors and stylistic deficiencies are of course my own.

D. H.

Steppenwolf

Editor's Preface

This volume contains the surviving notebooks of the man we used to call 'Steppenwolf' – an expression he himself employed on several occasions. Whether his manuscript is in need of a preface to introduce it is a moot point, but I at any rate feel the need to add to Steppenwolf's pages a few of my own in which I shall try to record my memories of him. Since I am wholly ignorant of his background and past life my actual knowledge of the man is scanty. I have, however, retained a strong and I must say, despite everything, congenial impression of his personality.

Steppenwolf was a man nearing fifty who one day some years ago called at my aunt's block of flats in search of a furnished room. Having rented the attic room up under the roof and the small bedroom next to it, he came back a few days later with two suitcases and a large book chest, and lodged with us for nine or ten months. He led a quiet life, keeping himself to himself, and had it not been for the odd chance meeting on the stairs or in the corridor, occasioned by the proximity of our bedrooms, we would probably not have become acquainted at all. For the man was not sociable; indeed he was unsociable to a degree that I had never observed in anyone before. He really was, to use the term he himself did on occasion, a Steppenwolf, or wolf of the steppes: an alien, wild but also timid – even very timid – creature from a world different to mine. Mind you, it was only after reading the notebooks he left here that I discovered how profoundly isolated a life he had, by virtue of his temperament and destiny, gradually made his own, and how consciously he recognized this isolation as his lot. Still, even before reading them, through meeting and talking with him briefly on a number of occasions, I did get to know him to some extent. And I found that the image I gained of him from the notebooks basically matched the admittedly paler and sketchier one derived from our personal acquaintance.

I happened to be there at the moment when Steppenwolf first set foot in our home and rented his rooms from my aunt. It was lunchtime when he arrived – the dishes were still on the table – and I still had half an hour to spare before getting back to the office. I well remember the odd and highly contradictory impression he made on me during this first encounter. He had rung the bell and entered by the glass door. In the dimly lit hall my aunt was asking him what he wanted, but he, Steppenwolf, had lifted his angular, close-cropped head upwards and was sniffing the surrounding air, his nose nervously twitching. And before he made to reply, or even to introduce himself, he said: 'My, it does smell good here.' He was smiling as he spoke, and my dear aunt smiled back, but I thought this was a peculiar way of greeting us if anything, and rather took against him.

'Well now,' he said, 'I've come about the room you have to let.'

Only when all three of us were climbing the stairs to the attic was I able to get a closer look at the man. Though not very big, he walked and held his head as men of some stature do. He was wearing a comfortable modern winter coat and was otherwise respectably if untidily dressed. He was clean-shaven and had extremely short hair with a slight glint of grey in it here and there. Initially I didn't like his walk one bit. There was something laborious and hesitant about it that clashed with the sharpness and severity of his profile as well as with the tone and vivacity of his speech. Only later did it come to my attention that he was ill, and that he had difficulty walking. He cast his eyes over the stairs, the walls, the windows and the old tall cupboards in the staircase with a peculiar smile on his face that I found equally unpleasant at the time. He appeared to like everything, yet at the same time find it somehow laughable. In general everything about the man suggested that he was a visitor from an alien world, from some lands overseas, say; and though he found everything here attractive, it all struck him as a bit comical too. He was, I have to say, polite, indeed friendly. He was also immediately happy with everything, hadn't a single objection to the building, the room, the rent, the price of breakfast or anything. And yet the whole man had an air about him that was alien and, so it seemed to me, hostile or ill disposed. He rented the room, taking the little bedroom in addition. He asked about heating, water, cleaning and the house regulations; he listened to everything in a friendly and attentive manner; he agreed to everything, immediately offering to pay an advance on the rent too. And yet he appeared to be remote from these proceedings; he himself seemed to find what he was doing comical and not to take it seriously. It was as if renting a room and speaking German to people were strange and novel activities for him, while in actual fact, deep inside, he was occupied with totally different matters. This, roughly, was my impression, and it would have been an unfavourable one, if a whole variety of little things hadn't contrived to make me modify it. It was above all the man's face that I found likeable from the start. I liked it in spite of its alien expression. It may have been a rather peculiar face, and a sad one too, but it was alert, very thoughtful and marked by experience, both intellectual and spiritual. And what, in addition, reconciled me to him even more was the fact that his politeness and friendliness, though they seemed not to come easily to him, were devoid of arrogance. On the contrary: there was an almost touching, imploring quality about them, for which I discovered the explanation only later, but which immediately went some way towards winning me over.

Before the two rooms had been viewed and the other arrangements completed my lunch break had come to an end and I had to go back to work. Taking my leave, I left the stranger in the hands of my aunt. When I came back in the evening she told me he had rented the rooms and would be moving in any day now. He had merely asked her not to register his arrival with the police because, as someone not in the best of health, he couldn't bear such formalities or the thought of being kept standing around in the duty officer's waiting room and the like. I can still distinctly remember suspecting something untoward about this proviso of his and warning my aunt against agreeing to it. It seemed to me that his reluctance to contact the police was all of a piece with the alien, unconventional nature of the man, and it was thus bound to make one suspect the worst. I explained to my aunt that she must under no circumstances consent to this request from a complete stranger, for it was not only rather bizarre in itself, but could possibly have quite dire consequences for her. However, as it turned out, my aunt had already agreed to grant the strange man's wish and, what's more, had allowed herself to be captivated and enchanted by him. You see, she never took in lodgers without being able to enter into some kind of humane, amicable and aunt-like, or rather motherly, relationship with them, which of course had led to many a previous lodger exploiting her to the hilt. It was thus no surprise that during the first few weeks I found much to criticize in our new lodger, while my aunt always spoke up warmly in his defence.

Since this business of omitting to register him with the police was not to my liking, I meant at least to find out what my aunt knew about the stranger, his background and his plans. And she did know a thing or two already, even though he had only stayed a short while after I left them at the end of my lunch hour. He had told her he was contemplating staying a few months in our city, using its libraries and viewing its historic remains. Such a short rental didn't actually suit my aunt, but he had evidently already won her over despite his rather odd manner. In short, the rooms were let, and any objections I had came too late.

'Why do you suppose he said that it smelled so good here?' I asked.

My aunt, whose instinct for such things is sometimes remarkably sound, replied: 'I know exactly why. Where we live there is a smell of cleanliness and order, of kindness and decency, and it appealed to him. By the look of him he's not used to that sort of thing any more, and he's missing it.'

Fair enough, I thought, if you say so. 'But,' I said, 'if he's not used to an orderly and respectable way of life, how is he to adapt to one? What will you do if he's unhygienic and makes a mess everywhere, or if he comes home drunk at all hours of the night?'

'We shall see, won't we,' she said, laughing, and I let the matter be.

And indeed, my fears proved groundless. Though by no means leading an orderly and sensible life, our lodger caused us no bother and did us no harm. We have fond memories of him even to this day. Yet inwardly, psychologically, the man did disturb and bother my aunt and me a great deal, and – to be frank – I've still not fully come to terms with him. Sometimes I dream of him at night, feeling fundamentally unsettled and perturbed by him, by the very existence of such a being, even though I grew positively fond of him.

*

Two days later, a haulier delivered the belongings of the stranger, whose name was Harry Haller. A very fine leather case made a good impression on me, while a large flat cabin trunk seemed to indicate long voyages made in the past. At any rate it was covered with the faded stickers of hotels and travel firms from various countries, including some overseas. Then he appeared in person, and the period in which I gradually got to know this unusual man began. Initially I did nothing on my side to further our acquaintance. Although I was interested in Haller from the moment I first set eyes on him, in those first few weeks I still made no move to encounter him or engage him in conversation. On the other hand, I must confess that I was observing him a bit right from the start, at times even entering his room during his absence, and generally snooping on him out of curiosity.

I have already given some indication of Steppenwolf's outward appearance. Even at first sight he gave every impression of being an important, a rare and unusually gifted individual. His whole face had the look of an intellectual about it, and the extraordinarily gentle and nimble play of his features was visual evidence of an interesting, highly agile, uncommonly delicate and sensitive life of the mind. If, in conversation, he went beyond the conventional niceties – which wasn't always the case – and uttered something personal and peculiar to him, arising from his alien nature, then the likes of you and me simply couldn't help but defer to him. He had thought more than other people and when it came to intellectual matters he had that almost cool objectivity, that secure knowledge based on careful reflection, which only truly intelligent people possess, being quite without ambition and never seeking to shine, to talk others round to their point of view, or always to be proved right.

I recall one such utterance from the last days of his stay with us, even though it wasn't even an utterance as such, but merely a look. A famous philosopher of history and cultural critic, a man with a big name throughout Europe, had announced a lecture in the great hall of the university, and I had managed to persuade Steppenwolf to go to it, though at first he had no desire to do so.

We attended it together, sitting next to each other in the lecture theatre. When the speaker mounted the podium and began his address, many in the audience, supposing him to be some sort of prophet, were disappointed by the rather polished and vain appearance he presented. And when, by way of introduction, he then made flattering remarks about the audience, thanking them for coming in such numbers, Steppenwolf cast a fleeting glance at me, a look critical of these remarks and of the speaker's whole person. And what a look it was! So unforgettable and terrible, you could write a whole book about its significance. His look wasn't just criticizing that particular speaker, reducing the famous man to ruins with its compelling though gentle irony. That was the least of it. It was a look of sadness much more than irony. What is more, it was immeasurably and desperately sad, its content a quiet despair which, to a certain extent, it had become habitual for him to express in this form. Such was the clarity of this despairing look that it was able at one and the same time to show up the speaker in all his vanity, to cast the present situation in an ironic light, to dash the expectations and mood of the audience and pour scorn on the rather pretentious title of the advertised lecture. But that was by no means all it did. No, Steppenwolf's look penetrated our whole age. It saw through all its hustle and bustle, all its pushy ambition, all its conceitedness, the whole superficial comedy of its shallow, self-important intellectualism. And sad to say, his look penetrated deeper still, well beyond the mere deficiencies and hopeless inadequacies of our age, our intellectualism and our culture. It went right to the heart of all things human. In a single second it eloquently expressed all the scepticism of a thinker – and perhaps of one in the know – as to the dignity and meaning of human life as such. His look seemed to say: 'Don't you see what apes we are? That's what human beings are like, just take a look!' and all celebrity, all cleverness, all intellectual achievements, all humanity's attempts to create something sublime, great and enduring were reduced to a fairground farce.

In telling you this I've got well ahead of myself. I have already – contrary to what I actually planned and intended – basically said all there is in essence to say about Haller, whereas my original intention was to unveil his portrait only gradually by recounting my acquaintance with him step by step.

Since I've anticipated so much, there is now no need to go on talking about Haller's enigmatic 'strangeness' or to report on the way I gradually sensed and recognized the reasons behind this strangeness, this extraordinary and terrible isolation, and what it variously signified. All the better, since as far as possible, I'd like to keep myself in the background. I've no desire to parade my own confessions, to play the literary storyteller, or indulge in psychology. I merely want to contribute something as an eyewitness to the portrait of the peculiar man who left behind these Steppenwolf manuscripts.

Even on that very first occasion, when I saw him enter my aunt's flat by the glass door and cock his head in bird-like fashion, praising the place because it smelled so good, I'd been struck by the peculiarity of the man, and my initial naive reaction had been to dislike him. I sensed (and my aunt, who in contrast to me isn't remotely intellectual, sensed almost exactly the same thing) that the man was ill, in some way or other mentally or temperamentally ill, and like all sane people my instinct was to defend myself against him. In the course of time, my defensiveness gave way to a sympathy based on great compassion for someone constantly and acutely suffering, a man whose progressive isolation and emotional decay I was witnessing with my own eyes. During that period I became increasingly aware that the illness he was suffering from didn't stem from any deficiencies in his nature. On the contrary, he had strengths and talents in abundance, but had never managed to combine them harmoniously, and that was his only problem. I came to realize that Haller had a peculiar genius for suffering, that he had, in the sense that Nietzsche intends in many of his aphorisms, trained himself to the point where his capacity for suffering was masterly, limitless, awesome. At the same time I realized that his pessimism wasn't based on contempt for the world but on self-contempt, for however ruthlessly critical he could be when condemning institutions or individuals, he never spared himself. He himself was always the first target of his barbed remarks, the prime object of his hatred and rejection.

At this point I can't help including a psychological comment. Although I know very little about Steppenwolf's life, I do have every reason to suppose that he was brought up by loving yet strict and very religious parents and teachers in that spirit which makes 'breaking of the will' the foundation of child-rearing and education. In the case of this pupil, however, their attempt to destroy his personality and break his will had not succeeded. He was far too strong and tough, far too proud and mentally alert for that to happen. Instead of destroying his personality they had only succeeded in teaching him to hate himself. Now, for the rest of his life, it was against himself, against this innocent and admirable target, that all his imaginative genius and brainpower was directed. For in one respect he was, despite everything, a Christian through and through, a martyr through and through. That is to say, he aimed every cutting remark, every criticism, all the malice and hatred he was capable of, first and foremost at himself. As far as others around him were concerned, he made the most heroic and earnest efforts to love them, to be fair to them, not to hurt them; for 'Love thy neighbour' had been drummed into him just as deeply as hatred of self. Thus his whole life was an example of how impossible it is to love one's neighbour without loving oneself, proof that self-hatred is exactly the same thing as crass egotism, and in the end leads to exactly the same terrible isolation and despair.

But the time has now come to put my own thoughts to one side and speak of actual facts. Well, the first thing I learned about Herr Haller, partly through my snooping, partly from observations made by my aunt, had to do with the way he led his life. It soon became apparent that he was not pursuing any practical profession but was a man of ideas and books. He always stayed in bed very late, often only getting up shortly before midday, when he would walk in his dressing gown the few steps from the bedroom across to his living room. A big, homely attic space with two windows, within a few days this living room already looked different from how it had when occupied by other tenants. It was filling up, and as time went by it got more and more packed with things. Pictures were hung, drawings stuck on the walls, sometimes illustrations cut from magazines, which were frequently replaced by others. There was a southern landscape hanging there, photographs of a small German country town, evidently Haller's home, and between them bright watercolours which, as we only discovered later, he had painted himself. Then came the photograph of a pretty young woman, or young girl. For a while there was a Siamese Buddha hanging on the wall, but a reproduction of Michelangelo's *Night* took its place, and it in turn gave way to a portrait of Mahatma Gandhi. There were books everywhere, not just filling the large bookcase, but lying around on the tables, on the fine old writing desk, on the divan, on the chairs, and on the floor. Slips of paper that constantly changed were inserted in them, marking the pages. And the number of books constantly grew because he brought whole bundles back from the libraries as well as very often receiving parcels of them in the post. The man occupying this room was quite possibly a learned scholar. The cigar smoke that enveloped everything fitted this picture, as did the ashtrays and cigar stubs that lay around everywhere. Yet a large proportion of the books was not academic in content, but literary. Works by great writers of all periods and nationalities made up the vast majority. On the divan, where he frequently spent whole days reclining, all six fat volumes of a late eighteenth-century work entitled *Sophia's Journey from Memel to Saxony* could be seen lying around for a time.* A complete edition of Goethe and one of Jean Paul[†] seemed to be much in use, as did the works of Novalis,[‡] but there were also editions of Lessing, Jacobi and Lichtenberg.[§] Some volumes of Dostoevsky were full of slips of paper with notes on them. Among the many books and papers on the fairly large table there was often a bunch of flowers. A set of watercolour paints lay around on it too, but it was always full of dust. Next to it were the ashtrays and – I see no reason why I should hide the fact – an array of bottles containing drink. One bottle woven in straw was usually filled with an Italian red wine he fetched from a small shop near by. Occasionally you would spot a bottle of burgundy or Malaga, and once I saw a squat bottle of kirsch being virtually emptied in next to no time, only to disappear in some corner of the room where it gathered dust without its remaining contents being reduced. Without wishing to justify my snooping, I openly confess that in the early days all these signs of a life being wantonly frittered away, however much it was occupied with intellectual pursuits, aroused loathing and suspicion in me. It's not just that I lead the orderly life of a solid citizen, keeping precisely to a timetable.

* An epistolary novel in sentimental vein by Johann Timotheus Hermes (1738–1821), one of the most read works of the eighteenth century.
† Jean Paul Friedrich Richter (1763–1825), humorous novelist of the Romantic period, greatly admired by Hesse, who wrote introductions to a number of twentieth-century editions of his works.
‡ Real name: Friedrich von Hardenberg (1772–1801), Romantic poet and thinker.
§ Gotthold Ephraim Lessing (1729–81), major dramatist and critic; Friedrich H. Jacobi (1743–1819), novelist and thinker, critical of rationalism; Georg Christoph Lichtenberg (1742–99), physicist, philosopher and satirist. These three writers indicate Haller's interest in the Enlightenment as well as Romanticism.

I'm also teetotal and a non-smoker, and the sight of those bottles in Haller's room was even less to my liking than the rest of his bohemian clutter.

When it came to food and drink, the stranger was just as irregular and capricious in his habits as he was when sleeping and working. Some days he didn't go out at all and apart from his morning coffee had absolutely nothing to eat or drink. At times, the only remaining trace of a meal my aunt found was a banana skin, yet on other days he would dine in restaurants, sometimes good, fashionable ones, sometimes small pubs in the suburbs. He didn't appear to be in good health. Apart from the difficulty with his legs – climbing the stairs to his room was often a real struggle – he seemed plagued by other infirmities. Once he remarked in passing that he hadn't managed to digest his food or sleep properly for years. Primarily I put this down to his drinking. Later, when I occasionally went along with him to one of his pubs, I witnessed him rapidly downing the wines as the whim took him, but neither I nor anyone else ever saw him really drunk.

I shall never forget our first encounter of a more personal kind. We knew each other only in the way next-door neighbours tend to in rented accommodation. Then one evening, coming home from work, I was astonished to find Herr Haller sitting on the stairs close to the landing between the first and second floors. He had sat down on the top step, and moved to one side to let me pass. Asking whether he was unwell, I offered to accompany him right to the top.

From the look Haller gave me I realized that I had roused him from some sort of trance. Slowly he began to smile that appealingly pitiful smile of his that so often saddened my heart. Then he invited me to sit down next to him. I declined to, saying I wasn't in the habit of sitting on the stairs outside other people's flats.

'Oh, quite so,' he said, smiling more intensely, 'you are right.

But wait a moment longer. You see, I must show you why I felt the need to stay sitting here for a while.'

As he spoke, he pointed to the landing outside the first-floor flat occupied by a widow. There, against the wall on the small area of parquet floor between the stairs, the window and the glass door, was a tall mahogany cupboard with old pieces of pewter on it. On the ground in front of it, resting on small squat stands, were two large plant pots, one containing an azalea, the other an araucaria. They were attractive-looking plants, always trim and immaculately well tended, and they had already made a favourable impression on me too.

'You see,' Haller continued, 'this little patio with the araucaria has such a fantastic smell, I often can't pass by without stopping for a while. Of course there is a good smell to your aunt's home too, and she keeps everything as tidy and clean as one could wish, but this spot with the araucaria is so spick and span, so well dusted, polished and washed down, so immaculately clean that it is positively radiant. I just have to take a deep breath and fill my nostrils with it every time. Can't you sense it too? The way the smell of floor polish and a faint after-scent of turpentine together with the mahogany, the moistened leaves of the plants and everything combine to produce a fragrance that is the ultimate in bourgeois cleanliness, a superlative example in miniature of meticulous care, conscientiousness and attention to detail. I don't know who lives there, but there must be a paradise of cleanliness and dust-free bourgeois existence behind that glass door, an Eden of order and painstaking devotion to little routines and chores that is touching.'

Since I remained silent, he went on: 'Please don't think I'm being ironic. The last thing I would want to do is pour scorn on this orderly bourgeois way of life. It's true, of course, that I myself live in a different world, not this one, and it may well be that I couldn't survive for even one day in a flat like that with its araucaria plants. Yet even though I'm an old Steppenwolf, inclined to snap at people, I am the son of a mother, and my mother too was a respectable housewife who grew plants and saw to it that the living room, the stairs, the furniture and the curtains were presentable. She always did her utmost to make her home and life as neat, clean and tidy as was humanly possible. That's what this whiff of turpentine, that's what the araucaria reminds me of, and that's the reason why every now and then I'm to be found sitting here, gazing into this little garden of order and rejoicing at the fact that such things still exist.'

He wanted to stand up but, finding it a struggle, didn't object to my giving him a bit of a helping hand. I still didn't break my silence, but I was under some sort of spell that this peculiar man was now and then able to cast on people, just as he had previously on my aunt. We made our way slowly up the stairs together and then, standing outside his door, the key already in his hand, he looked me full in the face again and in a very friendly manner said: 'You're just back from work? Well you see, that's something I have no knowledge of, living a bit apart as I do, a bit on the margin of things. But I believe you also take an interest in books and the like. Your aunt once told me you had been to grammar school and were good at Greek. As it happens, just this morning I found a sentence in Novalis. Can I show you it? I'm sure you'll be delighted with it too.'

Taking me with him into his room, where there was a strong smell of tobacco, he drew out a book from one of the piles and leafed through it, searching.

'This is good too, very good,' he said. 'Just listen to this sentence: "One ought to take pride in pain – all pain is a reminder of our exalted rank." Marvellous! Eighty years before Nietzsche! Only that's not the saying I had in mind – wait a bit – now I've got it. Here you are: "Most people have no desire to swim until they are able to."* Isn't that a laugh? Of course they don't want to swim! After all, they were born to live on dry land, not in water. Nor, of course, do they want to think. They weren't made to think, but to live! It's true, and anyone who makes thinking his priority may well go far as a thinker, but when all's said and done he has just mistaken water for dry land, and one of these days he'll drown.'

He had now captured my interest and I stayed in his room for a short while. From then on it was no rare thing for us to bump into one another on the stairs or in the street, when we would exchange a few words. To start with, just as when we met by the araucaria, I always had a slight feeling that he was poking ironic fun at me. But this wasn't the case. He had nothing but respect for me, positive respect, as for the araucaria plant. His isolation, his rootless existence 'swimming in water' had honestly convinced him that it was sometimes actually possible, without any hint of scorn, to regard with enthusiasm the everyday activity of normal citizens, for instance the way I went to work punctually in the office, or some expression used by a servant or the conductor of a tram. To begin with this struck me as a quite ridiculous and exaggerated response, the kind of whimsical sentimentality typical of a gentleman *flâneur*. However, I was increasingly forced to recognize that because of his very nature as alienated lone wolf, living as in a vacuum, he did in fact positively admire and love the small world most of us conventional people inhabit. It represented all that was solid and secure, homely and peaceful, but it was remote and unattainable since, for him, there was no road leading there. He showed genuine respect for our char-woman, the good soul, always raising his hat to her. And whenever my aunt had occasion to chat with him for a while,

* Both these aphorisms come from *Das Allgemeine Brouillon* or *General Rough Draft*, a vast collection of thoughts on science, philosophy and the arts that Novalis jotted down in the years 1798 and 1799.

pointing out to him some item of laundry that needed repairing, say, or a loose button on his coat, he would listen to her with remarkable attention, weighing her every word. It was as if he were making indescribable, desperate efforts to force his way through some tiny chink into her little peaceful world, hoping to find a home there if only for a brief hour.

As early as our first conversation by the araucaria he called himself Steppenwolf, and this too I found a bit off-putting and disturbing. What kind of way to talk was that, I wondered. However, force of habit taught me to accept the term as valid, and soon it was the only thing I myself called the man in my private thoughts. Even to this day I couldn't conceive of a more apt and accurate word for such a phenomenon. A stray wolf of the steppes, now part of the herd of city-dwellers – there could be no more compelling way of picturing him, his wary isolation, his wildness, his restlessness, his homelessness and his yearning for home.

Once I was able to observe him for a whole evening. I was at a symphony concert when, to my surprise, I saw him sitting close to me, though he hadn't noticed my presence. The concert began with some Handel, a fine and beautiful piece, but Steppenwolf sat there immersed in himself, cut off from both the music and his surroundings. He was looking down at his feet like someone who didn't belong there, a solitary and alien presence, his expression cool but careworn. Next came a different piece, a little symphony by Friedemann Bach, and I was quite astonished, after only a few bars, to see my strange loner start to smile and abandon himself to the music. He was completely absorbed, looking so engrossed in joyous reverie, so lost in contentment for what must have been a good ten minutes, that I paid more attention to him than to the music. When the piece came to an end he roused himself, sat up straighter and made as if to stand, apparently intent on leaving. However, he remained in his seat after all, listening to the final piece as well. This was a set of variations by Reger, a composition that many felt to be rather long and wearying. To begin with Steppenwolf showed willing, continuing to listen attentively, but he too switched off again, putting his hands in his pockets and withdrawing once more into himself. This time, however, there was no sign of joyous reverie. He appeared to be sad and, in the end, cross. His face was grey and lifeless, its expression again distant. He looked old, unwell and discontented.

After the concert I spotted him again in the street and followed in his footsteps. Hunched up in his coat, he was making his way tiredly and listlessly back towards our district of town. Outside a small, old-fashioned pub, however, he came to a halt and, glancing at his watch as if to make up his mind, went in. Obeying a momentary impulse, I followed him. There he was, sitting at the bar of this petit bourgeois establishment, being greeted by landlady and waitress as a familiar customer. I said hello to him too, joining him at the bar. We sat there for an hour, during which I drank two glasses of mineral water while he ordered half a litre of red wine, followed by another quarter. I told him I had been at the concert, but he didn't pursue the topic. Reading the label on my water bottle, he asked whether I wouldn't care for some wine too. It was on him, he said. When he heard that I never drink wine, his face again assumed a vacant expression and he said: 'I suppose you are right not to. For years I too lived abstemiously, even fasting for long periods, but at the moment I'm again under the sign of Aquarius, a dark and damp sign of the zodiac.'

When I now jokingly picked up on this reference, implying that I found it improbable that he of all people should believe in astrology, his response was to again adopt the polite tone of voice that I often found hurtful. 'Quite right,' he said. 'I'm afraid astrology is yet another branch of knowledge I can't believe in.'

Taking my leave of him, I went home. He didn't return until

the early hours, but his steps sounded the same as usual and as always he didn't go to bed immediately, staying up for another hour or so in his sitting room with the light on. Living next door to him, I could of course hear his every movement.

There was another evening that I haven't forgotten either. I was at home on my own, my aunt having gone out, when there was a ring at the front door. I opened it to find a pretty young lady standing there, and when she asked after Herr Haller I recognized her as the one in the photograph in his room. After showing her the door to his lodgings, I withdrew. She stayed up there for a while, then I heard them go down the stairs together and out of the building. They were engaged in lively conversation, cheerfully joking with one another. I was amazed to discover that this hermit of a man had a lover, and such a young, pretty and elegant lover at that. All I had assumed about him and the kind of life he led was again called into question. But scarcely an hour later he was already back home again, on his own, trudging up the stairs with sad steps, then quietly stealing to and fro for hours in his sitting room, just like a wolf in a cage. The lights were on all night in his room, almost till morning.

Though I know nothing of this relationship of his, I just want to add that I did see him with the woman once more. They were walking arm in arm along one of the streets in town, and he looked happy. Once again I was amazed to see how childlike and graceful his otherwise careworn and lonely face could appear. I could well understand the woman's feelings, just as I understood my aunt's affection for this man. Yet in the evening of that day too he came back home sad and miserable. Encountering him at the front door, I noticed, as was often the case, that he had his Italian wine bottle with him, under his coat. And he sat up there in his lair with it half the night long. I was sorry for him, but what else could he expect, having chosen to lead so miserably forlorn and vulnerable a life?

Well, I think that is enough of my gossiping. I feel no need to report further on Steppenwolf or add to my descriptions of him since what I have already said should suffice to demonstrate that he was leading a suicidal life. Nevertheless, I don't believe he did take his own life that day when, though he had settled all his outstanding debts, he quite unexpectedly left town and, without saying goodbye, disappeared without trace. We have never heard a thing of him since, though we still keep a few letters that arrived for him after his departure. He left nothing behind apart from his manuscript, written during his stay here, in which he penned a few lines, dedicating it to me and indicating that I could do with it whatever I liked.

I had no possible means of checking how far the experiences recounted by Haller in this manuscript corresponded to reality. That they are for the most part imaginative fictions, I don't doubt, but not in the sense of stories arbitrarily invented. I see them rather as attempts to express deeply felt psychological processes by presenting them in the guise of things actually occurring before our eyes. I suspect that the partly fantastical things that happen in Haller's writings originate from the last period of his stay here, and I have no doubt that they are based on his experience of some slice of external reality. During that period our lodger's behaviour and appearance did indeed change. He was away from home a very great deal, sometimes for whole nights, and his books lay untouched. On the few occasions I encountered him at that time, he seemed strikingly vivacious and rejuvenated, sometimes positively cheerful. True, this was immediately followed by a new spell of profound depression when he lay in bed all day without wanting food. And it was also during that time that an extraordinarily violent, indeed brutal row took place between him and his lover, who had reappeared on the scene. All the tenants were up in arms about this, and Haller apologized to my aunt about it the next day.

No, I am convinced that he didn't take his own life. He is still alive, somewhere or other still going up and down other people's stairs on his weary legs, staring somewhere at shiningly polished parquet floors and neatly tended araucaria plants, spending his days sitting in libraries and his nights in pubs. Or he is lying on a rented sofa, listening to all human life going by outside his windows and knowing that he is excluded from it. Yet he won't kill himself, because some remnant of faith tells him that he has to drink this bitter cup to the last dregs, go on suffering this vile heartache, because this is the affliction he must die of. I often think of him, though he didn't make my life easier, wasn't gifted with the power to cheer me up or reinforce what strengths I possess. Quite the opposite, I'm afraid. But I am not Haller, and I don't lead his kind of life, but my own. It is the insignificant life of a middle-class man, but it is a secure and thoroughly responsible one. As it is, my aunt and I can look back on Haller in a spirit of peace and friendship. She would be better placed to say more about him than me, but what she knows remains hidden within her kind heart.

*

Where Haller's notebooks are concerned, these bizarre, partly pathological, partly beautiful fantasies rich in ideas, I'm bound to say that if they had chanced to come into my possession without my knowing their author, I would certainly have thrown them away in indignation. But my acquaintance with Haller has made it possible for me to understand them in part, indeed to approve of them. If I merely regarded them as the pathological fantasies of some poor, mentally ill individual, I would have reservations about communicating their contents to others. However, I see something more in them. They are a document of our times, for today I can see that Haller's sickness of mind is no individual eccentricity, but the sickness of our times themselves, the neurosis of that generation to which Haller belongs. Nor does it by any means appear to afflict only those individuals who are weak or inferior, but precisely those who are strong, the most intelligent and most gifted.

It makes no difference how much or how little they are based on real life, these notebooks are an attempt to overcome the great sickness of our times, not by evading or glossing over the issue, but by seeking to make the sickness itself the object portrayed. They signify, quite literally, a journey through hell; a sometimes anxious, sometimes brave journey through the chaos of a mind in darkness. But the journey is undertaken with a strong determination to traverse this hell, to face up to the chaos and to endure the bad times to the limit.

The key to my understanding was provided by some remarks of Haller. Once, when we had been discussing so-called acts of cruelty in the Middle Ages, he said to me: 'What we think of as acts of cruelty are in reality nothing of the kind. Someone from the Middle Ages would still find the whole style of our present-day life abhorrent, but cruel, horrifying and barbaric in a quite different way. Every age, every culture, every ethos and tradition has a style of its own, has the varieties of gentleness and harshness, of beauty and cruelty that are appropriate to it. Each age will take certain kinds of suffering for granted, will patiently accept certain wrongs. Human life becomes a real hell of suffering only when two ages, two cultures and religions overlap. Required to live in the Middle Ages, someone from the Graeco-Roman period would have died a wretched death by suffocation, just as a savage inevitably would in the midst our civilization. Now, there are times when a whole generation gets caught to such an extent between two eras, two styles of life, that nothing comes naturally to it since it has lost all sense of morality, security and innocence. A man of Nietzsche's mettle had to endure our present misery more than a generation in advance. Today, thousands are enduring what he had to suffer alone and without being understood.'

Often, when reading Haller's notebooks, I couldn't help thinking of these words. For Haller is one of those people who end up caught between two eras, deprived of all security and innocence; one of those fated to experience to an intense degree, as a personal torment and hell, all that is questionable about human life.

That, it seems to me, explains the significance his notebooks may have for us, and it is why I resolved to make them public. Beyond that I wish neither to defend nor pass judgement on them. That is something for each individual reader to decide according to his or her conscience.

Harry Haller's Notebooks

For mad people only

The day had gone by as days tend to. I had whiled away the hours, gently killing time in the only way I know how to, unworldly and withdrawn as my life is. I'd spent a few hours working, poring over old books. For two hours I had been in pain, the way people getting on in years are. I had taken a powder and rejoiced at the outcome, for pain could be outwitted. I had lain in a hot bath, soaking up the welcome warmth. I had had three deliveries of post and flicked through all the letters and printed matter I could do without. I had done my breathing exercises but had skipped the mental ones, too idle for them today. I had been out walking for an hour and discovered fine, delicate, precious patterns traced in the sky by small wisps of cloud. This was very pleasing, just as reading the old books or lying in the warm bath had been. Yet, all in all, it had not exactly been a delightful or particularly glorious day, a day of happiness or joy. Instead, just one of those normal, routine days which for a long time now had been my lot: moderately pleasant, perfectly tolerable, reasonable, lukewarm days in the life of an elderly, discontented gentleman; days without exceptional pain, without exceptional worries, devoid of actual grief or despair. Days when, without getting upset or feeling anxious, it is even possible objectively and calmly to consider whether the time might not have come to follow the example of Adalbert Stifter by having an accident while shaving.*

Anyone who has experienced those other days, the nasty ones when you get attacks of gout or the sort of severe headaches, firmly lodged behind your eyeballs, which cast a diabolical spell on every activity of the eyes and ears, transforming all joy into agony; or the soulless days, bitter days when you feel empty inside and at the end of your tether, when, wherever you set foot on this devastated earth, sucked dry by joint-stock companies, the leering face of humanity and so-called culture will confront you in all its fake and vulgar, tinny fairground glitter, acting like an emetic, concentrated within your own sick self to the point where it becomes insufferable. Anyone who has tasted those hellish days will be more than content with normal half-and-half days such as today. All such people will sit thankfully by the warm stove and be grateful, on reading the morning paper, to find that today again no war has broken out, no new dictatorship has been set up, no particularly crass foul play has been discovered in politics or industry. Then, tuning the strings of their rusty lyre, they will intone a moderate, reasonably cheerful, almost happy psalm of thanksgiving to their silent, gentle, half-and-half god of content- ment who, somewhat sedated with bromide, will find it boring. And in the thick, lukewarm air of this contented boredom, this highly commendable painlessness, both of them – the bored, dozing half-and-half god and the slightly greying half-and-half human being singing the muted psalm – will look just as alike as twins.

It's a fine thing, this contentment, this painlessness, these toler- able days when you keep your head down, when neither pain nor desire dare to raise their voices, when you do everything at a whisper, stealing around on the tips of your toes. But my prob- lem, sad to say, is that precisely this kind of contentment doesn't

* Born in 1805, Stifter was an Austrian novelist and story-writer. The reference is to his suicide in Linz in 1868.

agree with me. After a short spell, finding it insufferably detestable and sickening, I have to seek refuge in other climes, possibly by resorting to sensual pleasures, but if necessary even opting for the path of pain. For a short time I can stand to inhale the lukewarm, insipid air of the so-called good days, free of desire and pain. But, childish soul that I am, I then get so madly sore at heart and miserable that I fling my rusty thanksgiving lyre in the smug face of the drowsy god of contentment and opt for a true, devilish pain burning inside me rather than this room temperature so easy on the stomach. At such times a savage desire for strong emotions and sensations burns inside me: a rage against this soft-tinted, shallow, standardized and sterilized life, and a mad craving to smash something up, a department store, say, or a cathedral, or myself. I long to do daringly stupid things: tear the wigs from the heads of a few revered idols, stand the fares of some rebellious schoolboys desperate to visit Hamburg, seduce a little girl, or twist the neck of the odd representative of the bourgeois powers that be. For of all things, what I hated, abhorred and cursed most intensely was just this contentment, this wellbeing, the well-groomed optimism of the bourgeois, this lush, fertile breeding ground of all that is mediocre, normal, average.

It was in such a mood that, as darkness fell, I ended this middling, run-of-the-mill day. I didn't succumb to the lure of my already-made bed with the hot-water bottle in it, as might be expected of a man who is slightly off-colour. Instead I irritably put on my shoes, slipped on my overcoat and – disgusted with my paltry day's labour – made my way through darkness and fog into town to drink what drinking men traditionally call 'a drop of wine' in a pub called the Steel Helmet. This entailed walking down the stairs from my garret, those alien stairs I find it hard to climb, the thoroughly bourgeois, well-swept, clean stairs of a highly respectable rented property with space for three families, in which I have my solitary retreat under the roof. I don't know how it comes about, but this rootless lone wolf of the steppes who detests the world of the petit bourgeoisie is forever living in true bourgeois housing. It's an old sentimental fad of mine. I don't make my home in palaces or working-class housing. No, of all places I prefer such highly respectable, highly boring, immaculately maintained refuges where there is a whiff of turpentine and soap, and where just closing the front door loudly or walking in with dirty shoes on is enough to give you a fright. No doubt my love of such an atmosphere stems from my childhood, and my secret longing for something like a true home from home keeps on leading me, when I am desperate, down these same old stupid paths. So it is, and I also like the contrast between my life – my solitary, loveless, hectic, utterly disordered way of life – and this bourgeois, family milieu. I like to savour the smell of peace and quiet, of cleanliness, decency and domesticity on these stairs. It never fails to move me, despite my hatred of the bourgeoisie. Then I like to cross the threshold of my room, where all that ceases to exist; where there are cigar butts and wine bottles lying around between the piles of books, where everything is an untidy mess, the opposite of homely. Here everything – books, manuscripts, ideas – is steeped in and marked by the anguish of those living alone, the problematic nature of human existence, and the strong desire to invest new meaning in this human life which has become meaningless.

And now I was passing by the araucaria plant. On the first floor, you see, our stairs go down via a little landing outside a flat that is certain to be even more immaculate, tidy and well swept than the rest because this little landing radiates a pride in housekeeping that is superhuman. It is a shining little shrine to tidiness. On a parquet floor you hardly dare set foot on there are two dainty stools, each with a large plant pot on it. One contains an azalea, the other a quite majestic araucaria, a healthy, strapping specimen of a dwarf tree, the very acme of perfection. And there isn't a single needle on a single one of its twigs that doesn't gleam as if freshly washed. Occasionally, when I know no one is watching, I use this place as a shrine. I sit down on one of the stairs above the araucaria, rest a while, fold my hands and look down into this little garden of order. The touching upkeep of it, its absurdly isolated location, somehow moves me to the depths of my soul. Beyond this landing, in the sacred shade, one might say, of the araucaria, there is, I suspect, a flat full of gleaming mahogany where lives full of decency and health are lived by people who rise early, do their daily duty, have moderately jolly family parties, go to church on Sundays, and are tucked up in bed early every night.

By now, putting on a brave face, I was crossing the damp asphalt of the roads at a trot. The street lamps, as if shedding tears of grief, shone through the cool, damp gloom, sucking inert reflections of themselves from the wet ground. The forgotten years of my youth came to mind. How I used to love dark and gloomy evenings like this in late autumn and winter! Then, I would eagerly and enthusiastically soak up their atmosphere of loneliness and melancholy as, wrapped in my overcoat, I spent half the night walking in rain and strong wind through hostile, leafless nature. I already felt lonely even then, but I deeply enjoyed my isolation and my head was full of verses which I wrote up afterwards by candlelight in my room, sitting on the edge of the bed. Well, that was over and done with now; I had drunk that cup dry, and it had not been replenished. Was it a matter for regret? No, it wasn't. Nothing that was over and done with was a matter for regret. What I did regret was the here and now, all the countless hours and days lost to me because I just endured them and they brought neither rewards nor profound shocks to my system. Yet, praise be to God, there were also exceptions. There were occasional, rare hours that were different, that did bring shocks and rewards, tearing down walls and taking me – lost soul – back again to the living heart of the world. Feeling sad, yet deeply moved, I tried to recall my last such experience. It had been during a concert in which a magnificent piece of early music was being played. Suddenly, between two bars of a passage played *piano* by the woodwind, the door to eternity had opened up for me again. I had flown through heavens, seen God at work. I had suffered blissful pains, no longer resisting or fearing anything the world had to offer. I had affirmed everything, surrendered my heart to everything. The experience had not lasted long, perhaps a quarter of an hour, but it recurred in the dream I had that night and ever since, through all the dismal days, its secret gleam had now and again resurfaced. Occasionally I saw it clearly for minutes, passing through my life like a golden trace of the divine, but it was almost always deeply buried under layers of filth and dust. Then it would shine forth afresh in a shower of golden sparks, apparently never to be lost again. Yet it was soon lost once more, totally. Once, lying awake at night, I found myself speaking lines of poetry, lines far too beautiful and strange for me to consider writing them down. In the morning I no longer knew them, yet they lay hidden inside me like the heavy nut inside an old, brittle shell. On another occasion it came back when reading a great writer, when thinking through an idea of Descartes or Pascal in my head. And once it shone forth again, its golden trace guiding me onwards up to the heavens, when I was with the woman I loved. Sadly, this trace of the divine is difficult to pick up in the midst of the life we now lead, this so extremely contented, so extremely bourgeois, so extremely shallow life, and faced with the kind of architecture, business, politics, human beings that are all around us. How can I help being a lone wolf and disgruntled hermit, surrounded by a world, none of whose aims I share, none of whose joys appeal to me? I can't bear to sit in a theatre or cinema for long, I can scarcely read a newspaper, hardly ever a modern book. I can't understand the pleasures or joys people now seek in crowded trains and hotels, in crowded cafés with their obtrusive hot-house music; in the bars and variety theatres of expensive, fashionable cities; at the world's fairs, at street carnivals, in the public lectures for those desperate to improve their education, or at large sporting venues. I am unable to understand or share any of these joys which thousands of other people jostle one another to experience, though they would of course be within my reach. On the other hand, what I experience in my own rare hours of joy, what invigorates, delights, uplifts me, and sends me into ecstasies, the world at large knows, looks for and loves if at all only in works of literary fiction. In real life they find it mad. And in fact, if the world at large is right, if the music in the cafés, these mass entertainments, these American-style people who are content with so little are all right, then I am wrong, I am mad. I am indeed the Steppenwolf that I often call myself, a beast that has strayed into an alien and incomprehensible world and is no longer able to find its home, the air it is used to breathing or the food it likes to eat.

Thinking these habitual thoughts, I carried on walking along the wet street, through one of the quietest and oldest districts of the city. Opposite me in the darkness, beyond the street itself, stood an old grey stone wall. It was always a pleasure to see it standing there so old and serene between a little church and an old infirmary. In daylight I would often look lingeringly at its rough surface since there were few such quiet, kind, silent surfaces in the inner city. Otherwise, every one and a half square foot of ground there was occupied by a shop, a lawyer, an inventor, a doctor, a barber, or a specialist in treating corns, all of them blaring out their names at you. This time too, the old wall looked quiet and peaceful, yet something about it was different. In the middle of it I noticed an attractive little portal with a Gothic arch and, scarcely able to believe my eyes, couldn't decide whether it had always been there or was a recent alteration. It certainly looked old, age-old. Presumably centuries ago this little closed gateway with its dark wooden door had been the entrance to some sleepy monastery courtyard, and it still was, even though no monastery now stood there. I had probably seen the gateway a hundred times, simply failing to take notice of it. Perhaps it caught my eye now because it was freshly painted. Whatever the case, I remained standing there, peering across at it. I didn't venture over the road – it was so deep in mud and rainwater – but stayed on the pavement, just gazing across. Everything was already shrouded in night, but it seemed to me that there was a garland or some other colourful thing draped around the gateway. And, striving to look more intently, I now saw above the portal a bright sign on which, so it seemed, something or other was written. Despite the mud and the puddles, having looked as hard as I could, I eventually walked across. Above the portal, on the greyish-green of the old wall, I could now see a dimly lit patch, and across this patch brightly coloured mobile letters were darting, only to quickly disappear, return again, and once more vanish. Now, I thought, they've even gone and abused this dear old wall by turning it into a neon advertising sign! Meanwhile I was trying to decipher some of the words that fleetingly appeared. They were difficult to read, had to be half guessed at because the letters came at unequal intervals and were so pale and feeble, fading rapidly from view. Whoever thought this was a good way to advertise his business was clearly incompetent. He was a Steppenwolf, poor chap. Why was he getting his neon letters to dart about here on this wall in the darkest alleyway of the Old Town, at this time of night, when it was raining and nobody was about? And why were they so fleeting, so random, so fitful and illegible? But wait, now I was getting somewhere, I was able to catch several words in sequence. They read:

MAGIC THEATRE
ADMISSION NOT FOR EVERYBODY
– NOT FOR EVERYBODY

I tried to open the door but the heavy old handle just would not budge. The display of letters was over. It had suddenly come to a halt, in a sad fashion, as if aware of its own pointlessness. I took a few steps backwards, landing deep in the mud. No more letters appeared. The display had vanished, but I remained standing there in the mud for a long time, waiting in vain.

Then, just as I was giving up, having already returned to the pavement, I saw, reflected drop by drop on the asphalt, a few coloured neon letters flit by in front of me.

I read:

FOR – – MAD – – PEO – – PLE – – ONLY

Although my feet had got wet and I was freezing, I stood there for quite a while, waiting. Nothing more appeared. But all at once, as I was still standing there, thinking how attractively the delicate coloured letters had flitted like will-o'-the-wisps across the damp wall and the gleaming black asphalt, something that I had been thinking of earlier came to mind again. It was the metaphor of the golden trace that shines forth only to vanish again so suddenly and irretrievably.

Chilled to the bone, I continued on my way, dreaming of that trace and filled with yearning for the gateway to a magic theatre, for mad people only. By now I had reached the area round the market where there was no shortage of nightlife. Every few yards there was a poster or billboard advertising an all-girl band, a variety show, a cinema, or a dance night, but none of this was for me. It was all for 'everybody', for normal people. And they were indeed the ones I saw thronging through the entrances. Nevertheless, I was no longer so sad. My mood had brightened up. After all, the other world had extended a hand of welcome to me. A few coloured letters dancing in front of my eyes had touched hidden chords in my soul. A glimmer of that golden trace had come into view again.

I called in at the little old-fashioned pub where nothing has changed since my first stay in this city some twenty-five years ago. It even had the same landlady then, and many of the present customers were already sitting there in the same places, with the same drinks in front of them. For me, this modest pub was a refuge. True, it was only a refuge like, say, the one on the stairs by the araucaria plant. I didn't find a home or a community there, just a quiet seat as a spectator in front of a stage on which unknown people were acting unknown plays. Yet even this quiet seat was of value. There were no crowds, no shouting, no music here, just a few peaceful citizens sitting at plain wooden tables (no marble, no enamel, no plush upholstery, no brass!), all of them enjoying their evening drink of good hearty wine. These few regulars, all of whom I knew by sight, may have been real philistines. At home perhaps, in their philistine dwellings, they had dreary shrines to the stupid false gods of contentment. But they may also have been solitary chaps like me who had gone off the rails, silent drinkers, pondering bankrupt ideals – lone wolves and poor devils, they too. I could not tell. They were all drawn here by some kind of homesickness, disappointment or need for surrogates. The married man was seeking the atmosphere of his bachelor days, the old civil servant echoes of his time at university. They were all fairly untalkative, all drinkers who, like me, preferred to sit in front of half a litre of wine from Alsace rather than an all-girl band. Here I cast anchor. It was bearable here for an hour, or even two.

I had scarcely taken a sip of my Alsace wine when I realized that I hadn't eaten a thing all day apart from some bread at breakfast. Strange, all the things human beings are able to swallow. I must have spent ten minutes reading a newspaper, allowing the spirit of some irresponsible individual – one of those who chews up the words of others in his mouth and spits them out again undigested – to enter me through my eyes. I ingested a whole column of the stuff. And then I wolfed down a fair portion of the liver cut from the body of a slaughtered calf. Strange! The best thing was the Alsace wine. I am not partial to those heady, powerful vintages that flaunt their charms and are famous for their special flavours, at least not for everyday drinking. Most of all I like perfectly clean, light, modest local wines without particular names. You can drink a lot of them, and they have a good, friendly taste of the countryside, of earth and sky and woodland. A glass of Alsace and a piece of good bread, that's the best of all meals. But now I already had a portion of liver inside me – an outlandish indulgence since I seldom eat meat – and a second glass of wine in front of me. Strange, too, to think that decent, healthy people in some green valley or other should take the trouble to grow vines and press grapes. Why? So that in some other place far away a few disappointed citizens and helpless lone wolves might sit in silence, soaking up a little courage or good humour from their wine glasses.

What did I care whether it was strange! It did me good. It helped to improve my mood. Relieved, I was able to raise a belated laugh at the soggy mess of words in the newspaper article, and suddenly the forgotten melody of that quiet passage in the woodwind came back to me. Like a little radiant soap bubble it rose up inside me, reflecting the whole world in colourful miniature, before gently dispersing again. If it had been possible for this heavenly little melody secretly to put down roots in my soul and one day to blossom forth in me again in all its lovely colours, could I be totally lost? Even if I was a stray animal, unable to understand its environment, my foolish life did have some meaning. There was something in me that responded to things, was receptive to calls from distant worlds above. My brain was a storehouse of a thousand images.

There were Giotto's hosts of angels from the small blue vault of a church in Padua. Next to them came Hamlet and Ophelia, she garlanded with flowers, beautiful allegories of all the world's grief and misunderstanding. Then there was Gianozzo the aeronaut,* blowing his horn as he stood in the burning balloon. And Attila Schmelzle,† his new hat in his hand. Or the Borobudur Temple‡ with its sculptures soaring to the skies like a mountain range. And though all these beautiful creations might be alive in a thousand other hearts, there were ten thousand other unknown images seen by my eyes and sounds heard by my ears that had their dwelling solely in me. The old weathered infirmary wall, stained greyish-green with age, the cracked, worn surface of which conjured up a thousand frescoes – who responded to it, who let it enter his soul, who loved it, who felt the magic of its gently fading colours? The ancient books of the monks with their delicately illuminated miniatures, the books by German writers of one or two hundred years ago, all those dog-eared volumes full of stains, forgotten now by their nation, or the prints and manuscripts of the old composers, those tough, yellowish scores in which their musical dreams found fixed form – who heard their witty, mischievous, wistful voices, who carried their spirit and charm in his heart through a different era, one estranged from them? Who still remembered that small tough cypress tree high on the mountain above Gubbio, bent and split by falling

---

* Central figure in *The Logbook of the Aeronaut Gianozzo*, a story of 1801 by Jean Paul. See p. 13 footnote †.

† Another Jean Paul character, this time from his 1809 story *Army Chaplain Schmelzle's Journey to Flätz*.

‡ Monumental Buddhist shrine in Java, erected in the eighth and ninth centuries AD.

rocks but clinging to life and managing to grow a new, sparse makeshift crown? Who was it gave the hardworking housewife with the gleaming araucaria on the first floor her full due? Who read the cloud messages in the mists swirling over the Rhine at night? It was Steppenwolf. And who, above the ruins of his life, was striving to locate some elusive meaning? Who was enduring a seemingly senseless, seemingly mad existence, yet still, at this last insanely chaotic stage, secretly hoping to find revealed truth and divine presence?

Holding on tight to the glass the landlady was about to refill for me, I stood up. I didn't need any more wine. The golden trace had suddenly lit up, reminding me of things eternal, of Mozart, of the stars. For an hour I was able to breathe again, to live, allowed to exist without suffering agonies, being afraid or feeling ashamed.

When I stepped out on to the now empty street the fine drizzle, agitated by the cold wind, was swishing around the street lamps, sparkling and flickering like crystal. Now where? If at that moment I'd had the magic power to wish for something, a small, attractive room in the style of Louis the Sixteenth would suddenly have appeared, and a few good musicians would have played two or three pieces by Handel and Mozart for me. In just the right mood for that now, I would have slurped the cool, noble music as gods do nectar. Ah, if only I'd had a friend at that time, a friend brooding by candlelight in some garret, his violin at his side! How I would have stolen up on him as he passed the night in silence! Quietly climbing the twisty stairs, I would have taken him by surprise, and we would have enjoyed a feast of conversation and music for a few heavenly hours of night. I had often tasted such happiness, once upon a time, in years gone by, but it too had gradually receded, finally deserting me. Since then there had only been lean years.

After some hesitation I set off home, turning up the collar of my overcoat and prodding the wet pavement with my walking stick. However slowly I covered the ground, all too soon I would be back there sitting in my garret, in the pseudo-home I did not like but could not do without, for the time was long past when I was able to spend a rainy winter's night out walking in the open air. Yet I swear to God I had no intention of letting anything spoil my good mood that night: neither the rain, my gout, nor the araucaria. And though no chamber orchestra was to be had, and no solitary friend with a violin either, still I could hear that sweet melody inside my head and I was able, quietly humming it to the rhythm of every breath I took, to play it to myself after a fashion. Deep in thought, I strode on. No, I could manage without the chamber music and without the friend. To allow myself to be consumed by an impotent desire for warmth was ridiculous. Solitude is independence. For years I had wished for it, and now it was mine. My solitude was cold, there was no denying that, but it was also serene, wonderfully serene and vast like the cold serene space in which the stars revolve.

As I walked by a dance hall a loud blast of jazz music hit me, hot and raw like the vapour raw meat exudes. For a moment I stopped. Much as I abhorred it, this kind of music had always held a secret attraction for me. I found jazz repellent, but it was ten times better than contemporary academic music. Naively and genuinely sensual, its breezy, raw savagery could even affect the likes of me at a deep instinctual level. I stood there a while sniffing, getting a whiff of the brash, raw music, wickedly and lecherously savouring the atmosphere of the dance floor. One half of the music, the lyrical one, was schmaltzy, sickly sweet and cloyingly sentimental; the other half was wild, quirky and energetic, and yet both combined artlessly and peaceably to form a whole. It was the music of an age in decline; similar music must have been played in Rome under the last emperors. Compared with Bach and Mozart and real music, it was of course an outrage.

But then so was all our art, all our thinking, all our pseudo-culture once it was measured against real culture. And the advantage of this music was its great honesty, endearing Negro sincerity and cheerful, childlike mood. There was something of the Negro in it, something of the American who with all his strength seems boyishly fresh and childlike to us Europeans. Would Europe become like that too? Was it already halfway there? Were we ageing connoisseurs and admirers of the Europe of old, of the genuine music and literature of yore, merely a small stupid minority of complicated neurotics who tomorrow would be forgotten and laughed to scorn? Was what we called 'culture', spirit, soul, or dubbed beautiful and sacred, merely a ghost, long since dead and thought to be real and alive only by us few fools? Had it perhaps never been real and alive at all? Had what we fools were striving for perhaps merely been a phantom from the start?

By now I was back in the fold of the city's old quarter. Its lights extinguished, the little church stood there in the greyness, looking unreal. Suddenly I recalled what I had experienced earlier that evening: the mysterious Gothic doorway and the mysterious sign above it, mocking me with its flickering neon letters. What message had they spelled out? 'Admission not for everybody.' And: 'For mad people only.' I stared intently across at the old wall, secretly wishing that the magic might start afresh, the written invitation might be meant for the madman that was me, and I might be allowed through the little portal. Perhaps I would find what I was yearning for there; there, perhaps, they were playing my music.

In the profound gloom the dark stone wall looked at me calmly, seemingly locked up in its own deep dream. And nowhere was there a gateway, nowhere a Gothic arch, just dark, motionless wall with not a hole in it. I walked on with a smile and a friendly nod to the old stonework: 'Sleep well, Wall, I won't wake you. There will come a time when they will tear you down or stick the greedy publicity for their firms all over you, but for now you are still there, still beautiful and peaceful, and I am very fond of you.'

Suddenly I was startled by a figure emerging without warning from the black depths of a street right in front of me. It was a man wearily going home late on his own. He was dressed in a blue smock, had a cap on his head, and was carrying a pole with a placard on it over his shoulder. Strapped in front of his belly was an open tray of the kind people use to sell things at fairs. He walked on wearily ahead of me without looking round, otherwise I would have greeted him and given him a cigar. In the light of the next street lamp I tried to read the device on his banner, the red placard, but it was swaying from side to side on the pole and I could not decipher anything. I called out to him, asking to be shown the placard. When he stopped, holding his pole fairly straight, I was able to pick out some flickering, swaying letters:

Anarchist evening show!

Magic Theatre!

Admission not for every . . .

'You are just the person I've been looking for,' I shouted, delighted. 'What is this evening show of yours? Where is it? When?'

He had already started walking on again.

'Not for everybody,' he said in a sleepy voice, as if he didn't care, and went on walking. He had had enough, he couldn't wait to get home.

'Stop,' I cried, running after him. 'What have you got in that tray of yours? I want to buy something from you.'

Without stopping, the man reached mechanically into his tray and took out a little booklet, which he held out to me. I took it quickly and put it in my pocket. As I was fumbling with my coat buttons, wanting to fish out some money, he turned aside into a gateway, pulled the gate to behind him and was gone. I could hear the sound of his heavy footsteps in the courtyard, first on flagstones, then on wooden stairs. After that I heard nothing more. And all at once I too was very tired. I felt as if it were very late, high time to go home. Walking faster, I had soon made my way through the sleeping suburban street to my area between the old ramparts of the city where, behind bits of lawn, the civil servants and people with small private incomes live in neat little ivy-covered blocks of rented accommodation. Walking by the ivy, the lawn and the little fir tree I came to the front door, found the keyhole, found the light switch, and crept up past the glass doors, the polished cupboards and the pot plants before unlocking the door to the attic, my little pseudo-home. The armchair and the stove, the inkwell and the box of paints, Novalis and Dostoevsky were waiting for me, just as other, normal people expect their mother or wife, the children, the maids, the dogs and cats to be waiting for them when they get back home.

When taking off my wet overcoat, I happened on the little book again. Removing it from my pocket, I saw it was one of those thin pamphlets, poorly printed on poor paper, which you see on sale at fairs. 'Tips for those born in January' or 'How to make yourself twenty years younger in a week', that kind of thing.

But when I had settled down in the armchair and put on my reading glasses, I was amazed and suddenly filled with foreboding to see on the cover of this cheap pamphlet the title: 'On Steppenwolf: A Tract. Not for everybody.'

The contents of this document, which I read with constantly increasing suspense at one sitting, were as follows:

On
Steppenwolf

A
Tract

For
mad people
only

♠ ♠

Once upon a time there was a man called Harry, otherwise known as Steppenwolf. He walked on two legs, wore clothes and was a human being, but in actual fact he was still a wolf of the steppes. He had learned a lot of the things sensible human beings are capable of learning, and he was a fairly clever man. One thing he had not learned, however, was to be satisfied with himself and his life. He was incapable of this; he was a dissatisfied human being. This was probably because in the depths of his heart he always knew (or thought he knew) that he wasn't actually a human being at all, but a wolf of the steppes. Wise minds might argue the point as to whether he really was a wolf; whether he had once, even before his birth, been transformed by magic from a wolf into a human being; whether he had been born a human being but endowed with and possessed by the spirit of a lone wolf; or, alternatively, whether his belief that he was in fact a wolf was merely a delusion or a form of sickness on his part. One possibility, for instance, would be that he was wild, boisterous and disorderly in his youth. Those responsible for his upbringing had then tried to stifle the beast in him, but precisely by doing so had led him to imagine and believe that he really was in fact a beast, clothed in only a thin veneer of education and humanity. It would be possible to go on discussing this at length, entertainingly so; or even to write whole books on the subject. However, that would be of no help to Steppenwolf because to him it was a matter of complete indifference whether the wolf had been instilled in him by magic spells, by beatings, or whether it was merely a product of his imagination. Whatever other people might think about it, and even what he himself might think, was of no use to him at all. He certainly wasn't going to get the wolf out of his system by speculation of that kind.

Steppenwolf's nature was thus twofold, partly human, partly wolfish. This was his fate, and it may well be that such a fate was nothing special or unusual. There have been quite a number of reported sightings of human beings with a great deal of the dog or fox, the fish or snake in their make-up, yet they had no special difficulties on that account. In their cases, the human being and the fox, or the human being and the fish simply coexisted without either of them harming the other. The one was even of help to the other, as can be seen from many an instance of men who are envied because of their great success in life. They owe their good fortune more to the fox or the monkey in them than to the human being. This is of course common knowledge. Harry's case, on the other hand, was different. In him the human being and the wolf went their own separate ways. Far from helping one another, they were like mortal enemies in constant conflict, each causing the other nothing but grief. When two mortal enemies are locked in one mind and body, life is a miserable business. Well, to each his lot. None of us has it easy.

In Steppenwolf's case, the fact is that, like all hybrid creatures, he lived with the feeling of being sometimes a wolf, sometimes a human being. However, as a wolf he was forever conscious of his human side lying in wait, observing, judging and condemning him; just as the wolf did when he was a human being. For example, whenever Harry in his capacity as human being had some lovely idea, experienced some fine and noble sentiment, or did a so-called good deed, the wolf in him would bare its teeth and laugh him utterly to scorn, indicating how ludicrously out of character all this fine play-acting was in a wild animal of the steppes, a wolf who at heart knew perfectly well that his real pleasure lay in stalking alone across the plains, occasionally quaffing blood or pursuing a she-wolf. Seen thus from the wolf's point of view, every human action became frighteningly comic and self-conscious, vain and inane. But it was exactly the same when Harry felt and behaved like a wolf, when he showed other people his teeth or became murderously hostile to humankind as a whole, hating all its hypocritical and degenerate manners and customs. For then it was the human side of him that lay in wait, observing the wolf, calling him a brute and a beast, spoiling and souring all the pleasure he was taking in the straightforward life of a healthy untamed wolf.

This was the way of things for Steppenwolf, and one can imagine that Harry's life was not exactly a pleasant and happy one. However, this doesn't mean to say that he was unhappy to some quite unusual degree (even though this did seem to him to be the case, all human beings tending to consider their share of suffering to be the greatest). That ought never to be said of anyone. Even those without a trace of wolf in them are not necessarily happy. And even the unhappiest of lives has its hours of sunshine, small flowers of contentment that dot its sandy, stony ground. And so it was for Steppenwolf too. He was usually very unhappy, there is no denying that, and he was capable of making others unhappy too; the ones he loved, that is, and those who loved him, for all those who grew fond of him only ever saw the one side of the man. Some took a liking to him as a refined, intelligent and exceptional person, only to react with horror and disappointment on suddenly discovering the wolf in him. And this was inevitable because Harry, wishing his whole self to be loved, as everybody does, was for that very reason incapable of denying the wolf or concealing its existence from those whose affection meant a lot to him. There were, however, others who of all things loved the wolf in him, precisely the side of him that was free, wild, untameable, dangerous and strong. And they in turn were of course extraordinarily disappointed, indeed miserable, when the wild, wicked wolf suddenly turned out to be human too, still felt a strong desire to be kind and gentle, still wanted to listen to Mozart, read poetry and keep faith with the ideals of humanity. More than any others, these people were especially prone to react with anger and disappointment, and thus Steppenwolf transmitted to all the strangers whose lot it was to come into contact with him something of his own dual, divided nature.

Any readers now thinking they know Steppenwolf and can imagine what his wretched life, lived at odds with himself, was like, are mistaken, however, because they don't know the half of the story. Just as there are exceptions to every rule, and one lone sinner may under certain circumstances be more pleasing to God than ninety-nine righteous people, there were, though we haven't mentioned them yet, exceptions and strokes of luck in Harry's case too. At times he had no difficulty breathing, thinking and feeling purely as a wolf, at other times purely as a human being. On very rare occasions, the two even made peace with one another, lived for each other's sake, so that it was no longer the case that one of them slept while the other was on watch. Rather, they reinforced one another, each acting as the other's double. Moreover, as happens all over the world, there were also times in this man's life when all things habitual, everyday, familiar and routine seemed only to exist in order to be put on hold for a matter of seconds, momentarily disrupted so as to make way for something extraordinary and miraculous, for grace. It is of course debatable whether these rare and brief periods of happiness made up for and alleviated Steppenwolf's otherwise wretched lot so that his happiness and suffering eventually balanced one another out. Perhaps the fleeting but potent happiness of these rare moments even absorbed all his suffering, leaving a positive residue. This is one more question that those with time to spare might care to brood upon. The wolf frequently did brood upon it, and the days he spent doing so were wasted, pointless days.

There is one more thing to be said about this. There are quite a lot of human beings of a similar kind to Harry; many artists, in particular, are members of the species. All such people have two souls within them, two natures. Divine and devilish elements; maternal as well as paternal blood; a capacity for happiness and suffering can be found side by side and intermingled in them in just as hostile and confused a manner as were the wolf and human being in Harry. And in their rare moments of happiness these people, whose lives are very unsettled, now and then experience something powerful and ineffably beautiful, lifting them like dazzling spray so high above the sea of suffering that the fleeting glow of their happiness can radiate outwards, touch others and enchant them. It is in such moments of elation, fleeting and precious like spray over a sea of suffering, that all those works of art have their origins in which suffering individuals have managed to rise above their personal fates to such a degree that their happiness radiates like a star. To all those viewing it, it seems like something eternal, like the happiness they themselves have been dreaming of. All people of this kind, however their actions or works are defined, actually have no lives at all; that is to say their lives have no being, no shape. They are not heroes or artists or thinkers the way other people are judges, doctors, shoemakers or teachers. Instead, their lives are an eternal ebb and flow full of suffering; unhappy, ghastly, riven lives that are without meaning unless one is prepared to see their meaning in precisely those rare experiences, actions, thoughts and works that, rising above the chaos of such lives, suddenly shine forth. It is among people of this kind that the dangerous and frightening idea originated that human life as a whole may be merely a dreadful mistake, the botched outcome of a serious miscarriage suffered by some primeval mother, an experiment of nature gone wildly and horrifyingly wrong. However, it is also from among their ranks that a very different idea arose: the idea that human beings may not merely be moderately rational creatures, but rather children of the gods, destined for immortality.

Every human type has its hallmarks, its personal signatures. Each has its virtues and vices, its own deadly sin. Steppenwolf was a nocturnal creature; that was one of the things that marked him out. Morning was a bad time of day for him, a time to dread because no good ever came of it. In his whole life there wasn't a single morning when he felt really cheerful. In the hours before noon he never achieved anything of value, never had good ideas, never managed to bring joy to himself or others. Only in the course of the afternoon did he slowly warm up and come to life. And only towards evening, on his good days, did he spring into action and become productive, at times passionate and excited. His need for solitude and independence was also linked to this. No one has ever had a more profound and passionate need for independence than he did. In his youth, when he was still poor and having difficulty earning his daily bread, he would rather wear tattered clothes and go hungry if only to salvage some small fragment of his independence. He never sold himself in exchange for money or a good life, never became a slave to women or people in power. To preserve his freedom he was prepared on countless occasions to throw away or reject things the world at large saw as advantages or blessings. He could not imagine anything more detestable and horrifying than having to follow some profession, keep strictly to a daily and yearly timetable, and obey others. He utterly loathed the idea of an office, secretariat or legal chambers, and his worst nightmare was to be confined in army barracks. He was able to avoid all such predicaments, though it often meant sacrificing a great deal. This was the man's great virtue and strength. In this respect he was incorruptible, unwilling to compromise, steadfast and unwavering in character. On the other hand, this virtue was inextricably linked to his suffering and eventual fate. The same thing happened to him as to everyone. The thing he most compulsively desired, most stubbornly searched and strove for, was granted to him, but more abundantly than is good for a human being. Initially all he dreamed of and wished for, it later became his bitter lot. Those who live for power are destroyed by power, those who live for money by money; service is the ruin of the servile, pleasure the ruin of the pleasure-seeker. Thus it was Steppenwolf's independence that proved his downfall. He achieved his goal; he became more and more independent. He took orders from no one; he was required to comply with no one's rules. He alone could freely determine what he did or did not do, for all people of strength unfailingly achieve whatever they are compulsively driven to search for. But, having achieved his freedom, Harry suddenly realized when experiencing it to the full that it was a living death. His position was a lonely one; it was uncanny the way the world left him to his own devices. Other people were no longer of concern to him; he wasn't even concerned about himself. The air around him was getting thinner and thinner the more solitary he became, severing all contact with others, and he was slowly suffocating as a result. For the situation now was different. No longer his desire and goal, solitude and independence were a fate he was condemned to. He had made his magic wish and there was no going back on it. However strongly he yearned to re-establish contact with others, however willing he was to hold out his arms to embrace them, it was of no avail: they now left him alone. Yet there was no indication that people hated him or found him repugnant. On the contrary; he had lots of friends. Lots of people liked him. But friendliness and sympathy were the only reactions he ever encountered. People would invite him to their homes, give him presents, write him nice letters, but nobody got close to him, no attachments were ever formed, nobody was able or willing to share his life. He was now breathing the air that the lonely breathe, living in an atmosphere that was still, adrift from the world around him. No amount of yearning or goodwill had any effect on his inability to form relationships. This was one of the significant hallmarks of his life.

Another was his suicidal nature. At this point it has to be said that it is wrong to use the term 'suicide case' solely to designate those people who actually take their own lives. Even many of the latter to some extent become suicide cases only by chance. They are not necessarily suicidal by nature. Among the ranks of people devoid of personality or individual stamp, sheep-like people leading run-of-the-mill lives, destined for nothing of strong significance, there are many who end up committing suicide. Yet nothing in their whole character and make-up qualifies them as typical suicide cases, whereas conversely many of those who are by nature suicidal, perhaps the majority of them, never in fact lay a finger on themselves. The typical 'suicide case' – and Harry was one – need not necessarily live in a particularly close relationship to death. It is possible to do that without being a suicide case. What is, however, peculiar to all suicide cases is the sense that their own selves, rightly or wrongly, are particularly dangerous, questionable and endangered natural growths. It seems to them that they are in an extraordinarily exposed and vulnerable position, as if they are standing on the narrowest of all cliff ledges where a slight push from someone else or some minute weakness on their part will be enough to plunge them into the void. People of this kind typically have written in their line of life the message that they are most likely to meet their death by suicide, or at any rate they imagine this to be the case. Their cast of mind almost always becomes apparent when they are still quite young, remaining with them for the rest of their lives, but it is not, as one might think, conditioned by any unusual lack of vital energy on their part. Quite the opposite: extraordinarily tenacious, voracious and also audacious characters can be found among these 'suicide cases'. However, just as there are people prone to develop a temperature whenever they have the slightest ailment, those we call 'suicide cases', by nature always sensitive and highly strung, tend to react to the mildest distress by giving serious consideration to suicide. If we had a branch of science courageous and conscientious enough to occupy itself with human beings rather than simply the mechanisms of life's phenomena; if we had an anthropology or a psychology worthy of the name, these matters of fact would be common knowledge.

It goes without saying that all these pronouncements of ours on the subject of suicide cases only scratch the surface of the matter. They are psychology, and therefore belong to physical science. From a metaphysical point of view, the issue looks different, much clearer. Viewed from such an angle, 'suicide cases' appear to us to be suffering from guilt feelings with regard to their very individuality. They are those individuals who no longer see self-development and fulfilment as their life's aim, but rather the dissolution of self, a return to the womb, to God, to the cosmos. Very many people of this kind are utterly incapable of really committing suicide because they have a profound insight into the sinful nature of the act. In our eyes they are nevertheless suicide cases because they see death as their saviour, not life, and they are prepared to jettison, abandon and extinguish themselves in order to return to their origins.

Just as every strength can turn into a weakness (indeed *must* do so under certain circumstances), the converse is true. Typical suicide cases can often make their apparent weaknesses into strengths and means of support; what is more, they manage to do so with remarkable frequency. Harry, our Steppenwolf, is just such a case. For him, as for thousands of his kind, the notion that death was an option available to him at any time had become more than just the melancholy play of an adolescent imagination. It was from this very idea that he derived his consolation, his main support in life. As is the case with all people of his kind, every shock to his system, every pain, every bad situation he experienced in life did indeed arouse in him the desire to choose death as an escape. Yet gradually he was able to turn this of all tendencies to his advantage by deriving from it a useful philosophy of life. As he grew accustomed to the idea that an emergency exit from life was always to hand, it gave him strength, made him curious to experience painful and wretched conditions to the full. And occasionally, when his life was a real misery, he might take a kind of perverse and grim delight in gleefully feeling: 'Why not go on? I'm curious to see just how much a human being can bear! Once I reach the limit of what is bearable, all I need to do is open the door and I'll have escaped it all.' Very many suicide cases derive extraordinary strength from this idea.

On the other hand, all suicide cases also know what a struggle it can be resisting the temptation to take their own lives. In some small corner of their minds they all know that suicide, though it offers a way out, is nevertheless merely a shabby and illegitimate emergency exit. At bottom, the nobler and finer course is to let oneself be defeated and laid low by life itself rather than by one's own hand. This knowledge, this bad conscience – which can be traced to the same source as the bad conscience, say, of so-called self-abusers – forces most 'suicide cases' to engage in a constant fight against temptation. They fight against it just as kleptomaniacs fight against their vice. This battle was something Steppenwolf also knew well; he had fought it with a whole range of different weapons. Eventually, at the age of roughly forty-seven, he hit on a good idea that was not without its humorous side and often filled him with delight. He decided on a firm date when he would allow himself to commit suicide: his fiftieth birthday. He agreed with himself that he should be free to use the emergency exit, or not, depending on the mood he was in that day. Whatever might happen to him in the meantime, whether he fell ill, experienced poverty, grief or suffering, it was all only for a limited period. At the most it could only last these few years, months and days, and their number was getting smaller with each day that passed! And in fact he did now find it easier to put up with many trials and tribulations that would previously have caused him deeper and longer agonies, perhaps even shaken him to the core. If for some reason or other he was going through an especially bad patch; if in addition to his usual bleak, solitary and turbulent life he was suffering some particular pain or loss, he was now able to respond to the pain by saying: 'Just you wait, two more years to go, then I'll get the better of you!' Then he would take deep delight in imagining all the cards and congratulatory letters arriving on his fiftieth birthday just when, sure in the knowledge that his razor wouldn't let him down, he was bidding farewell to all pain and closing the door behind him. Then the gout in his joints, all the bouts of depression, the headaches and the pangs in his stomach could find some other poor devil to torment.

It still remains to us to explain Steppenwolf's individual case, and his curious relationship to the bourgeoisie in particular, by relating these phenomena to the basic laws that govern them. Since it seems the obvious place to begin, let us take that relationship of his to things 'bourgeois' as our starting point.

According to his own understanding Steppenwolf was a total outsider to the world of the bourgeoisie since he knew no family life and had no ambition to climb the social ladder. He felt himself to be an out-and-out loner, now an eccentric and unhealthy recluse, now an individual of potential genius, far superior to the petty average. Conscious of despising the average bourgeois, he took pride in not being one. And yet in many respects his own life was thoroughly bourgeois. He had money in the bank and gave financial support to poor relatives; he dressed casually, but respectably and modestly; he sought to remain on a good footing with the police, the taxman and suchlike authorities. Beyond this, however, an intense, secret yearning constantly attracted him to the small world of the middle classes, to respectable family houses with their neat little gardens, their spotlessly clean staircases and their totally unassuming atmosphere of orderliness and good repute. He took pleasure in his little vices and extravagances, liked to feel that he was a creature apart from the bourgeois world, an eccentric or genius, yet he never, if we can put it this way, chose to settle in any of those areas where bourgeois respectability is now non-existent. He never felt at home in the atmosphere of misfits or people prone to violent behaviour; never sought the company of criminals or social outcasts. No, the sphere he always lived in was that of respectable citizens, for he could constantly relate to their atmosphere, their customs and standards, if only in a spirit of opposition and revolt. Moreover, his own upbringing had been of a narrow, middle-class kind, and he still adhered to a whole host of ideas and stereotypical notions inculcated in him when he was growing up. In theory he hadn't the slightest objection to prostitution, but he would have been personally incapable of taking any whore seriously or actually regarding her as his equal. Those the state and society made outlaws of, political criminals, revolutionaries, persuasive demagogues, he was capable of loving as brothers, but he would have had no idea how to react to a thief, burglar or sex killer other than disapproving of them in a rather conventional bourgeois manner.

So it was that in all he thought and did one half of his being was forever recognizing and affirming the things the other half fought against and rejected. He had grown up in a cultivated middle-class household where the social and moral proprieties were religiously observed, and deep down part of him still constantly clung to the prescribed norms of that world. This even continued to be the case long after he had established his own individual identity to a degree that would have been impossible within the confines of the bourgeoisie and had long since liberated himself from the burden of its ideals and beliefs.

Now, what we call 'the bourgeois' is an ever-present aspect of the human condition. It is nothing more than an attempted compromise, a striving for a balanced middle ground between the countless extremes and binary opposites of human behaviour. If we take any one of these binary opposites as an example, say that of the saint and the profligate, the sense of our metaphor will be immediately apparent. It is possible for human beings to devote themselves totally to things spiritual, to aspire to something approaching the divine, the ideal of sainthood. Conversely, they may devote themselves totally to their carnal urges, the demands of their senses, investing all their energy in the pursuit of instant gratification. One of these routes leads to the saint: the martyr to things spiritual, self-surrender to God. The other leads to the profligate: the martyr to carnal urges, self-surrender to corruption of the flesh. Members of the bourgeoisie will typically try to lead a life in the temperate zone between the two. They will never surrender themselves, never devote themselves either to dissipation or to asceticism. They will never be martyrs, never acquiesce in their own destruction; on the contrary: their ideal is not self-surrender but self-preservation. Neither sanctity nor its opposite is the goal they strive for; for them absolute goals are intolerable. They do wish to serve God, but they also give Bacchus his due, and although they want to be virtuous they are not entirely averse to earthly pleasures and creature comforts. In short, they attempt to put down roots midway between two extremes, in a bland and temperate zone without strong winds and rainstorms. Their attempt succeeds too, yet at the expense of all those intense experiences and emotions that only a life devoted to absolute and extreme goals can afford. Intensity of life is only possible at the expense of self. But there is nothing members of the bourgeoisie value more highly than self, albeit only at a rudimentary stage of development. Thus, at the expense of intensity, they manage to preserve their selves and make them secure. Instead of possession by God, an easy conscience is the reward they reap; instead of desire, contentment; instead of liberty, cosiness; instead of life-threatening heat, an agreeable temperature. Members of the bourgeoisie are therefore essentially creatures weak in vital energy, timid individuals, afraid ever to abandon themselves, easy to govern. That is why they have replaced power by majority rule, replaced force by the rule of law, and replaced responsibility by the ballot box.

It is clear that these weak and timid creatures, however high their numbers, cannot sustain themselves. By virtue of their characteristics the only role they could possibly play in the world is that of a flock of sheep among free-roaming wolves. Yet although members of the bourgeoisie are the first to go to the wall in periods when very forceful natures hold power, we never witness their extinction. At times they even seem to rule the world. How is this possible? Neither their numerical strength, nor their virtue; neither what the English call their 'common sense', nor their organization would be strong enough to save them from extinction. People of their sort, whose vital energy is so sapped from the outset, cannot be kept alive by any medicine known to man. And yet the bourgeoisie survives, is strong, thrives. – Why?

The answer is because of the lone wolves. The fact is that the vital strength of the bourgeoisie is by no means based on the characteristics of its normal members, but rather on those of the extraordinarily numerous 'outsiders', as the English call them, that it manages to bring within its embrace because its ideals are so vague and elastic. The bourgeoisie constantly has a whole host of strong, untamed characters living in its midst. Harry, our Steppenwolf, is a typical example.

This man, whose individuality has evolved to a degree far beyond what is possible for any member of the bourgeoisie; who is familiar with both the ecstasy of meditation and the dark delights of hatred and self-hatred; who despises the law, virtue and 'common sense', is nonetheless a prisoner of the bourgeoisie, and unable to escape from it. Deposited around the hard core of the genuine bourgeoisie there are thus extensive layers of humankind; thousands of lives and minds, every one of whom has outgrown the bourgeoisie and would, it is true, be ideally suited to a life of absolute freedom. Yet every one of them, still attached to the bourgeoisie by infantile sentiment, infected to some degree by its weakened vitality, nevertheless somehow remains stuck in its ambit, is still in bondage to it, is committed to it and at its service. For the fundamental principle of the great applies in reverse to the bourgeoisie: Those who are not against us are for us!

If in the light of this we examine the mind of the Steppenwolf, what we find is a human being destined, if only because of his high degree of individuality, to lead a non-bourgeois life. This is because all highly developed individuality eventually turns against the self, tending to work towards its destruction. We see that he is driven by strong desires in the direction of both the saint and the profligate, yet as a result of some loss of vitality or a kind of inertia has not been able to propel himself into the freedom of untamed outer space. Instead he remains under the gravitational spell of the maternal star that is the bourgeoisie. This is his cosmic location, and he is tied to it. The vast majority of intellectuals, most artist figures are of the same type. Only the strongest of them manage to thrust their way through the atmosphere of the bourgeois earth and enter the cosmic realm. All the others end in resignation or make compromises, despising the bourgeoisie but nonetheless belonging to it. And they end up strengthening and glorifying it because, in order to be able to go on living, they cannot help but approve of it. These numerous individuals may lack the stuff of tragedy, but they are dogged by considerable misfortune, live under an unlucky star, and their talents only flourish after a slow roasting in the furnace of that star's

hell. The few who manage to tear themselves away and discover absolute freedom meet their ends in admirable fashion. They are the truly
tragic ones, and their numbers are small. As for the others, however,
the ones who remain tied to the bourgeoisie and often bring honour
to it by dint of their talents, there is a third realm open to them, an
imaginary but sovereign world: that of humour. To those restless lone
wolves who, forever in torment, lack the propulsion required to break
through into starry outer space and attain tragic status; who feel destined
for absolute freedom yet are unable to live in it, humour can, if their
spirit is tough and flexible, offer an optimistic way out. Humour always
remains somehow or other bourgeois even though the true bourgeois
is incapable of understanding it. In its imaginary realm, the convoluted
and enigmatic ideals of every Steppenwolf can become reality. Here it
is not only possible to take a positive view of the saint and the profligate
at one and the same time, to bring the opposite poles into contact, but
also to include the bourgeois as an object of approval. It may be perfectly
possible for those possessed by God to view lawbreakers positively, and
vice versa, but both groups – and all other such uncompromising types
– will be quite incapable of also giving their approval to that neutral,
lukewarm middle way that constitutes life for the bourgeois. Only
humour – the splendid invention of those highly talented but unfortunate individuals who are frustrated in the pursuit of the highest ideals,
figures bordering on the tragic – only humour (possibly the most original and brilliant of humankind's achievements) can accomplish the
otherwise impossible feat of uniting all spheres of human life by bathing
them in the iridescent light of its prisms. To live in the world as though
it were not the world, to respect the law but to remain above it, to have
possessions 'as if not possessing', to renounce things as though it were
no renunciation: – all the things asked of us in such well-loved and
frequently expressed words of wisdom can only be put into practice
through humour.

And if Steppenwolf, who shows signs of being capable of and blessed
with the gift of humour, should in the torrid chaos of his private hell
one day manage to concoct and distil this magic potion then he would
be saved. In many respects, he still lacks what it takes for this to happen.
However, the possibility, the hope is there. Anyone who likes him and
has his welfare at heart will want him to find salvation in this way. In
doing so he would of course remain forever confined to the bourgeois

sphere, but his suffering would be bearable, indeed would become fruitful. His love–hate relationship with the world of the bourgeois would cease to be sentimental, and what he regards as the disgrace of being tied to that world would no longer constantly torment him.

To succeed in this, or in the end perhaps even be capable of venturing the great leap into outer space, such a Steppenwolf would need for once to be confronted with himself, would have to look into the chaos of his own psyche and become totally self-aware. Then his questionable existence would be revealed to him as something utterly inalterable. It would be impossible for him in future again and again to escape the hell of his basic instincts by indulging in the consolations of sentimental philosophizing, or in turn to seek refuge from these in the blind frenzy of his wolfish appetites. The human being and the wolf would be compelled to recognize each other without the distorting masks of emotion, to look each other nakedly in the eye. They would then either explode and go their separate ways for ever, Steppenwolf thus ceasing to exist, or, in the rising light of humour, they would enter into a marriage of convenience.

One day, perhaps, Harry will be given this latter opportunity. One day, perhaps, he will learn to know himself, whether by coming into possession of one of our little mirrors, or by encountering the Immortals, or perhaps by finding in one of our magic theatres what he needs to liberate himself from his badly troubled state of mind. A thousand opportunities of this sort are waiting for him. Because of the plight he is in they are irresistibly drawn to him. The atmosphere that all such outsiders on the fringes of the bourgeoisie live and breathe is full of magic opportunities of this kind. It takes very little for lightning to strike.

And even if he never gets to read this sketch of his inner biography Steppenwolf is well aware of all these things. He senses what his place is in the structure of the universe; deep down he is no stranger to the Immortals; he is dimly aware of – and fears – the possibility of a confrontation with his own self. And though he knows the mirror he so desperately needs to look into exists, the thought of looking into it fills him with mortal dread.

There is still one last fiction, one fundamental delusion that needs to be laid to rest before we bring our study to a close. All 'explanations', all psychological analysis, all attempts at understanding are reliant upon theories, myths, falsehoods for support. And where possible no respectable author ought to round off his portrayal without exposing such falsehoods. If I say 'above' or 'below' it is in itself an assertion that calls for explanation because an above and a below only exist as objects of abstract thought. The world itself is ignorant of any above or below.

Thus, to come straight to the point, 'Steppenwolf' is a fiction too. If Harry feels himself to be a hybrid of wolf and human being, thinks he consists of two hostile and conflicting entities, that is merely a simplification, a myth. Harry is nothing of the kind. If when attempting to consider and interpret him as an actual hybrid, as a Steppenwolf, we appeared to adopt the tale he himself tells and believes in, we were resorting to deceit in the hope of making ourselves more easily understood. What now follows is an attempt to put things straight.

The division into wolf and human being, body and mind or spirit, by means of which Harry tries to make his destiny more comprehensible to himself, is a very crude simplification. It does violence to reality in favour of a plausible but false explanation of the contradictions that this human being discovers in himself and which seem to him to be the source of his not inconsiderable suffering. Harry finds a 'human being' in himself, that is to say, a world of ideas, feelings, culture, domesticated and sublimated nature. Besides this he also finds a 'wolf', that is to say, a dark world of instincts, savagery, cruelty, nature unsublimated and raw. Yet despite this ostensibly clear division of his being into two mutually hostile spheres he has time and again experienced happy moments when the wolf and the human being got on well together for a while. Were Harry to attempt at every single moment of his life, in everything he did and felt, to determine the part played by the human being and that played by the wolf, he would immediately be in a fix. All his fine theory of the wolf would go to pieces, for there are absolutely no human beings, even primitive Negroes, even idiots, who are so pleasingly simple that their characters can be explained as the sum of only two or three principal elements. And to attempt to explain someone as subtly complex as Harry, of all people, by naively splitting him into wolf and human being is too childish for words. Harry is not made up of two characters, but of hundreds, of thousands. His life, like that of every human being, does not oscillate between two poles only – say between the body and the mind or spirit, between the saint and the profligate – but between thousands, between innumerable polar opposites.

We should not be amazed at the fact that a man as learned and clever as Harry is able to consider himself a 'Steppenwolf', that he thinks he can encapsulate his life's richly complex design in such a simple, brutal, primitive formula. Human beings' thinking capacity is not very highly developed, and even the most intellectual and educated of them constantly view the world and themselves – for the most part themselves! – through the distorting lenses of very naive and simplistic formulae. For it seems that all human beings are born with an absolutely compulsive need to imagine their selves as unified wholes. No matter how often and how drastically this illusion is shattered, they always manage to patch it up again. The judge who, sitting opposite a murderer and looking him in the eye, momentarily hears the murderer speaking with his own (the judge's) voice and discovers within his own self all the emotions, capabilities and potential actions of the murderer is in the very next moment his old unified self again. Retreating swiftly into the shell of his imagined identity, he is again a judge doing his duty, and he sentences the murderer to death. And whenever it begins to dawn on specially talented and highly strung souls that they have multiple selves, when they, like every genius, see through the delusion of the unified personality and feel themselves to be multifaceted, a bundle of many selves, they only need to assert the fact for the majority to lock them up on the spot. Scientific experts called in to help will diagnose schizophrenia, thus ensuring that the rest of humanity will never have to hear a cry of truth from the mouths of these unfortunate people. But why should we go to great lengths to express self-evident truths that any thinking person should recognize, but which it is not the done thing to express? – Now, even if some human beings advance only to the point where they replace the imagined unity of the self with a broader twofold entity they are already close to being geniuses, or at any rate interesting exceptions. In actual fact, however, no self, even the most naive, is a unity. Rather, it is an extremely diverse world, a miniature firmament, a chaos of different forms, different states and stages of development, different legacies and potentialities. All individuals nevertheless endeavour to view this chaos as a unity and speak of their selves as if they were simple, firmly shaped, clearly defined phenomena. It would seem that this delusion, which is common to all human beings, even those of the highest order, is a necessity, just as essential to life as eating and breathing.

The delusion is based on a straightforward instance of transference. As a body every human being is a single entity, as a soul never. Traditionally literature too, even at its most sophisticated, operates with ostensibly whole, ostensibly unified characters. In literature as we know it so far, the genre most highly regarded by experts and connoisseurs is drama. Rightly so, for drama offers the greatest opportunity to represent the self as multiple, or might do so, if only outward appearances didn't contradict this impression, each individual character being deceptively portrayed as a unity because he or she is inevitably encased in a unique, unified and self-contained body. This of course also explains why aesthetically naive judges value the so-called character play most highly, in which every figure appearing on stage is a quite discrete and recognizable entity. Only remotely and gradually is it beginning to dawn on some individuals that this aesthetic approach may be shoddy and superficial, that it is a mistake to apply ancient Greek concepts of beauty to our own great dramatists. Splendid though these are, they are not native to us. We have been talked into adopting them from Greek thinkers who, taking the visible body as their starting point, were the real originators of the fiction of the individual self or character. This concept is totally unknown in the literary works of ancient India. The heroes of the Indian epics are not single characters but tangled knots of character, serial incarnations. In our modern world too, some works of literature exist in which, though the author is probably scarcely conscious of the fact, an attempt is being made to portray a multiplicity of souls behind the veil of individual character depiction. Anyone wishing to appreciate this must for once resolve to view the characters in such a work not as individual entities but as parts, as facets, as different aspects of a higher unity, if you like, of the mind of the author. Anyone considering Goethe's *Faust* in this way, for example, will make of Faust, Mephistopheles, Wagner and all the other figures a unity, a super-character. And only from this higher unity, not the individual characters, can one glean some hint of the work's true soul. When Faust makes the pronouncement – on the tongue of every schoolteacher and apt to make philistines shudder with admiration – 'Two souls, alas, dwell in my breast!' he is forgetting Mephisto and a whole host of other souls that are just as much part of him. Our Steppenwolf also thinks he is bearing the burden of two souls (wolf and human being) within his breast, and that his breast is painfully constricted as a result. The fact is that the breast, the body, is always one, yet the souls that it houses are neither two nor five but countless in number. A human being is an onion consisting of a hundred skins, a fabric composed of many threads. The Asians of old had exact knowledge of this; Buddhist Yoga invented a precise technique for exposing the personality as a delusion. But then humankind moves in all sorts of comic ways: the delusion that for a thousand years India made such great efforts to expose is the self-same delusion that the West has been at equally great pains to bolster and reinforce.

If we consider Steppenwolf from this point of view we can see clearly why he suffers so much from his ludicrous sense of himself as twofold. Like Faust he thinks that even two souls are too much for a single breast to contain and ought by rights to tear that breast asunder. Yet they are, on the contrary, far too few, and Harry is doing terrible violence to his poor psyche by seeking to comprehend it with the help of so primitive an image. Harry may be a highly educated human being, but he is acting like some savage, say, who is incapable of counting beyond two. Calling one bit of himself human being, another wolf, he thinks that is the end of the story and all his possibilities have been exhausted. Into the 'human' half he packs all intellectual or spiritual attributes, all things sublimated or cultivated that he finds in himself, and into the wolf everything instinctual, savage and chaotic. Yet in real life things are not as simplistic as in our thinking, not as crude as in the poor simpletons' language we use, and Harry is doubly deluding himself when applying this primitive model of the wolf to his own case. We fear that whole areas of Harry's psyche which he attributes to the 'human being' are by no stretch of the imagination human, while parts of his character that he assigns to the wolf have long since progressed beyond the merely wolf-like.

Like all human beings Harry thinks he knows perfectly well what human beings are, yet he most certainly doesn't know, even though the truth dawns on him quite often in his dreams or in other states of consciousness he has difficulty in controlling. If only he could memorize these fleeting insights, could as far as possible make them his own! Of course human beings are not fixed, enduring forms – which was, despite suspicions to the contrary on the part of their leading thinkers, the ideal view of the ancient Greeks – but rather experiments, creatures in transition. They are no less than the perilously narrow bridge between nature and spirit. Their innermost destiny drives them in the direction of spirit, towards God, while their most heartfelt yearning pulls them back towards nature, to their mother. Wavering between these two powerful poles, human beings live their lives in fear and trembling. What they understand by the term 'human being' at any given time is never more than a transient agreement entered into by a majority of respectable citizens. Under this convention certain extremely crude physical impulses are rejected, declared taboo; a degree of consciousness, cultured behaviour and de-bestialization is a requirement; a modicum of spirituality is not only permitted but even insisted upon. The 'human being' of this convention is, like all bourgeois ideals, a compromise. It is a timid and naively cunning attempt to dodge the powerful demands of both the wicked primeval mother, nature, and the irksome primeval father, spirit, and to make one's home in the lukewarm atmosphere of the middle ground between the two. That is why conventional citizens permit and tolerate what they call 'personalities' yet are prepared to hand over these personalities to that Moloch, the 'state', and constantly to play the one off against the other. It also explains why those they declare heretics can today be burned at the stake, those deemed criminals can be hanged, only for monuments to be erected to them the day after tomorrow.

'Human beings' are not already created entities but ideal figures that spirit demands we should strive to become, remote possibilities that are both longed for and feared. The road leading to them can only ever be covered in very short stages, accompanied by terrible experiences of torment and ecstasy. And those advancing along it are precisely the rare individuals for whom the scaffold is made ready today, the monument in their honour tomorrow. All these truths Steppenwolf is dimly aware of. However, what he calls 'human being' in himself, as opposed to 'wolf', is for the most part nothing more than that mediocre 'human being' of respectable bourgeois convention. Harry does instinctively sense which road to take to become a true human being, the road that leads to the Immortals; indeed now and then he hesitantly advances a tiny bit of the way along it, paying the price in terms of intense suffering and painful isolation. Yet in the depths of his being he is afraid to face the highest of all challenges posed by spirit: that of striving to become fully human, and venturing along the sole narrow road leading to immortality. He senses only too clearly that this route leads to even greater suffering, to the life of an outcast, to the ultimate sacrifice, perhaps to the scaffold. And for this reason, even though the prize that beckons at the end of the road is immortality, he is unwilling to suffer all these ills, to die all these deaths. Though he is much more aware than the average bourgeois of what becoming truly human entails, he still closes his eyes to the truth, refusing to acknowledge that clinging desperately to the notion of self, desperately wanting not to die, is the surest route to eternal death. On the other hand, the ability to die, to slough off one's skin like a snake, to commit oneself to incessant self-transformation is what leads the way to immortality. If Harry worships his favourites among the Immortals, for example Mozart, it is because he is still seeing him through bourgeois eyes, tending to explain the composer's consummate art, just as a schoolmaster would, in terms of highly specialized talent. He thus ignores Mozart's commitment, his willingness to suffer, his indifference to all bourgeois ideals, and his ability to endure the kind of extreme isolation that transforms the bourgeois atmosphere surrounding those suffering in the process of becoming fully human into the much thinner, ice-cold air of the cosmos. This is the isolation of Christ in the Garden of Gethsemane.

Still, our Steppenwolf has at least discovered a Faustian duality within himself, has found out that no unified soul inhabits the single entity that is his body and that at best he is just starting out on a long pilgrimage towards such an ideal inner harmony. He would like either to become wholly human by conquering the wolf in himself, or conversely to renounce his human side in order at least to live an integrated, undivided life as a wolf. He has presumably never observed a real wolf closely, otherwise he might have seen that animals too have no such things as unified souls; that the beautiful, taut frames of their bodies house a whole variety of aspirations and states of mind; that wolves suffer too, having dark depths within them. Oh no, human beings are always desperately mistaken and bound to suffer when they try to get 'back to nature'. Harry can never fully become a wolf again, and if he did he would realize that even wolves are not simple and primitive creatures but complex and many-sided. Wolves also have two and more than two souls in their wolves' breasts, and anyone desiring to be a wolf is guilty of the same kind of forgetfulness as the man who sings 'What bliss still to be a child!'* The likeable but sentimental chap with his song about

* Part of a refrain in the 1837 comic opera *Zar und Zimmermann* (*Tsar and Joiner*) by the popular Berlin composer Albert Lortzing (1801–51).

the blissfully happy child would also like to get back to nature, to his innocent origins, but he has totally forgotten that children are by no means blissfully happy. Rather, they are capable of many conflicts, a host of contradictory moods, suffering of all kinds.

There is no way back at all, either to the wolf or the child. Things do not begin in innocence and simplicity; all created beings, even the ostensibly simplest, are already guilty, already full of contradictions. Cast into the muddy stream of becoming they can never, never hope to swim back up against the current. The road to innocence, to the state before creation, to God, doesn't run backwards, either to the wolf or the child, but forwards, further and further into guilt, deeper and deeper into the experience of becoming fully human. Nor is suicide, poor Steppenwolf, a serious solution to your problem. You will just have to go down the longer, more onerous, more difficult road to becoming truly human. You will frequently have to multiply your two selves, make your already complex nature a great deal more complicated. Instead of making your world more confined and your soul simpler you are going to have to include more and more world, ultimately the entire world in your soul as it painfully expands, until one day, perhaps, you reach the end and find rest. This, in so far as they succeeded in the venture, is the path taken by Buddha, by all great human beings, some knowingly, others unconsciously. Every birth entails separation from the cosmos, enclosure within limits, isolation from God, painful self-renewal. Returning to the cosmos, overcoming the painful experience of individuation, achieving God-like status: all these entail an expansion of the soul to the point where it is once again able to contain the whole cosmos within itself.

We are not now talking about human beings as educationalists, economists and statisticians understand them. We are not concerned with the millions of them that roam our streets. They are just like so many grains of sand or the spray from waves breaking on the shore. Whether there are a few million more of them, or fewer, is unimportant. They are mere material, nothing more. No, we are talking about human beings in the ideal sense of the term, about the goal reached at the end of a long process of becoming fully human, about sovereign human beings, about the Immortals. Genius is not as rare a phenomenon as often seems to us the case, although it is of course not as common as histories of literature or the world, not to mention newspapers, would have us believe. Harry the Steppenwolf would, it seems to us, be blessed with sufficient genius to venture along the road to becoming fully human instead of pitying himself whenever he encounters the slightest difficulty and, as an excuse, falling back on the stupid notion of himself as Steppenwolf.

The fact that individuals of such potential can fall back on Steppenwolf imagery and clichés like 'two souls, alas' is just as surprising and depressing as the cowardly affection they often have for things bourgeois. Any human being capable of understanding Buddha, who has some idea of the heights and depths of human experience, ought not to be living in a world where 'common sense', democracy and middle-class culture prevail. It is only cowardice that makes him live there, and whenever he finds his confines oppressive, whenever his poky little middle-class room becomes too cramped for him, it is the 'wolf' he blames, refusing to acknowledge that at times the wolf is the best part of him. 'Wolf' is the name he gives to all the wild elements in himself. He feels them to be wicked, dangerous, apt to frighten the life out of respectable citizens, yet – despite thinking himself a highly sensitive artist – he cannot see that apart from the wolf, behind the wolf, there are a lot more creatures living inside him. Nor is every creature with sharp teeth a wolf. Harry is home to the fox, the dragon, the tiger, the ape, and the bird of paradise too. He can't understand that by sticking to his fairy-tale of the wolf he has turned his whole world, this Eden full of creatures lovely and terrifying, great and small, strong and gentle, into an oppressive prison house. In much the same way, the pseudo 'human being' of bourgeois convention is suppressing and shackling the true human being within him.

Just imagine a garden with hundreds of different trees, thousands of different flowers, hundreds of different fruits and herbs. Now, if the only botanical distinction the gardener knows is that between edible things and weeds, he will not know what to do with nine tenths of his garden. He will uproot the most enchanting flowers, fell the finest trees, or at any rate detest and frown upon them. This is just what Steppenwolf is doing with the thousand blooms in his soul. He is totally ignoring anything that doesn't come under the heading of 'human being' or 'wolf'. And there is no end to the things he counts as 'human'! All things cowardly, vain, stupid and mean are classed as 'human' if only because they are not exactly wolf-like, just as all strong and noble qualities are attributed to the 'wolf' simply because Harry hasn't yet managed to master them.

It is time for us to take leave of Harry and allow him to continue his journey on his own. Just suppose he were already in the realm of the Immortals, had already reached what seems to be the goal of his arduous quest. How amazed he would be to observe Steppenwolf's wild meandering, as he zigzags here and there, unable to make up his mind as to the best course to take. How he would smile at him – both encouragingly and reproachfully, with compassion as well as amusement.

When I had finished reading it occurred to me that a few weeks ago during the night I had once written out a rather strange poem, also on the subject of Steppenwolf. I searched for it among the jumble of paper that took up the whole of my desk, found it and read:

Steppenwolf is on the prowl,
the world is covered in snow.
Up in a birch I spot an owl,
but no hare is in sight and no roe.
On tender hinds I love to prey,
the nicest things in wood or heath.
If only one would come my way,
I'd grasp her with my claws and teeth.
I'd treat my sweetheart really well:
Give her thighs a good deep bite,
of her bright red blood I'd drink my fill,
then howl all alone through the night.
A hare would be better than nothing –
of a night their warm flesh tastes so sweet –
but sadly I seem to be lacking
all that once made my life such a treat.
The hairs on my tail are now grey,
my eyesight's no longer so clear.

It's years since my wife passed away,
now I prowl, and my dreams are of deer,
or sometimes of hares as well
when, hearing the winter wind blow
and slaking my thirst with the snow,
I haul my poor soul down to hell.

*

Now I had two portraits of myself to hand, one a self-portrait in crude rhyming doggerel, sad and anxious just like me, the other cool and, it would seem, highly objective, the work of someone uninvolved, picturing me from the outside and from above. Whoever wrote it knew more than I myself did, yet in some senses also less. And both these portraits together, my melancholy, halting words in the poem and the clever study by some unknown hand, caused me pain. Both of them were right, both painted an unvarnished picture of my desperate existence, both clearly revealed just how intolerable and unsustainable a state I was in. This Steppenwolf had to die, he had to put an end to his detestable existence by his own hand. Either that, or he must undergo the deadly flames of further self-scrutiny till melting point, then transform himself, tear off his mask and enter upon a new stage of self-development. Alas, I was no stranger to this process. I knew it of old; I had already experienced it several times, always in periods of extreme despair. In the course of this deeply disturbing experience my then self had on each occasion been shattered in fragments; each time profound forces had shaken and destroyed it; each time I had been deserted by and lost a cherished and particularly dear part of myself. In one such instance, as well as my worldly wealth, I had lost my reputation as a respectable citizen, and had to learn to live without the esteem of those who previously had raised their hats to me. A second time my family life had collapsed overnight. My wife, falling mentally ill, had driven me out of house and comfortable home; love and trust had suddenly turned into hatred and mortal combat; the neighbours watched me go with a mixture of sym-pathy and disdain. That had been the beginning of my progressive isolation. And once more, after a period of years, cruelly hard years when I had been able, in strict isolation and by means of harsh self-discipline, to construct a new life based on ascetic and spiritual ideals and to regain a certain degree of calm and sovereign control, this rebuilt existence, dedicated to exercises in abstract thought and strictly regulated meditation, had also collapsed, having all at once lost its noble and lofty purpose. Something launched me on mad, strenuous journeys around the world again, leading to new suffering and new guilt in abundance. And each time, before tearing off one of my masks and witnessing the collapse of one of my ideals, I had experienced the same dreadful emptiness and silence, the same sense of being caught in a mesh, isolated, without human contact, the same empty and barren hell, bereft of love and hope, that I was now obliged to go through once again.

Every time my life had been shattered in this way I had, there is no denying it, ended up gaining something or other; something in the way of liberty, intellectual and spiritual refinement, profundity, but also in the way of loneliness, since I was increasingly misunderstood or treated coldly by others. From a bourgeois point of view my life had been, from each shattering blow to the next, one of steady decline, a movement further and further away from all things normal, acceptable and healthy. Over the years I had lost my profession, my family and my home, and now I stood alone, an outsider to all social circles, loved by no one, viewed with suspicion by many, in constant, bitter conflict with public opinion and public morality. And even though I still lived in a bourgeois setting, everything I thought and felt nevertheless made me a stranger among the respectable people of that world. For me religion, fatherland, family and state, having been devalued, were no longer matters of concern. I was sickened by the pompous antics of those involved in academic life, the professions and the arts. My opinions, my tastes, my whole way of thinking, which had once upon a time made me popular, a man of talent who shone in conversation, were now so degenerate and decadent that people found them suspect. I may have gained something as a result of my painful series of transformations, something invisible and incalculable, but I had been made to pay dearly for it, my life having on each occasion become harsher, more difficult, more isolated, more at risk. Believe me, I had no cause to want this journey of mine to continue since, like the smoke in Nietzsche's autumn poem,* it was heading for regions where the air would become thinner and thinner.

Ah yes, I knew these experiences, knew them all too well, these transformations that fate has in store for its problem children, the most awkward of its progeny. I knew them as an ambitious but unsuccessful hunter may know the various stages of an expedition or an old stock-exchange gambler the sequence of speculating, making a profit, losing confidence, wavering, going bankrupt. Ought I really to go through that whole process yet again? All that torment, the terrible distress, all the insights into one's own vile and worthless self, all the awful fear of failure, all the mortal dread? Wasn't it wiser and easier to avoid any repetition of so much suffering by getting the hell out? Certainly, that was the easier and wiser thing to do. Whether the arguments about 'suicide cases' in the Steppenwolf pamphlet were correct or not, nobody could deny me the satisfaction of ending my life with the help of carbon monoxide, a cut-throat razor or a pistol, thus sparing myself any repetition of the bitterly agonizing process that I had, believe me, been obliged to endure all too often and too intensely. No, damn

* The reference is to a poem of autumn 1884, unpublished in Nietzsche's lifetime, which he variously entitled 'Vereinsamt' ('Isolated') and 'Abschied' ('Departure').

it all, no power in the world could require me to endure the mortal dread of another confrontation with my self, another reshaping of my identity, a new incarnation, the aim and outcome of which was never, of course, peace and quiet, but simply renewed destruction of the self followed by yet more self-redevelopment! Suicide might well be stupid, cowardly and shabby, it might be an inglorious and shameful emergency exit, but any exit from this grinding mill of suffering, even the most ignominious, was devoutly to be wished. My life was no longer a stage for heroes and the noble-minded; what I now faced was a simple choice between a slight, momentary pain and unimaginably agonizing, endless suffering. In the course of my so difficult, so crazy life I had played the noble Don Quixote often enough, preferring honour to comfort and heroism to reason. Enough was enough!

When I finally got to bed, morning was already gaping in through the window panes, the leaden morning, curse it, of a rainy winter's day. I took my decision to bed with me. However, at the very last moment, at the extreme limit of consciousness just before falling asleep, that remarkable passage from the Steppenwolf pamphlet flashed before my mind's eye in which the 'Immortals' were mentioned. In connection with this I suddenly remembered that on a number of occasions, and only recently, I had felt close enough to the Immortals to be able to savour in a few notes of early music all their cool, bright, harshly smiling wisdom. The memory of it surfaced, shining brightly, only to fade again when sleep, as heavy as a mountain, descended on my brow.

Waking towards midday, I was soon able to view my situation clearly again. The little booklet was there on my bedside table together with the poem, and my decision still stood. Overnight, as I slept, it had become firm and rounded, and now, emerging from the chaos that had been my life in recent times, it was taking a cool but kind look at me. There was no need to rush things.

My decision to die was no passing whim, but a fruit that had ripened and would keep. It had grown slowly and was heavy now, gently rocked by the wind of fate and bound to fall when the next gust came along.

In my travelling medicine chest I had an excellent painkiller, a particularly strong opiate that I only rarely resorted to, often denying myself for months on end the relief it brought. Only when racked by pain to the point where my body could no longer stand it did I take this potent analgesic. Unfortunately it was not suitable for committing suicide. I had tried it out years ago when once again engulfed in despair. I had swallowed a fair old quantity of it, enough to kill six people, and still it did not kill me. It did put me to sleep, and I lay there fully anaesthetized for a few hours, but to my terrible disappointment I was then half wakened by strong stomach convulsions. Without fully coming to, I brought up all the poison and went to sleep again, only finally waking up midway through the next day. I felt horribly sober, burned out and empty-headed, scarcely able to remember a thing. Apart from a spell of sleeplessness and irritating stomach pains the poison had no after-effects.

This means was therefore out of the question. But I now formulated my decision as follows: as soon as my condition was again bad enough to make me reach for that opiate, I should be allowed, instead of slurping it in search of fleeting relief, to seek lasting salvation in death – and a certain and reliable death, what's more, either by a bullet or the blade of a razor. This clarified the situation. To wait until my fiftieth birthday, the solution oddly suggested in the booklet about Steppenwolf, seemed to me far too long. After all, there were still two years to go till that date. Whether it was a matter of a year or a month, whether tomorrow even – the door was now open.

★

I cannot say that the 'decision' greatly changed my life. It made me a little more indifferent to ailments, a little more careless in my consumption of opium and wine, a little more curious about the limits of what I could bear, but that was all. The other experiences of that evening had stronger after-effects. I read through the Steppenwolf tract once more, now with rapt attention and gratitude as if I knew that some invisible magician was wisely determining my fate, now with scorn and contempt against the tract's cool objectivity which, so it seemed to me, totally failed to understand the tenor and tension of my life. The points made in it about lone wolves and suicide cases, for all their accuracy and intelligence, were ingenious abstractions, valid only for the general category and type. However, it seemed to me that my person, my real psyche, my own unique, individual destiny could not be caught in so wide-meshed a net.

However, what preoccupied me most was that hallucination or vision I had had at the church wall, the dancing illuminated letters with their inviting message that tallied with some of the things intimated in the tract. I had been promised much then, the voices from that strange world had greatly aroused my curiosity, and I often spent hours on end deeply absorbed in contemplation of the matter. In the process, the warnings contained in those inscriptions became more and more clear to me: 'Not for everybody!' and 'For mad people only!' So I had to be mad and quite remote from 'everybody' if those voices were to reach me, those worlds to communicate with me. My God, had I not long since been living at a sufficient remove from everybody, from the lives and minds of normal folk? Had I not been enough of an outsider, mad enough, for years? And yet, deep down inside me, I fully understood this summons, this invitation to go mad, to jettison all reason, inhibition and bourgeois respectability, and to surrender myself to the fluctuating, anarchic world of the soul, of the imagination.

One day, after yet again searching the streets and squares in a vain attempt to find the man with the placard on a pole and roaming several times on the lookout past the wall with the invisible portal, I encountered a funeral procession in the suburb of St Martin. Contemplating the faces of the mourners who were trudging along behind the hearse, the thought went through my head: Where is there anyone in this city, in this world, whose death would be a loss to me? And where is there anyone to whom my death might matter? True, there was Erika, the woman I loved. Well yes, but we had been in a very unsteady relationship for ages, rarely seeing one another without falling out, and at that moment I didn't even know where she was staying. From time to time she would come to me or I would travel to see her and since we are both solitary and difficult people, to some degree like each other in mentality and mental sickness, some sort of bond continued to exist between us despite everything. But might she not breathe a sigh of relief if she heard of my death? I didn't know, nor could I guarantee my own feelings with any certainty. To have any knowledge of such matters you have to live a normal, practical life.

In the meantime I had, on a whim, joined the funeral procession, jogging along behind the mourners as far as the cemetery, an up-to-date concrete affair, complete with crematorium and all mod cons. However, our deceased one was not cremated. Instead, his coffin was unloaded in front of a plain hole in the ground and I watched the clergyman and the remaining vultures, employees of some undertaker, going about their business. Attempting to invest their activities with a semblance of solemnity and grief, they overdid things to the point where, through sheer theatricality, awkwardness and insincerity, they ended up being comic. Dressed from head to foot in flowing black robes, the uniform of their profession, they were doing their utmost to instil the right mood in the assembled mourners, hoping to force them to their knees before the majestic spectacle of death. But all their efforts were in vain; nobody wept; none of them seemed to miss the deceased at all. Nor could anyone be persuaded to adopt a solemnly religious air. Again and again the clergyman addressed the assembly as 'dear brothers and sisters in Christ', but all these silent shopkeepers, master bakers and their wives merely looked at the ground in front of them, forced expressions of seriousness on their tradespeople's faces. They were awkward and insincere, wishing for nothing more than a rapid end to this uncomfortable ceremony. Well, it did come to an end and the two Christian brethren standing furthest forward, having shaken hands with the speaker, went to the edge of the nearest bit of lawn to rub the damp clay, in which their deceased had been laid, from their shoes. Without the slightest delay they resumed their normal, human appearance, the face of one of them suddenly striking me as familiar. It seemed to me to be the same man who had carried the placard that night and thrust the pamphlet into my hand.

The very moment I thought I recognized him he turned round, bent down and busied himself with his trousers, painstakingly rolling them up above his shoes. Then he rapidly walked off, an umbrella tucked under his arm. Walking after him, I caught him up and nodded to him, but he seemed not to recognize me.

'Is there no show tonight?' I asked, attempting to give him a wink, as people who are in on some secret do. However, the time when such knowing facial expressions came naturally to me was all too long past. After all, I had almost forgotten how to speak, so secluded a life did I lead. I myself sensed that I only managed a stupid grimace.

'Show tonight?' the man snarled, looking me in the eye as if he didn't know me from Adam. 'The Black Eagle's the place to go, for goodness' sake, if that's what you are in need of.'

In fact I was no longer certain that he was the man. Disappointed,

I continued on my way, not knowing where to go. For me there were no goals, nothing to strive for, no responsibilities. Life had a dreadfully bitter taste. I felt the nausea that had been mounting for a long time reach its peak, felt myself cast out by life, thrown on the scrap heap. I walked through the grey city in a rage. Everything seemed to me to have an odour of damp earth and burial about it. I wasn't having one of those vultures standing at my graveside in his black clergyman's robes, oh no, nor any of that sentimental twaddle about brothers and sisters in Christ! Sad to say, wherever I looked, whatever I turned my thoughts to, there was no joy to be found, no one to call out my name. Nothing felt the least bit attractive; everything had the smell of stale second-hand goods, of stale, lukewarm contentment. It was all old, faded, grey, listless, worn out. My God, how was it possible? What had managed to reduce me – inspired youth, man of letters, lover of the arts, widely travelled man and ardent idealist – to such a sorry state? How had this paralysis so slowly and stealthily come over me, this hatred of myself and everyone else, this emotional constipation, this profound, evil disgruntlement? How had I ended up, my heart empty, in this filthy hellhole of despair?

As I was going by the library, I bumped into a young professor with whom I had earlier had occasional conversations. When I was last staying in this city, I had even visited him several times in his flat in order to discuss oriental mythologies, an area of study I was much occupied with at the time. Walking stiffly in my direction, this learned scholar, who was rather short-sighted, only recognized me as I was already about to pass him by. Hurling himself at me, he greeted me most warmly, for which I, given the lamentable state I was in, was moderately grateful. Pleased to see me, he became animated, reminding me of detailed points from our former conversations and assuring me that he had benefited a great deal from my suggestions and had often thought of me. Since then, he said, he had rarely had such lively and productive exchanges with colleagues. He asked me how long I had been in town – only a few days, I lied – and why I hadn't looked him up. As I gazed into the charming fellow's learned, kind face I actually found the scene ridiculous, but like a starving dog I nevertheless enjoyed the scrap of warmth, the sip of love, the morsel of recognition it brought me. Steppenwolf Harry was so touched that he began to grin; his parched gullet filled with saliva and, against his will, sentimentality made him grovel. I did indeed grovel, lying through my teeth, saying I was here only briefly, to do some research, and in any case I didn't feel particularly well, otherwise I would of course have paid him a visit. And when, despite everything, he then warmly invited me to spend the evening at his home I gratefully accepted, asking him to give my best wishes to his wife. What with all this energetic smiling and talking my cheeks, no longer accustomed to such exertions, were now aching. And while I, Harry Haller, caught unawares and feeling flattered, courteous and anxious to please, stood there in the street, smiling back at the kind face of this friendly, short-sighted man, the other Harry was standing next to me, a grin on his face too. And as he stood there grinning, he was thinking what a strange, twisted and two-faced chap I was, since only two minutes ago I had been fiercely baring my teeth against the whole damned world. Now, as soon as I heard someone call my name, immediately upon being innocuously greeted by some solid respectable citizen, I was so moved that I couldn't wait to give my blessing and consent to everything. Like a little pig in muck, I was wallowing in the minimal benevolence, respect and friendliness shown to me. Thus the two Harrys, neither cutting a particularly sympathetic figure, stood facing the worthy professor, mocking each other, observing each other and spitting at one another's feet. As always in such situations, they were once again wondering whether their behaviour was simply a sign of stupidity and weakness, a common feature of human nature, or whether such sentimental egoism, such spinelessness, emotional dishonesty and ambivalence were merely personal characteristics of a peculiarly Steppenwolf kind. If this disgraceful behaviour was a common feature of human nature, I was justified in hurling my contempt in humanity's face with even greater force than before; if it was just a personal weakness, then I had reason to indulge in an orgy of self-contempt.

As a result of the dispute between the two Harrys the professor almost got forgotten. Suddenly finding him tiresome again, I rid myself of him as fast as I could. For a long time I watched him go off along the avenue of leafless trees. He had the good-natured, slightly comical walk of an idealist, a man who believed in something. The battle inside me was still raging. Mechanically bending my stiff fingers and stretching them out again in an effort to combat the pangs of gout that were secretly torturing me, I had to admit that I had just allowed myself to be duped. I had now landed myself with an invitation to dinner at half past seven with all that entailed in the way of responsibility to be polite, to indulge in academic chit-chat and to observe the happy family life of others. Making my way angrily back home, I mixed myself a brandy and water, washed down my gout pills with it, lay down on the sofa and tried to read. When I had finally managed a few pages of *Sophia's Journey from Memel to Saxony*,* an enchanting eighteenth-century romance, I suddenly remembered the invitation, and realized that I needed to shave and get dressed. God knows why I had lumbered myself with this! Now then, Harry, on your feet, put the book away, lather your chin and scrape it till it bleeds, dress up and take pleasure in the company of human beings! And while brushing my chin with shaving soap my thoughts turned to that muddy hole in the cemetery into which earlier today they had lowered the stranger's coffin. Thinking of

* See p. 13, footnote *.

the pinched faces of the bored brothers and sisters in Christ, I was unable even to raise a laugh. It seemed to me that what I had witnessed there by that muddy hole in the ground, surrounded by the stupid, awkward words of the clergyman, the stupid, awkward expressions on the faces of the assembled mourners, all the dreary crosses and plaques in metal and marble, all the artificial flowers made of wire and glass, was more than just the demise of that stranger. Not only would I myself perish too, tomorrow or the next day; end up being interred in the mud, surrounded by awkward and insincere onlookers, no – that was how everything would end up, all our aspirations, our whole civilization, all we believed in, all the joy and delight we took in life. It would soon be laid to rest there too, so terminally sick had it become. Our whole cultural world was a cemetery in which Jesus Christ and Socrates, Mozart and Haydn, Dante and Goethe were now nothing more than faded names on rusting metal plaques, surrounded by awkward and insincere mourners, who would have given a great deal to have their faith in these once sacred plaques restored to them. They would also have given a lot to be able to utter just one single sincere, serious word of mourning and despair over the demise of this world, instead of which they had no alternative but to stand with awkward grins on their faces around its grave. In my fury I managed to cut my chin with the razor in the same old place again. I spent some time cauterizing the wound, but I still had to replace the clean collar I had just put on. I had absolutely no idea why I was doing all this since I hadn't the least desire to go to the professor's. However, one part of Harry was putting on an act again, calling the professor a likeable chap, yearning for a whiff of humanity, a chance to chat, and good company. Recalling that the professor had a pretty wife, this part of Harry was, in spite of everything, basically cheered up by the thought of spending the evening with such friendly hosts. He helped me stick a plaster on my chin and put on a decent tie, thus gently persuading me to abandon my real wish, which was to stay at home. At the same time I was thinking to myself: just as I am now getting dressed, going out to visit the professor and exchange polite remarks with him – all the opposite of what I really want to do – so most human beings spend their lives acting compulsorily, day after day, hour after hour. Without really wanting to, they pay visits, hold conversations, work fixed office hours – all of it compulsorily, mechanically, against their will. It could all be done just as well by machines, or not done at all. And it is this perpetual mechanical motion that prevents them from criticizing their own lives in the way I do, from realizing and feeling just how stupid and shallow, how horribly, grotesquely questionable, how hopelessly sad and barren their existence is. And oh, how right they are, these people, a thousand times right to live the way they do, playing their little games and pursuing what seems important to them instead of resisting this depressing machinery and staring despairingly into the void as individuals who have gone off the rails do, like me. If from time to time I seem to despise and even pour scorn on such people in these pages, let no one think that I wish to accuse others of being responsible for my personal misery or put all the blame on them. However, once you have got to the point where you are standing on the very edge of life like me, gazing down into a dark abyss, it is wrong and dishonest to attempt to deceive yourself and others into believing that life's machinery is still running smoothly, that you can still be a party to that blissful, childlike world of endless game-playing.

As it turned out, my evening at the professor's was a marvellous example of this whole problem. Before entering, I paused for a moment outside my acquaintance's home, looking up at the windows. This is where the man lives, I thought, going on with his work year after year, reading and commenting on texts, trying to discover connections between Near Eastern and Indian mythologies. And it gives him pleasure since he thinks what he is doing is of value, believes in academic research, is its servant. He believes in the value of knowledge for its own sake, and in the need to store it up, because he has faith in progress, in evolution. He did not experience the war or the shattering effect Einstein's theories had on the foundations of all previous scientific thinking. (He thinks they are only a matter for mathematicians.) He is blind to the fact that, all around him, preparations are being made for the next war; he considers Jews and Communists to be detestable; he is a good, unthinking, contented child who sets great store by himself. He is much to be envied. Pulling myself together, I went in to be welcomed by a maid in a white apron. I must have sensed something or other because I took exact note of where she put my coat and hat before I was taken into a warm, brightly lit room and asked to wait. There, in obedience to a playful urge, instead of saying a prayer or taking a nap, I picked up the first object that lay to hand. This was a small, framed picture that was kept on the round table, a stiff cardboard flap obliging it to stand at an angle. It was an etching, a portrait of the writer Goethe as an old man with handsomely moulded features and hair swept back with a flourish, the mark of a genius. The artist hadn't neglected to include the famous blazing eyes and had taken particular trouble to convey a hint of loneliness and tragedy behind the thin veneer of the courtier. Without detracting from the profundity of the daemonic old writer in any way, he had managed to give him an air of self-control and solid respectability that had something of the professor about it, or even the actor. All in all he had succeeded in transforming him into a truly handsome old gentleman, fit to adorn any bourgeois household. I suppose the picture was no sillier than all the rest of its kind: all those comely images of Christ the Saviour, Apostles, heroes, intellectual giants and statesmen diligently produced by skilled craftsmen. It may just have been a certain degree of virtuosity in its execution that provoked me so much. Whatever the case, this conceited and self-satisfied portrayal of the ageing Goethe immediately shrieked out at me, striking a fatal false note. As if I wasn't already irritated and furious enough, it demonstrated to me that I had come to the wrong place. Beautifully stylized old masters and the nation's great and good were at home here; it was no place for a Steppenwolf.

If the man of the house had entered at this moment I might have managed, after making some acceptable excuses, to beat a retreat. However, it was his wife who came in and I surrendered to my fate even though I sensed that nothing good would come of it. As we exchanged greetings, the first dissonant note was followed by a whole series of others. The professor's wife congratulated me on how well I was looking, whereas I was only too aware of the extent to which I had aged in the years since our last meeting. The pain in my gout-ridden fingers as we shook hands had been an embarrassing enough reminder of the fact. Yes, and when she then asked how my dear wife was I had no alternative but to tell her that my wife had left me and that we were now divorced. We were pleased to see the professor come in. He too greeted me warmly, only for the whole awkwardness and comedy of the situation to emerge at once and in the most striking form imaginable. He was carrying a copy of the newspaper he subscribed to, a publication of the militarist and warmongering party, and, after shaking my hand, he pointed to it, saying there was something in it about a namesake of mine, a journalist called Haller who must be a dastardly figure, one of those chaps without any allegiance to the Fatherland. Haller had, he said, made fun of the Kaiser and publicly declared that his Fatherland was no less responsible for starting the war than the enemy countries. What a nasty piece of work he must be! Well, he said, now the fellow was getting his comeuppance. The paper's editor had well and truly pilloried the pest, made short work of him. However, when he saw that I was not interested in the subject we went on to talk of other matters. It didn't remotely occur to either of them that the monster in question might be sitting there in front of them, yet this was indeed the case: I myself was that monster. Ah well, why upset people by making a song and dance about it? I was laughing inwardly, but by now I had abandoned all hope of still having a pleasant evening. I can remember clearly the moment when I did so. You see, precisely when the professor was talking about that traitor to the Fatherland Haller the awful feeling of depression and despair that had been building up in me ever since the scene at the funeral, getting stronger and stronger, reached maximum intensity. Its pressure was terrible; I experienced it physically as an acute abdominal pain, a harrowing, fearful sense that my fate was sealed. I felt something was lying in wait for me, some threat stealing up on me from behind. Fortunately we were now informed that dinner was served. We went into the dining room where, constantly making an effort to say or ask something quite harmless, I ate more than I was accustomed to. Feeling more wretched by the moment, I kept wondering why on earth we make such efforts. It was clear to me that my hosts too were feeling anything but comfortable, that their cheerfulness was forced, whether because they were inhibited by me, or else were out of sorts for some domestic reason. They only asked me questions it was impossible to give an honest answer to and, as a result, I had soon lied myself into such a corner that every word I uttered almost made me sick. Eventually, in an effort to distract them, I started to tell them about the funeral I had witnessed that day, but I struck the wrong note. My attempts at humour did nothing to improve the general mood, and we were increasingly at odds with one another. Inside me, Steppenwolf was laughing and baring his teeth and, by the time dessert was served, we had all three fallen quite silent.

We went back into the first room for coffee and schnapps,

which, I thought, might buck us up a bit. But there, although he had been put to one side on a chest of drawers, the prince among writers caught my eye again. Unable to tear myself away from him, I again picked up his portrait and, despite hearing warning voices inside me, started to discuss its merits. The situation was, I had convinced myself, so intolerable that in order to rescue it I would either have to win over my hosts by rousing their enthusiasm to the same pitch as mine; or to cause a major explosion.

'Let's hope,' I said, 'that the real Goethe didn't look like this! This conceited aristocratic pose; this dignified courting of the assembled ladies and gentlemen; and under the veneer of masculinity all this sugary sweet sentimentality! You can certainly find a great deal to criticize about the man – I myself often find fault with lots of things the pompous old ass got up to – but no, to picture him like this really is taking things too far.'

With an intensely pained expression on her face, the lady of the house finished pouring the coffee, then rushed out of the room. Half embarrassed, half reproachfully, her husband revealed to me that the Goethe portrait belonged to his wife and that she was especially fond of it. 'And even if, objectively speaking, you were right, which incidentally I would dispute, you oughtn't to have expressed your opinion in so crass a fashion.'

'You are right,' I conceded. 'Unfortunately it's a bad habit of mine, one of my vices. I'm always opting for the crassest form of words possible, something Goethe, by the way, also did in his better moments. Of course this sugar-sweet, petit bourgeois, front-parlour Goethe would never have used a crass, genuine, direct expression of any kind. I beg your and your wife's forgiveness. Please tell her that I am a schizophrenic. And with that, if I may, I'll take my leave.'

The embarrassed professor raised a few more objections, then again mentioned how agreeable and stimulating our former discussions had been. Indeed he had been profoundly impressed at the time by my theories about Mithras and Krishna and had, he said, been hoping that today too . . . and so on. Thanking him, I said it was very kind of him to say all this, but that unfortunately my interest in Krishna as well as my desire to take part in academic discussions had completely worn off. I had, I said, lied to him on several occasions today. It was not true, for example, that I had been in town for just a few days. I had been here for many months but, now living my own life apart, I was not the ideal person to invite to a better class of home. For one thing, I was constantly in a bad mood and plagued with gout; and secondly I was drunk most of the time. What's more, just to get things straight and in order not to go away a liar, I needed to make it clear to the honourable gentleman that he had today insulted me most grievously. How? By siding with the verdict of a reactionary rag on the views expressed by Haller – a stupid, bull-necked verdict worthy of an unemployed army officer, not an academic scholar. However, this Haller 'fellow', this chap lacking any allegiance to the Fatherland, was none other than me; and our country and the whole world would be a lot better off if at least the few people capable of thinking would stand up for reason and love of peace instead of blindly and fanatically heading towards a new war. Now he knew, and with that I wished him goodbye.

And thus rising from my chair, I took my leave of Goethe and the professor, hastily grabbed my things from the coat hook outside, and beat a fast retreat. Full of malicious joy, the wolf within me was howling loudly; the two Harrys were acting up for all they were worth. For I realized immediately that this disagreeable evening meant far more to me than it did to the indignant professor. For him it was a disappointment, a minor irritation, but for me it was the hour of ultimate failure when I turned and ran. It was my farewell to the world of bourgeois respectability, morality and academic scholarship, a total triumph for Steppenwolf. And I was parting from all this as a refugee, admitting defeat, declaring myself bankrupt in my own eyes. There was no consolation in my going, and no humour: I had taken leave of my former world – home, bourgeois respectability, morality, scholarship – just as a man with a stomach ulcer says goodbye to roast pork. I walked along under the street lamps in a rage, in a rage and terribly dejected. What a miserable, shameful, vile day it had been from morning to evening, from the cemetery to the scene at the professor's! To what end? Why go on? Was there any point in saddling myself with even more days like this, swallowing even more of these bitter pills? No! And so I was going to put an end to the farce that night. Harry, take yourself home and cut your throat! You've been putting it off for long enough.

I walked back and forth through the streets, driven on by despair. It had of course been stupid of me to go spitting on one of the knick-knacks those good people chose to deck out their drawing room with, stupid and bad-mannered. But try as I might, there was nothing else for it: I simply could not stand that tame, insincere, well-behaved way of living any more. And since, as it seemed, I was now unable to stand loneliness either, since even my own company had become unspeakably abhorrent, indeed nauseating to me; since I was flailing around, close to choking in the airless sphere of my private hell, what possible way out was there for me? There was none. O Father and Mother, O far-off sacred fires that burned in my youth, O all you countless joys, labours and goals of my life! Nothing now remained of all this for me, not even regret; just nausea and pain. Never, it seemed to me, had the mere obligation to go on living been so painful as at this hour.

I took a moment's rest in a dreary pub on the outskirts of town, drinking brandy and water, then walked on again, hounded by my demons, up and down the steep, crooked lanes of the Old Town, along the tree-lined avenues, across the station square. Get away from here, I thought, and went into the station where

I stared at the timetables on the walls, drank some wine and tried to gather my thoughts. I could see the spectre that was haunting me drawing closer and closer, becoming more and more distinct. It was the fear of going back home, returning to my garret and having to face my despair in silence. Even if I spent many more hours wandering around town, I could not avoid that moment when, returning to the door of my flat, to my desk with its books, to the sofa with the picture of the woman I loved above it, I had to sharpen my razor and cut my throat. This was the prospect that revealed itself to me more and more clearly and, my heart beating at a furious rate, I experienced more and more clearly that fear to end all fears, the fear of death. Yes, I was terribly afraid of dying. I could see no other way out; nausea, pain and despair were piled up around me; nothing was now capable of attracting me or giving me joy and hope. Nevertheless, the thought of executing myself, of that final instant as the cold blade cut deeply into my own flesh, filled me with inexpressible dread.

I could see no way of escaping the thing I feared. Even if today, in the battle between despair and cowardice, cowardice were perhaps to win again, despair would confront me afresh tomorrow and every day, and it would be further increased by self-contempt. I would go on taking the razor in my hand and throwing it aside again until one day the deed was finally done. In that case, better to get it over with today. I was talking sensibly to myself as to a frightened child, but the child didn't listen. Wishing to go on living, it ran off. Seized with panic, I was driven on through the town. I walked round and round my home in wide circles, constantly meaning to go back there, constantly putting it off. Now and then I ended up in a pub, long enough for one glass, long enough for two, before I felt compelled to walk on, again in a broad arc around my destination, around the razor, around death. Tired out, I sat from time to time on a bench, on the rim of a fountain, on a kerbstone, listening to my heart beating and wiping the sweat from my brow. Then I set off walking again, filled with mortal dread; filled too with a flickering desire for life.

Thus, in the early hours, in a remote outlying district of town that I hardly knew, I found myself entering a pub where, behind the windows, I could hear loud dance music. As I went in, I read on the old sign above the entrance: 'The Black Eagle'. Drinking hours were unrestricted that night, and inside the place was packed with people, full of smoke, the smell of wine and the loud cries of the drinkers. In the large room at the back people were dancing; the music was in full swing there. I stayed in the room at the front where the customers were without exception ordinary folk, some of them poorly clad, whereas in the ballroom at the rear I also glimpsed the odd fashionably dressed figure. Carried along by the throng of people, I found myself pushed across the room and ended up squashed against a table near the bar. There, on the bench by the wall, sat an attractive, wan-looking girl in a thin, low-cut little ball-dress, a faded flower in her hair. When she saw me coming the girl gave me a friendly, attentive look, then smiled as she moved a bit to one side to make room for me.

'May I?' I asked, sitting down beside her.

'Certainly, dear,' she said. 'And who are you, then?'

'Thanks,' I said. 'I can't possibly go home, I can't, I can't. I want to stay here, next to you, if you'll let me. No, I can't go home.'

She nodded as if understanding me and, as she nodded, I contemplated the lock of hair that ran down from her forehead past her ear, noticing that the faded flower she wore there was a camellia. Over in the back room the music was blaring out, while at the bar the waitresses were hastily calling out their orders.

'Just you stay here,' she said in a soothing voice. 'Why is it you can't go home, then?'

'I can't. There is something waiting for me at home. I just can't. It's too terrible.'

'Then let it wait, and stay here. Come on, give your glasses a clean first; you can't see a thing like that. There, give me your hanky. Now what shall we have to drink? Burgundy?'

She cleaned my glasses for me. Only now could I see her clearly: her pale, firm face with the lips painted blood-red, her bright grey eyes, her smooth, cool forehead, the short, tight lock of hair in front of her ear. In a kind, though slightly mocking, manner she took me under her wing, ordering the wine. Then, as we clinked glasses, she looked down at my shoes.

'My God, where have you been, then? You look as though you've walked it here from Paris! You don't go to a dance looking like that!'

I answered yes and no, laughed a little, and let her talk. I was amazed to find that I liked her a lot since until now I had avoided young girls like her, if anything viewing them with suspicion. The way she behaved towards me was exactly what I needed at this point to make me feel good, and in fact it has been like that whenever we have been together since. She treated me with precisely the degree of protectiveness I required, but poked fun at me too, just as judiciously. Ordering a sandwich, she commanded me to eat it. Pouring me a glass of wine, she told me to take a drink from it, but not too quickly. Then she praised me for being so obedient.

'There's a good boy,' she said, encouraging me. 'That wasn't so difficult, was it? I bet it's a long time since you last had to obey orders from somebody, isn't it?'

'You win. How did you know that?'

'Easy. Obeying orders is like eating and drinking; anyone who has gone without either for a long spell will think there's nothing quite like it. It's true, isn't it: you like obeying me?'

'Very much. You know everything.'

'That's not difficult in your case, my friend. I might even be able to tell you just what it is you are so afraid of, waiting for you there at home. But you yourself know what it is, so we don't need to talk about it, do we? What nonsense! People either hang themselves, in which case – well, they go ahead and hang themselves, no doubt for a good reason. Or they remain alive, in which case all they have to worry about is living. It's as simple as that.'

'Oh, if only it were that simple!' I cried. 'I swear to God I've done enough worrying about living, and it's got me nowhere. Hanging oneself may be difficult, I don't know, but living is much, much more difficult. God only knows how difficult it is.'

'On the contrary, it's child's play, as you will see. We've already made a start: you've cleaned your glasses and had something to eat and drink. Now we'll go and give your trousers and shoes a bit of a brushing; they could certainly do with it. And then you're going to shimmy with me.'

'You see, I was right after all!' I exclaimed eagerly. 'Nothing grieves me more than being unable to carry out one of your orders, but this one is beyond me. I can't shimmy; I can't waltz or do the polka either, or any of those things, whatever you call them. In all my life I've never learned how to dance. Not everything is as simple as you say it is. Don't you see that now?'

A smile appeared on the blood-red lips of the beautiful girl as she shook her firm head of boyish hair. Looking at her, it seemed to me at first that she resembled Rosa Kreisler, the first girl I had fallen in love with as a young boy, and yet she had been swarthy and dark-haired. No, I couldn't tell who this stranger of a girl reminded me of; all I knew was that it was someone from my very early youth, my boyhood days.

'Don't be so hasty,' she cried. 'Gently does it! So you can't dance? Not at all? Not even a one-step? And yet you claim to have gone to heaven knows how much trouble to make something of your life! You were telling a fib when you said that, my lad, and at your age people shouldn't still be telling fibs. Come on, how can you say you've gone to a lot of trouble to make something of your life when you don't even want to dance?'

'But what if I just can't? I've never learned how to.'

She laughed.

'But you have learned to read and write, haven't you, and you've learned arithmetic; probably Latin and French too, all sorts of stuff like that? I bet you spent ten or twelve years at school, then quite possibly went to university into the bargain. For all I know, you may even have a doctorate and can speak Chinese or Spanish. You see? But you've never managed to spare a bit of time and money for a few dance lessons! There, I told you so!'

'It was my parents,' I said, trying to justify myself. 'They got me to learn Latin and Greek and all that stuff. But they never made me learn to dance; it wasn't the fashionable thing to do in our family. My parents themselves never went dancing.'

She gave me a really icy look, full of disdain. Again I saw something in her face that reminded me of the earliest days of my youth.

'I see, so it's your parents who must take the blame! Did you also ask their permission to come to the Black Eagle tonight? Did you? They are long since dead, you say? Well then! If from sheer obedience to them you refused to learn to dance in your youth, that's all right with me, though I don't believe you were such a model son back then. But what about afterwards, what did you get up to in all the years afterwards?'

'Oh,' I confessed, 'I'm not sure myself now. I went to university, made music, read books, wrote books, travelled –'

'You have strange ideas of what it means to live! So you've always done difficult and complicated things, never once learning how to do the simple ones? No time for them? No desire? Well, fair enough, I'm not your mother, thank God. But then to pretend that you've given life a serious try and found it worthless, that simply won't do!'

'Don't take me to task,' I pleaded. 'I don't need you to tell me I'm mad.'

'Go on with you! Don't try to fool me. You're not the least bit mad, Herr Professor; indeed, you're nowhere near mad enough for my liking! You strike me as clever in a stupid kind of way, as true professors are. Come on, have another sandwich. Afterwards you can tell me more about yourself.'

She got me another sandwich, put some salt on it and a little mustard, cut a bit off for herself and ordered me to eat. I ate. I would have done anything she ordered me to, anything apart from dancing. It did me a power of good to obey someone, to sit next to someone who was questioning me, giving me orders and taking me to task. If only the professor and his wife had done that to me a few hours ago, I would have been spared a great deal. But no, it was a good thing they hadn't, because then I would have missed a great deal too!

'By the way, what's your name?' she suddenly asked.

'Harry.'

'Harry? That's a little boy's name! And a little boy is what you are, Harry, in spite of the odd grey patch in your hair. You're a little boy, and you should have somebody to keep a bit of an eye on you. I won't mention dancing again, but what about the state of your hair? Haven't you got a wife, or a sweetheart?'

'I've no wife now; we're divorced. I do have a sweetheart, but she doesn't live here. I very rarely see her; we don't get on very well with one another.'

She whistled softly through her teeth.

'It strikes me you must be a really difficult man if no woman can stick it out with you. But tell me now, what went wrong tonight specially? What made you wander the streets in a daze like that? Did you have a row? Had you gambled away all your money?'

I had some difficulty explaining why.

'You see,' I began, 'it was actually something or nothing. I'd been invited to dinner at the home of a professor – though I'm not one myself – and I ought really not to have gone. I'm not used to that kind of thing any more, sitting and chatting with people. I've forgotten how. What's more, even as I entered the place I sensed that things would turn out badly. When hanging up my hat, the thought already occurred to me that I might need to take it back again in no time at all. And you see, at this professor's, there happened to be a picture on the table, a stupid picture that annoyed me –'

'What sort of picture?' she asked, interrupting me. 'Why were you annoyed?'

'Well, it was supposed to represent Goethe, you know, the great writer Goethe. But it wasn't Goethe as he looked in real life – actually we have no idea how he looked exactly, he's been dead a hundred years. No, some modern artist or other had produced a smart, well-groomed version of Goethe as he imagined him, and his picture annoyed me. I'm not sure whether you can understand why, but I found it horribly repugnant.'

'Don't worry, I can very well understand why. Go on.'

'I was already at loggerheads with the professor. He's a great patriot, as nearly all professors are, and during the war he did his bit to help deceive the nation's people – all in good faith, of course. But I'm an opponent of war. Well, no matter, let me go on. Of course, I needn't have looked at the picture at all –'

'You can say that again.'

'But in the first place, I felt really sorry for Goethe. You see, I'm very, very fond of him. And then one way or another I thought – I um . . . the thing is I thought, or rather felt, something along the lines of: Here I am, sitting in the home of people I regard as like-minded, who I assume will have a similar liking for Goethe and pretty much the same image of him as me, and I now find they've got this tasteless, adulterated, saccharine picture on display. And, oblivious to the fact that the spirit of the picture is exactly the opposite of Goethe's, they find it splendid. They think it is wonderful – fair enough, they are of course entitled to their opinion – but as for me, any faith I have in these people, any friendship with them, any feeling of kinship or solidarity is immediately over and done with. Besides, we weren't such great friends anyway. So at that point I became really angry and sad, realizing that I was entirely on my own and that no one understood me. Do you see what I mean?'

'Of course, Harry, it's not difficult. And then what? Did you fling the picture at them, hit them on the head with it?'

'No, I cursed and swore, then I rushed off, intending to go home, but –'

'But there would have been no mummy waiting there to comfort her stupid baby boy, would there, or to give him a good telling-off. Oh dear, Harry, you almost make me feel sorry for you. You're a real big baby if there ever was one!'

I certainly was. I could see that now, or so it seemed to me. She gave me a glass of wine to drink. She was really mothering me, but from time to time I noticed momentarily how beautiful and young she was.

'So,' she began again, 'so famous old Goethe died a hundred years ago and our Harry, who is very fond of him, conjures up this wonderful picture of him in his head, imagining how he may have looked, as Harry is of course perfectly entitled to, that's right, isn't it? But the artist, who is also mad about Goethe and creates his own image of him, isn't entitled to; nor is the professor or anyone else at all, because that doesn't suit Harry. That's something he can't put up with. It makes him curse and swear, then he rushes off! If he had enough sense, he would simply laugh at the artist and the professor. If he were mad, he would chuck their picture of Goethe straight back in their faces. But since he's just a little boy he runs off home, meaning to hang himself . . . I can well understand your story, Harry. It's a funny story. It makes me laugh. Hey, hold on, don't drink so quickly. You should take your time with burgundy, otherwise you'll get too hot. But then you need to be told everything, don't you, my little lad?'

She had a look of strict admonition on her face, just like that of a sixty-year-old governess.

'Indeed I do,' I said contentedly. 'Go on, tell me, just tell me anything.'

'What am I supposed to tell you?'

'Anything you like.'

'All right, I'll tell you something. For an hour now you've been listening to me using the familiar form "du", yet you are still addressing me formally as "Sie". Just like your blessed Latin and Greek, always making things as complicated as you possibly can. If a girl says "du" to you, and you don't exactly find her loath-some, you say "du" back to her. There, you've learned something new. And secondly: for half an hour now I've known that you're called Harry. Because I asked you your name, that's why. But you've no desire to know what I'm called.'

'Oh yes I have, I want very much to know your name.'

'Too late, little man! If we ever meet again, you can ask me once more. I'm not going to tell you today, so there you are. And now I fancy a dance.'

Since she moved as if to get up, I suddenly felt my spirits sink. I feared she would go and leave me on my own, and I would be back where I started. Just as a toothache that has fleetingly vanished can resurface, burning like fire, my anxiety and dread were back again in a trice. Lord only knows how I had managed to forget what was lying in store for me. Had anything really changed?

'Stop,' I cried. 'I beg you, young lady, not to . . . uh, sorry . . .

I mean, don't leave me, dear. Of course you can dance, dance as much as you like, but don't stay away too long. Come back again, dear. Come back again.'

With a laugh, she stood up. I had imagined her to be bigger, but now that she was standing I could see that she was slim but not tall. Again she reminded me of someone, but who? I couldn't put my finger on it.

'You'll come back?'

'I'll come back, but I may be gone a while, half an hour or even an hour. I'll tell you what to do. Close your eyes and get a bit of sleep. That's just what you need.'

I made room for her to go. Her little dress brushed against my knees; then, as she walked away, I saw her glance at herself in a tiny round pocket mirror, raise her eyebrows and dab her chin with a miniature powder puff before disappearing into the ball-room. Looking around me, I saw strange faces, men smoking, spilled beer on the marble-topped table. All around I could hear shouting and shrieking, and from the next room the noise of dance music. She had told me to get some sleep. What an innocent child! Little did she know how shy a creature sleep was in my experience, even less likely to keep me company than a weasel. And she wanted me to sleep in this funfair of a place, sitting at a table with the clatter of beer mugs on all sides! I sipped at my wine, took a cigar out of my pocket and looked around for matches, but feeling no really strong desire to smoke, I put the cigar down in front of me on the table. 'Close your eyes,' she had said. Heaven knows where the girl had got that voice of hers from, that slightly deep, kind voice, like a mother's. It was good to obey that voice, as I had already discovered. Obediently closing my eyes, I leaned my head against the wall and, with hundreds of raucous sounds ringing in my ears, smiled at the thought of trying to sleep in this of all places. I decided to make my way to the ballroom door and steal a glance inside – after all, I couldn't miss seeing my beautiful girl dance. But only now realizing, as I moved my legs under the table, just how immensely tired I felt after wandering the streets for hours, I remained seated. And before I knew it I was already asleep, following mother's orders to the letter. I slept my fill, unable to get enough of it, and was thankful. And I dreamt, dreamt more clearly and beautifully than I had dreamt for ages. What I dreamt was this: –

I was sitting waiting in an old-fashioned anteroom. All I knew at first was that I had an appointment to see some dignitary or other. Then I suddenly realized that it was none other than Herr von Goethe who was to receive me. Unfortunately I was not there in a private capacity, but as the correspondent of a magazine. I found this very disturbing, unable as I was to understand what had landed me in such a situation. I was also worried by a scorpion that only a moment ago I had seen trying to climb up my leg. Although I had warded off the little black creepy-crawly by shaking myself, I didn't know where it was now, and I didn't dare make a grab for it.

I was not sure either whether I'd been granted an audience with Matthison* rather than Goethe, but in my dream I must also have confused Matthison with Bürger,† since I ascribed the Molly poems to him. I would, by the way, have been delighted to meet Molly, whom I imagined to be a wonderful woman: soft, musical, nocturnal. If only I hadn't been sent there by the editor of that damned magazine! I was getting more and more annoyed at this, and bit by bit my annoyance shifted to Goethe too. Suddenly I found all manner of things to question and criticize

---

* Friedrich von Matthison (1761–1831), once popular, now almost totally forgotten writer of neoclassical verse.

† Gottfried August Bürger (1747–94), poet of the 'Storm and Stress' period, noted for his ballads. The 'Molly' poems were written for Auguste, younger sister of his then wife, Dorette. After Dorette's death he entered into a short-lived second marriage with Auguste.

him for. A fine audience this might turn out to be! But as for the scorpion, it was perhaps not so bad, even if it were a possible threat lurking somewhere quite close to me. You could, it seemed to me, put a more friendly interpretation on it. Perhaps, I thought, it had something or other to do with Molly. It might be some sort of harbinger of her, or the creature on her crest: a beautiful, dangerous heraldic creature representing femininity and sin. Might not this creature's name perhaps be Vulpius?* However, at this point, a servant threw open the door and, rising from my seat, I went in.

Standing there stiffly was the small, ageing Goethe and – sure enough – the venerable Classic was sporting the sizeable star of some Order on his chest. It seemed he was still in a position of power, still granting audiences, still exercising control over the world from his Weimar museum. For scarcely had he cast eyes on me when, jerkily nodding his head like an old crow, he solemnly declared: 'Well, I suppose you youngsters find precious little to agree with in our person and all that we are striving to accomplish?'

'Quite right,' I said, chilled to the core by the ministerial look in his eye. 'We youngsters are indeed unable to agree with you, ageing Sir. You are much too solemn for our liking; too vain and pompous; not honest enough, Your Excellency. Not honest enough, that is probably the nub of the matter.'

The little old man thrust his stern face slightly towards me. Suddenly his harsh, tight-lipped official mien gave way to a little smile and he came charmingly alive. All at once my heart beat faster as I remembered the poem 'Dusk descended from above',† realizing that the words of this poem had come from this man

---

* Christiane Vulpius (1765–1816) was for many years Goethe's lover and eventually his wife.

† The first line of the untitled eighth poem from Goethe's late cycle 'Chinese-German Hours and Seasons' of 1827.

and these lips. At that moment, in fact, I was totally disarmed and unnerved, within an ace of kneeling down in front of him. But I held myself erect as his smiling lips uttered the words: 'Aha, so you're accusing me of being dishonest, are you? A fine thing to say, I don't think! Would you mind going into more detail?'

I was pleased to do so, only too pleased.

'Just how problematic and desperate a thing human life is, you, Herr von Goethe, like all great minds, clearly recognized and felt: how the splendour of the moment fades miserably; how it is only possible to experience the heights of emotion at the expense of an everyday life lived in a prison house; how this prison-house routine is the mortal enemy of our equally ardent and equally sacred passion for the lost innocence of nature; all the terrible sense of being left hanging in a void, uncertain about everything and condemned to experience things fleetingly, never to the full but always in an experimental, dilettantish fashion; in short, human existence in all its hopelessness, absurdity and heartfelt despair. You recognized all this, from time to time you even confessed to believing that it was so. Yet you spent your whole life preaching the opposite, expressing faith and optimism, and deluding yourself and others into believing that our intellectual and spiritual endeavours are meaningful and of lasting value. You dismissed those who believed in penetrating to the depths, suppressed those voices speaking the desperate truth, your own voice as well as those of Kleist and Beethoven.* For decades you acted as if accumulating knowledge and collections of things, writing and hoarding letters, as if the whole life you led in Weimar

---

* Goethe was not without admiration for the dramatist and story-writer Heinrich von Kleist (1777–1811), but he shied away from the more pessimistic aspects of his work, which he regarded as self-destructive. Kleist committed suicide in 1811. Similarly, though less strongly, the 'Classical' Goethe seems to have deplored the wilder aspects of Beethoven's personality and his compositions.

in your old age really was a way of preserving momentary experiences for all eternity and lending spiritual meaning to things natural. Yet you only succeeded in mummifying the moment and turning nature into a stylized masquerade. That is what we mean when accusing you of dishonesty.'

Deep in thought, the old privy counsellor looked me in the eyes, a smile still playing on his lips.

Then, to my amazement, he said: 'In that case you must, I suppose, find Mozart's *Magic Flute* utterly abhorrent.'

And, even before I had time to protest, he went on: 'The *Magic Flute* pictures life as an exquisite song; it extols our feelings, which are after all transient, as something eternal and divine. Far from agreeing with Messrs von Kleist or Beethoven, it preaches optimism and faith.'

'I know, I know!' I cried in a rage. 'Lord only knows what made you hit on the *Magic Flute* of all things. It is dearer to me than anything on earth! But Mozart didn't live to be eighty-two. And in his personal life he never aspired to lasting significance or to the well-ordered existence of a stuck-up dignitary like you. He wasn't so full of his own importance. He sang his divine melodies, was poor, died an early death, impoverished and unappreciated . . .'

I had run out of breath. Ideally I would have needed to say a thousand things in ten words. Sweat was starting to appear on my brow.

However, Goethe replied amiably: 'It may well be unforgivable of me to have lived to the age of eighty-two, but I derived less pleasure from doing so than you may think. You are correct in saying that I was always filled with a great desire for lasting significance, and I did constantly fear and battle against death. It is my belief that the struggle against death, the stubborn, unconditional desire for life is what has driven all outstanding human beings to act and live their lives as they did. On the other hand, my young

friend, the fact that one must nevertheless ultimately die is something that I proved at the age of eighty-two just as conclusively
as if I had died as a schoolboy. And by way of self-justification,
if it helps, I'd like to add that there was a great deal in my make-
up that was childlike, a lot of curiosity and playfulness, much
delight taken in wasting time. There, and the fact is it took me a
fair amount of time to realize that one day the playing had to
stop.'

As he said this he smiled slyly, looking positively like a rogue.
His figure had grown larger, his stiff posture and his forced expression of dignity had disappeared. And now the air around us was
full of nothing but melodies, all of them settings of Goethe
poems. Among others I clearly detected Mozart's 'The Violet'
and Schubert's 'To the Moon'. And Goethe's face was now young
and rosy. He was laughing, now looking so like Mozart, now so
like Schubert that he could have been their brother. And the star
on his breast was made up entirely of wild flowers, a cowslip
bursting forth joyfully and juicily from its centre.

Since the old man's attempts to evade my questions and accu-
sations in such a jocular manner were not quite to my liking, I
gave him a disapproving look. At this point he bent forward,
placing his mouth, now completely transformed into the mouth
of a child, close to my ear, and whispered softly into it: 'You are
taking old Goethe far too seriously, my lad. Old people who have
already died shouldn't be taken seriously, it's unfair on them. We
Immortals don't like taking things seriously, we like to have fun.
Seriousness, my lad, is a function of time. It arises – this much
I'll divulge to you – when the value of time is overestimated. I
too once overestimated the value of time; that's why I wanted
to live to be a hundred. But, you see, there is no time in eternity.
Eternity is an instant, just long enough for a prank.'

From now on, in fact, it was quite impossible to talk seriously
to the man. He was taking great pleasure in prancing lithely up

and down, making the cowslip in the centre of his star shoot out one moment like a rocket, the next shrink to nothing and disappear. Watching him execute such brilliant steps and figures, I couldn't help thinking that here at any rate was a man who had not neglected to take dancing lessons. He could dance wonderfully well. Then, suddenly thinking of the scorpion again, or rather of Molly, I called out to Goethe: 'I say, is Molly not here?'

Goethe laughed out loud. Walking to his desk, he opened a drawer, took out a valuable case made of leather or velvet and, opening it, held it up to my eyes. There, small, immaculate and sparkling on a bed of dark-coloured velvet, lay a tiny woman's leg, an enchanting leg, slightly bent at the knee, the stretched foot pointing downwards and culminating in the daintiest of toes.

Utterly enamoured, I held out my hand, intending to take hold of the little leg, but just as I was about to seize it with two fingers, the toy limb seemed to make a tiny jerking movement and at once I suspected that it might be the scorpion. Goethe appeared to understand my reaction, seemed indeed deliberately to have placed me in a deep quandary, making me wince, as desire fought inside me against fear. Dangling the charming little scorpion really close to my face, he saw me both yearn for and shrink back from it, and this seemed to give him the greatest of pleasure. While taunting me with this charming, dangerous object he had aged again. He was really ancient now, a thousand years old, his hair white as snow, his withered old man's face silently laughing. Without making a sound, he was chortling away to himself with the dark, inscrutable kind of humour typical of the very old.

*

When I woke I had forgotten the dream. Only later did I recall it. I suppose I had slept for about an hour at the pub table. I would never have thought that possible, what with the noise of the music and the hustle and bustle all around. The dear girl was standing in front of me, one hand on my shoulder.

'Give me two or three marks,' she said. 'I've had a bite to eat over there.'

I gave her my purse. She went off with it, returning again soon.

'There, now I can sit with you a little while longer. Then I'll have to go. I've arranged to meet someone.'

I was startled. 'Who?' I quickly asked.

'A gentleman, Harry my boy. He's invited me to the Odeon Bar.'

'I see. I was thinking you wouldn't leave me on my own.'

'In that case you ought to have invited me yourself. Someone else has beaten you to it. Never mind, this way you're saving a fair amount of money. Do you know the Odeon? Nothing but champagne on offer after midnight, leather armchairs, a Negro band, the finest of the fine.'

All this had been far from my thoughts.

'Oh, why don't you let me take you out somewhere!' I begged. 'I thought it went without saying. After all, we've become friends, haven't we? Let me take you out, anywhere you like, please.'

'That's very sweet of you, but don't you see, a promise is a promise. I've agreed to go and I'm going. Don't you go to any more trouble. Come on, have a bit more to drink, there's still some wine left in the bottle. Drink it up, then go home like a good boy and get some sleep. Promise me you will.'

'No, dear. I can't go home, I just can't.'

'Oh you and your stories! Have you still not got that man Goethe out of your system?' (It was at this juncture that I remembered my Goethe dream.) 'But if you really can't go home, stay the night here, they have rooms to let. Shall I ask about one for you?'

Happy with this arrangement, I asked her where we could

meet each other again. Where did she live? She didn't tell me. I only needed to search a little, she said, and I would find her all right.

'Can't I invite you out somewhere?'

'Where?'

'Anywhere you like, anytime you like.'

'All right. Tuesday, for dinner in the Old Franciscan, first floor. Goodbye.'

She held out her hand. Only now did I notice it. It was a hand that matched her voice perfectly, beautiful and fully rounded, shrewd and kind. When I kissed it she gave a mocking laugh.

And at the last moment, turning round to me again, she said: 'To go back to that Goethe story of yours, there's one more thing you ought to know. You see, what you felt, not being able to stand that picture of him, is exactly what I sometimes feel about the saints.'

'The saints? Are you so religious?'

'No, I'm not religious, sadly, but I was once and will be again one day. Being religious takes time, and of course that's something nobody has enough of nowadays.'

'Enough time? Does it really require time?'

'Yes, of course. To be religious you need time. You even need something more. You need to be independent of time. You can't be seriously religious while living in the real world and, what's more, taking the things of the real world seriously – time, money, the Odeon Bar and all that.'

'I see. But what is it that you feel about the saints?'

'Well, there are quite a few saints that I'm particularly fond of: St Stephen, St Francis and some others. Occasionally I see pictures of them or of Our Saviour and the Virgin Mary, such fake, dishonest travesties that I can't stand them any more than you could stand that picture of Goethe. Whenever I notice some such stupid sentimental Saviour or St Francis and see that other people find pictures of this sort beautiful and uplifting it strikes me as an insult to the real Saviour and I ask myself why, oh why did he live and suffer so terribly if all it takes to satisfy people is a stupid picture like that! Yet, in spite of this, I know that my own image of Our Saviour or of St Francis is merely a human image too, one that falls short of the original. If he could see the image I have of him in my mind, Our Saviour would find it just as stupid and inadequate as I do those sickly, sentimental portrayals. That's not to say that you are right to be so depressed and furious about the Goethe picture, not at all: you are wrong. All I'm saying is that I can understand you. You scholars and artists may well have your minds full of outlandish things, but you are just as human as the rest of us. We others have our dreams and fancies too. You see, learned Sir, I couldn't help notice that you were slightly embarrassed when it came to telling me your Goethe story. To explain your grand ideas to a simple lass like me, you had to make a great effort, didn't you? Well now, I'd just like you to know that you needn't go to such lengths. I do understand, believe me. There, and now we must stop. Bed's the place for you.'

She left, and an aged servant took me up two flights of stairs, or rather, having first asked about my luggage, on hearing that I hadn't any, made me pay in advance what he called 'bed money'. Then he led me up an old dark staircase into a bedroom and left me there alone. There was a plain wooden bed, very short and hard. On the wall hung a sabre, a coloured portrait of Garibaldi and also a withered wreath, left over from the festive gathering of some club or other. I would have given anything for a nightshirt. At least there was water and a small towel, so I was able to wash. Then, leaving the light on, I lay down fully clothed on the bed with ample time to think. Well, I had now set the record straight with Goethe. How marvellous it had been, his appearance in my dream! And this wonderful girl – if only I'd known her name! All at once a human being, a live human being, shattering the clouded glass cloche that covered my corpse-like existence and holding out her hand to me, her beautiful, kind, warm hand! All at once things that mattered to me again, things I could take joy in, worry about, eagerly anticipate! All at once an open door through which life could get in to me. Perhaps I could start to live again, perhaps I could again become a human being. My soul, having almost frozen to death in hibernation, was breathing again, drowsily flapping its small, frail wings. Goethe had been in my presence. A girl had ordered me to eat, drink and sleep, had been kind to me, had made fun of me, calling me a silly little boy. She had also, this wonderful girlfriend, told me about the saints, shown me that even with regard to my most eccentric and outlandish preoccupations I was by no means alone and misunderstood. I was not a pathologically exceptional case, but had brothers and sisters. People could understand me. Would I see her again, I wondered? Yes, certainly, she could be relied on. 'A promise is a promise.'

And before I knew it I was asleep again, went on sleeping for four or five hours. It was gone ten o'clock when I woke, feeling battered and weary. My clothes were all crumpled; and the memory of something horrible from the previous day was going around in my head. Yet I was alive, full of hope, full of good thoughts. On returning to my flat I felt none of the terrible dread that such a homecoming had held for me the day before.

On the staircase, above the araucaria plant, I bumped into the 'aunt', my landlady. Although I seldom set eyes on her, I was very fond of the kind soul. I was not best pleased to encounter her now, though. After all, I was bleary-eyed and a bit dishevelled; my hair was unkempt and I hadn't shaved. I wished her good morning and was on the point of going by. As a rule, she always respected my desire to remain alone and unnoticed, but today it really did seem that between me and the people around me a veil had been torn apart, or a barrier had fallen, for she stopped and laughed.

'You've been gadding about, Herr Haller. I don't suppose you got to bed at all last night. You must be feeling pretty weary!'

'Yes,' I said, and couldn't help laughing myself. 'Things got a bit lively last night and since I didn't want to lower the tone of your home I slept the night in a hotel. I hold the tranquillity and respectability of this place you inhabit in such high esteem that I sometimes feel very much like a foreign body in it.'

'Don't mock, Herr Haller.'

'Oh, I was only mocking myself.'

'That's just the thing you oughtn't to do. I won't have you feeling like a "foreign body" in my home. I want you to live as you please, get up to anything you like. I've had any number of very, very respectable lodgers in my time, gems of respectability, but none was quieter or less of a disturbance to us than you are. Now then, how about a cup of tea?'

I didn't say no. I was served tea in her lounge with its beautiful pictures and furniture, venerable objects of a past age. As we chatted a little, the kind woman, without actually asking, got to know this and that about my life and my ideas. She listened to me with that mixture of respect and motherly reluctance to take one wholly seriously that intelligent women reserve for the eccentricities of men. There was also talk of her nephew. In one of the adjoining rooms she showed me the latest thing he had been constructing in his spare time, a wireless set. The industrious young man, utterly fascinated by the idea of wireless communication, sat there of an evening, painstakingly assembling a machine of that sort; going down on his knees to worship the god of technology, the deity who after thousands of years has finally managed to discover and – in a highly imperfect manner – portray things that every serious thinker has always known about and put to more intelligent use. We talked about this since the aunt, who was a little bit religiously inclined, was not averse to discussing such matters. I told her that the ancient Indians had been fully cognisant of the omnipresence of all forces and actions. Technology had merely managed to make people in general aware of a fraction of this truth by constructing, as far as sound waves were concerned, an as yet terribly imperfect receiver and transmitter. However, the principal insight of that ancient body of knowledge, the fact that time was unreal, had so far escaped the notice of technicians. Of course, it too would eventually be 'discovered' and engineers would put their eager fingers to work on the problem. They would, perhaps very soon, discover that we are not only constantly surrounded by a flood of current, present-day images and happenings – in the way that now makes it possible to hear music from Paris or Berlin in Frankfurt or Zurich – but that everything that has ever happened is recorded and available in precisely the same way. With or without wires, with or without interfering noises off, we would one day no doubt be able to hear King Solomon or Walther von der Vogelweide speaking.* And, just like the beginnings of radio today, all this would, I said, only serve to make human beings surround themselves with an ever-more dense network of distraction and pointlessly fevered activity, thus deserting their true selves and destiny. However, rather than holding forth on these familiar topics in my usual embittered tone of voice, full of scorn for modern times and technology, I spoke in a playful, joking manner. The aunt smiled, and we sat for what must have been an hour together, contentedly drinking tea.

Having arranged to take the remarkable, beautiful girl from the Black Eagle out on Tuesday evening, I had considerable difficulty killing the time in between. And by the time Tuesday finally arrived it had become frighteningly clear to me just how important

* Walther von der Vogelweide (*c.*1170–1230) is the most important German lyric poet of the Middle Ages.

my relationship with the unknown girl was. Without being the least bit in love with her, I nonetheless thought of nothing but her, expected everything of her, was willing to sacrifice everything for her and lay it at her feet. I only needed to imagine her breaking our date, or possibly forgetting it, in order to realize what a state that would leave me in. The world would be empty again, one day as grey and worthless as the next. Again I would be surrounded by that whole terribly still, death-like atmosphere from which there was no escape except by cutting my own throat. And the last few days had done nothing to make this way out more appealing. The razor had lost none of its dread for me. This was precisely what I found so abhorrent: the fact that I was profoundly, agonizingly afraid of cutting my own throat, dreaded the thought of dying with a force just as wild, tenacious, self-protective and obstinate as if I had been the healthiest of human beings and my life a paradise. Fully aware of my state of mind, I recognized with merciless clarity that what made the pretty little dancer from the Black Eagle so important was this intolerable tension between my inability to go on living and my inability to die. She was the tiny little window, the minute chink of light in the dark cave of my fear. She was my salvation, my one way out into the open air. She had to teach me how to live or teach me how to die. With her firm and pretty hand she had to touch my frozen heart and by such vital contact either make it spring to life again or reduce it to ashes. How she had come by such powers, where she had acquired her ability to work magic, what the mysterious reasons were for her having become so profoundly important to me – these were all imponderables. Not that it mattered, for I had no desire to know. I no longer had the slightest desire for any kind of knowledge or insight. After all, that was precisely what I'd had my fill of. The very fact that I could see my own state of mind clearly and was conscious of it to such a degree was what was causing me the most acute and ignominious torment and shame.

I could see this chap, this Steppenwolf creature, before my eyes like a fly caught in a spider's web. I watched him moving closer to the point where his fate would be decided, watched him hanging there entangled and defenceless, the spider ready to close its jaws around him, but a rescuing hand seemingly just as near. I would have been capable of making the most intelligent and discerning observations about the circumstances and causes of my suffering, my mental ailment, my bedevilment and neurosis. Their mechanisms were quite transparent to me. However, knowledge and understanding were not what I needed. Instead, what I was desperately longing for was experience, decisive action, the cut and thrust of life.

Although I never once during those few days of waiting doubted that my friend would keep her word, I was nevertheless very agitated and uncertain on the day itself. Never in my whole life have I waited more impatiently for evening to arrive than on that day. And, while my impatience and the tension within me became almost unbearable, at the same time they did me a power of good. For someone like me, accustomed to leading such a sober life, for a long time now never having anything to wait for or look forward to, it was an unimaginably new and beautiful experience. To spend this whole day in a state of utter restlessness, anxiety and eager anticipation; rushing to and fro, picturing to myself in advance our encounter, our conversations and whatever else the evening together might bring; shaving and dressing for it (taking particular care over this with new shirt, new tie, new shoelaces) – all this was wonderful. What did I care who this shrewd and mysterious girl was or how she had managed to get involved with me? It didn't matter. She existed. A miracle had happened. I had once again found a human being and a new interest in living. All that mattered was to keep the relationship going, to surrender to this magnetic attraction, to follow this star.

What an unforgettable moment when I saw her again! Sitting

at a small table in the old, comfortably appointed restaurant, having needlessly booked in advance by phone, I was studying the menu. In the water jug in front of me were two beautiful orchids that I had bought for her. Though I had to wait quite a while for her I felt sure she would come and was no longer agitated. And now she did come, pausing at the coat stand and merely casting an attentive, somewhat quizzical look of her light-grey eyes at me by way of a greeting. Suspicious, I checked carefully on the waiter's behaviour towards her. Not a trace of familiarity, thank goodness. No, maintaining just the right degree of aloofness, he was politeness itself. And yet they knew each other; she addressed him as Emil.

When I gave her the orchids she laughed in delight. 'How sweet of you, Harry. You wanted to give me a present, didn't you, and weren't quite sure what to choose. Not knowing how entitled you were to go buying me something, you wondered whether I'd be offended, and in the end you opted for orchids, just some flowers, and yet mighty expensive ones. Well, thanks very much, but I ought incidentally to tell you without further ado that I don't want you buying me presents. I may earn my living from men, but I've no desire to be kept by you. But anyway, just look at you! How you've changed! I'd hardly have recognized you. The other day you looked like something just cut down from the gallows and now you are already almost a human being again. Have you carried out my orders, by the way?'

'What orders?'

'Can't you remember anything? What I mean is: have you now learned to do the foxtrot? You said there was nothing you would like more than to receive orders from me, nothing better than to obey them. Do you remember?'

'Indeed I do, and I stick by what I said. I meant it seriously.'

'And yet you still haven't learned how to dance?'

'What, that quickly? Is it possible in just a few days?'

'Of course. You can learn the foxtrot in an hour, the Boston in two. The tango takes longer, but you've absolutely no need of that.'

'But what I do need, after all this time, is to know your name!'

She looked at me for a while in silence.

'You may be able to guess it. It would please me no end if you could. Just pay attention and take a good look at me. Hasn't it occurred to you yet that I sometimes have a boy's face? Now, for instance?'

So it was. On now taking a close look at her face, I couldn't help thinking that she was right. It was that of a boy. And as I allowed myself to contemplate it for a minute or so, her face began to speak to me, reminding me of my own boyhood and of my then friend whose name had been Hermann. For a moment she seemed to have changed completely into this boy Hermann.

'You ought, if you were a boy, to be called Hermann,' I said in amazement.

'Who knows? Perhaps I am a boy, only in disguise,' she said playfully.

'Is your name Hermione?'

She nodded, beaming with joy at the fact that I had guessed correctly. The soup was just arriving and, as we started our meal, she began to take a childlike pleasure in everything. Of all the things that I liked and found fascinating about her, the most charming and idiosyncratic was her ability to switch from being deeply serious to extremely funny. Yet she remained entirely herself, just as gifted children do, showing no signs of strain. She was now funny for a while, teasing me about the foxtrot and even giving me the odd kick under the table. She was lavish in her praise of the food, remarked that I had gone to some trouble to look my best, but still found a great deal to criticize in my appearance.

Amid all this I asked her: 'How did you manage to look like a boy all at once, and get me to guess your name?'

'Oh, you managed all that on your own. Can't you get it into your head, my learned friend, that you've taken a liking to me and feel that I matter because I'm like a kind of mirror for you, because something in me responds to you and understands you? Actually, all human beings ought to be such mirrors for one another, responding and corresponding to each other in this way, but the thing is that cranks like you are oddities. You easily get led astray, bewitched into thinking that you can no longer see or read anything in the eyes of other people, that there is nothing there that concerns you any more. And when a crank of your sort suddenly discovers a face again that really looks at him, in which he senses something akin to a response and an affinity, it naturally fills him with joy.'

'You know all there is to know, Hermione,' I cried in amazement. 'It's exactly as you say. And yet you're so utterly different from me! You're my opposite, after all, you have everything that I lack.'

'That's how it looks to you,' she said laconically, 'and it's as well it does.'

And now a heavy cloud of seriousness passed over her face, which really was a kind of magic mirror for me. All at once her whole face spoke only of seriousness now, of tragedy emerging as it were from the hollow, fathomless eyes of a mask. Slowly, as if word after word had to be prized from her lips, she said:

'Mind you don't forget what you told me, my dear. You told me to give you orders and that you'd be delighted to obey them all. Don't forget! I must tell you, Harry my boy, that just as you feel that my face responds to you, that there is something in me that comes halfway to meet you and inspires you with confidence, I feel exactly the same thing with regard to you. When I saw you coming into the Black Eagle recently, so weary and absent-minded, almost having departed this world already, I immediately sensed: there's someone who will obey me; he's just longing for me to order him about. And I intend to do just that. That's why I spoke to you, that's why we've become friends.'

She uttered these words in such deadly earnest, they poured forth from the depths of her soul with such force that I couldn't fully grasp their meaning. I tried to calm her down, to take her mind off the subject, but she merely shook off my attempt with a twitch of her eyebrows, gave me a forceful look and continued in a tone of voice devoid of all warmth: 'You'd better keep your word, my lad, I'm telling you, otherwise you'll be sorry. You'll receive lots of orders from me, and you'll obey them – orders that are so appealing, so agreeable that you'll be only too delighted to obey them. And at the end, Harry, you'll carry out my final order too.'

'I shall,' I said, half surrendering to her will. 'What will you order me to do finally?' I asked, although, God knows why, I already sensed what she had in mind.

Trembling, as if suffering a slight fit of shivering, she seemed slowly to awake from her deep trance. Her eyes remained fixed on me. All of a sudden her mood became even more sombre.

'The sensible thing to do would be not to tell you. But I don't want to be sensible, Harry, not this time, anything but sensible. Listen carefully. You'll hear what it is, then forget it again. It will make you laugh, then make you cry. Take note, my lad. We're going to play for high stakes. It's a matter of life and death, dear brother. And I want to lay my cards on the table even before we begin.'

How beautiful her face looked as she said this, how ethereal! A knowing sadness lay coolly and clearly on the surface of her eyes, eyes that seemed to have endured every sorrow it is possible to imagine and to have acquiesced in it. Words came from her mouth with difficulty, as if she had a speech impediment. She spoke roughly, as people do whose faces have been numbed by severe frost, yet – in apparent contradiction to the expression on her face and the tone of her voice – between her lips, in the corners of her mouth and in the movements of the tip of her tongue, only rarely caught sight of, all was sweet, playful, free-flowing sensuality and intense carnal desire. A short curl was hanging down on to her smooth, motionless forehead and the corner of her brow where the curl rested was the source from which that wave of boyishness, of hermaphroditic charm flowed from time to time like the breath of life. I listened to her full of anxiety, yet as if sedated, only half there.

'You are fond of me,' she said, 'for the reasons I've already mentioned. It's because I've made inroads into your isolation, thrown you a lifeline when you were on the very threshold of hell, and reawakened you to life. But I want more from you, much more. I want to make you fall in love with me. No, don't try to contradict me; let me have my say. I can sense that you're very fond of me, that you're grateful for what I've done, but you aren't in love with me. I intend to make you be in love with me. After all, it's my job: I earn a living by being able to make men fall in love with me. But mark you, I'm not doing this because I find you of all people particularly charming. I'm not in love with you, Harry, any more than you are in love with me. But I need you, as you need me. You need me now, at this moment, because you are desperately in need of someone to push you into the water and bring you back to life. You need me in order to learn how to dance, to learn how to laugh, to learn how to live. However, I need you for something that is also very important and beautiful – not today, but later. When you are in love with me I shall give you my final order, and you'll obey, which will be a good thing for you and for me.'

She lifted one of the brownish-mauve, green-veined orchids a little in the water jar and, bending her head over it for a moment, stared at the flower.

'It won't be easy for you, but you will do it. You will carry out my order *and will kill me*. That's what I have in mind. Don't ask me anything more.'

Still gazing at the orchid, she fell silent. Her face relaxed and, like the bud of a flower unfolding its petals, all pressure and tension went from it. Suddenly there was a delightful smile on her lips, whereas her eyes, as if spellbound, remained frozen for a moment. And now she shook her head with its little boyish curl and, taking a sip of water, suddenly became aware again of being in the middle of a meal and tucked into the food with a gleeful appetite.

Having clearly heard her eerie speech word for word, having even guessed her 'final order' well before she uttered it, I was no longer horrified by the statement: 'You will kill me.' Everything she said sounded convincing to me, destined to happen. I accepted it without resistance and yet, despite the horrifyingly earnest manner in which she had stated it all, none of it struck me as fully real or serious. One part of my being soaked up her words, believing them; another part, nodding sagely, noted that even the ever so clever, sane and confident Hermione had her semi-conscious moments of wild fantasy. Scarcely had she finished speaking before a layer of unreality and ineffectuality descended on the whole scene.

I, at any rate, found it impossible to leap back into the realm of reality and probability, as Hermione had done, with the ease of a tightrope-walker.

'So one day I'm going to kill you?' I asked, still slightly in a trance, whereas she was already laughing again and busily engaged in cutting up the roast duck on her plate.

'Of course,' she replied with a dismissive nod. 'But enough of that, it's time to eat. Order me a little more green salad, Harry, there's a dear. What's wrong with you, have you no appetite? I think you need to learn all those things that come naturally to other people, even the enjoyment of food. Just look at this, for instance. It's the leg of a duck, dear boy, and easing the lovely light-coloured flesh from the bone is an act of celebration. You have to savour the excitement of it, feel with all your heart as thankful for it as a man in love does when first helping his girl-friend out of her jacket. Do you see? No? You're a dunce. Pay attention, I'll give you a bit of this lovely duck leg, then you'll see. There, open your mouth. – Oh, what a silly fool you are! I don't know, now he goes sneaking a look at the other people, afraid that they might see him taking a titbit from my fork! Don't worry, you prodigal son, I'm not going to show you up. But you really are a poor devil if you need the permission of other people before you can enjoy yourself.'

The scene just before this seemed more and more divorced from reality. It was increasingly difficult to believe that only minutes ago these eyes of hers had been staring at me so gravely and frighteningly. In this respect, alas, Hermione was like life itself, forever fickle as the moment, never predictable in advance. Now she was eating, and the duck leg and the salad, the gateau and the liqueur were taken seriously, objects to rejoice in and pass judgement on, to discuss and go into flights of fancy about. Each plate that was taken away marked the beginning of a new chapter. This woman, who had seen through me so comprehen-sively, who seemed to know more of life than any wise men, was so skilled in behaving as a child, so adept at playing whatever little game life momentarily offered, that I automatically became her pupil. Whether it was wisdom of the highest order or the simplest form of naivety, it did not matter. Anyone knowing how to live for the moment, to live in the present as she did, treasuring every little wayside flower with loving care and deriving value from every playful little instant, had nothing to fear from life. How was I supposed to believe that this cheerful child with her healthy appetite and her playful attitude to wining and dining was at one and the same time a dreamer, a hysterical woman wishing herself dead, or a vigilant, calculating woman who deliberately and cold-bloodedly intended to make me fall in love with her and become her slave? That couldn't possibly be the case. No, she was simply such a total creature of the moment that she was exposed not just to any amusing idea that occurred to her, but equally to any fleeting dark tremor from remote depths of the soul. And she lived both to the full.

The Hermione I was seeing for the second time today knew all there was to know about me. It seemed impossible to me that I could ever keep anything secret from her. It might be that she had not fully understood my intellectual life, would not perhaps be able to keep up with me where my interests in music, in Goethe, in Novalis or Baudelaire were concerned – but even this was doubtful; she would probably have no difficulty with these things either. And even if she couldn't – what, I asked myself, remained of my 'intellectual life'? Wasn't it all in ruins, devoid of meaning? But as for my other, personal problems and interests, she would understand them all, of that I had no doubt. Soon I would talk to her about Steppenwolf, about the Tract, about each and every thing that until now had existed only for me, matters I had never spoken a word about to any human being. I could not resist making a start on this straight away.

'Hermione,' I said, 'something really odd happened to me the other day. A stranger gave me a little printed booklet, the kind of cheap pamphlet you get at fairgrounds, and in it I found the whole story of my life, everything of importance to me, described in exact detail. Don't you think that's remarkable?'

'And what's the title of the booklet?' she asked casually.

'It's called "On Steppenwolf: A Tract".'

'Oh, "Steppenwolf" is marvellous! And that's what you're supposed to be? You are Steppenwolf?'

'Yes, it's me. I'm somebody who is half human and half wolf, or imagines he is.'

She didn't respond. As she gazed intensely, searchingly into my eyes and inspected my hands, the look on her face was for a moment deeply serious and sombrely passionate again, as it had been before. I felt I could guess what she was thinking. She was wondering whether I was wolf enough to carry out her 'final order'.

'Of course it's something you've imagined,' she said, reverting suddenly to her cheerful self. 'Or, if you like, a poetic fancy. But there is something to it. You're not a wolf today, but when you walked into that ballroom the other day, looking like a zombie, there was indeed something of the beast about you. That's exactly what appealed to me.'

An idea must suddenly have occurred to her because she interrupted herself, then added, as if shocked: 'Words like "beast" and "predator" sound so stupid. We shouldn't talk of animals like that. I grant you they are often frightening, but they are nonetheless truer than human beings.'

'Truer? What do you mean by that?'

'Well, just take a look at any animal, a cat, a dog, a bird or even one of those beautiful big creatures in the zoo, a puma, say, or a giraffe. Surely you can't help noticing that they are all true, that not a single animal is at a loss to know what it should be doing or how it should behave. They have no desire to make an impression. They are not play-acting. They are as they are, like stones and flowers, or like stars in the sky. Do you see?'

I did.

'Animals are usually sad,' she continued. 'And when human beings feel very sad, not because they've got toothache or have lost money, but because for once in a while they sense what everything, the whole of life, is like and are truly sad, then they always look a bit like an animal. At such times they look sad, but truer and more beautiful than they normally look, believe me. And that's how you looked, Steppenwolf, the first time I saw you.'

'So, Hermione, and what do you think about that book with the description of me in it?'

'Oh, you know, I'm not one to spend all my time thinking. We'll talk about it some other time. You can simply give it me to read one day. No, on second thoughts, if I should ever get round to reading again, give me one of the books you've written yourself.'

Asking for some coffee, she seemed inattentive for a while and absent-minded, but then, having apparently thought her way through to some satisfactory conclusion, she suddenly beamed at me.

'Hey, listen!' she exclaimed joyfully. 'It's come to me now!'

'What has?'

'What I was saying about the foxtrot. I couldn't get it out of my head the whole time. Tell me, have you got a room that the two of us can dance in for an hour or so every now and then? It needn't be very big, that doesn't matter, but there mustn't be anyone living below you who is just the sort to come up and make a scene if the ceiling starts to shake a bit above. Yes? That's fine then, very good. In that case you can learn to dance at home.'

'Yes,' I said shyly, 'so much the better. But I thought you needed music to do it to.'

'Of course you do. Listen, you'll buy your own music, at most it will only cost as much as paying some woman for a course of dancing lessons. You're saving on the teaching. I'll do that myself. That way we'll have music as often as we want, and we can keep the gramophone into the bargain.'

'The gramophone?'

'Yes, of course. You simply buy one of those small gramophones and a few dance records to go with it . . .'

'Splendid,' I cried, 'and if you really succeed in teaching me to dance, then you can have the gramophone as your fee. Agreed?'

Although I said this with considerable force, it didn't come from the heart. I couldn't imagine a contraption like that, for which I had absolutely no liking, in my study with its books, and there were lots of things about dancing that I also objected to. I had thought I might give it a try one day if the opportunity arose, although I told myself I was far too old and stiff now ever to learn properly. However, embarking on it straight away like this was a bit too swift and sudden for my liking. Everything in me combined to resist the idea, all the objections I, as an old, spoiled connoisseur of music, had to gramophones, jazz and all kinds of modern dance music. To expect me to tolerate the sound of American hit-tunes in my room, my refuge, my thinker's den with its volumes of Novalis and Jean Paul, and to dance to them, was simply too much to ask. But it wasn't just anyone doing the asking. It was Hermione, and it was her business to give orders. It fell to me to obey. And I obeyed, of course I did.

We met in a café the next afternoon. When I arrived, Hermione, already sitting there drinking tea, smiled and showed me a newspaper in which she had discovered my name. It was one of those reactionary, mud-slinging rags from my home country that from time to time would publish defamatory articles against me. I had been an opponent of the war as it was taking place, and when it was over I had occasionally urged calm and patience, the need to behave humanely and self-critically, while combating the nationalistic hate campaign that was becoming more shrill, mindless and unrestrained by the day. Now here was yet another attack of that sort, badly written, partly the work of the editor himself, partly cobbled together by lifting passages from the many similar pieces that papers sympathetic to the same line had already published. It is well known that nobody writes as badly as those seeking to defend ideologies that have outlived their time. None ply their trade with less effort or attention to detail. Having read the piece, Hermione had learned that Harry Haller was a harmful pest, a wretch without any allegiance to the Fatherland. And it went without saying that the Fatherland was bound to be in a sorry state as long as people like him, with ideas like his, were tolerated, and the nation's youth was being taught to embrace sentimental humanistic ideas instead of being trained to take warlike revenge on the hereditary foe.*

'Is this you?' Hermione asked, pointing to my name. 'If so, Harry, it seems you haven't half made some enemies. Does it bother you?'

I read a few lines. It was the same old stuff. For years I had been familiar with every single one of the hackneyed phrases used to defame me, to the point where I was sick and tired of them.

'No,' I said, 'it doesn't bother me, I got used to it long ago. On a few occasions I've expressed the view that all nations and indeed all individual human beings, instead of rocking themselves to sleep by mulling over false political questions as to who was the "guilty party", ought to be taking a searching look at themselves, asking to what extent they themselves, by their mistakes, their failure to act and their habitual bad practices have a share in the responsibility for the war and all the rest of the world's miseries. Only in this way, I argued, could the next war perhaps be avoided. Of course, the reason they can't forgive me for saying this is that they themselves are totally innocent. The Kaiser, the generals, the big industrialists, the politicians, the press – none of them are in the least to blame, none of them is guilty of anything! You might think all is wonderfully well with the world, if it weren't for the fact that over ten million slaughtered men are lying buried in the ground. And look, Hermione, even if articles full of smears like this no longer have the power to annoy me, they do sometimes make me sad. Two thirds of my fellow Germans read newspapers of this kind, every morning and night they read

* The 'Erbfeind', that is to say, France, traditionally regarded by the Germans as their arch rival and enemy.

articles written in these strident tones. They are being manipulated every day, admonished, incited, made to feel anger and discontent. And the aim and purpose of it all is yet again war; the next, coming war, which will probably be even more horrific than this last one was. All this is clear and simple enough for anybody to grasp; anyone could reach the same conclusion after merely an hour's reflection. But nobody wants to, nobody wants to avoid the next war, none of them want to spare themselves and their children the next bloody slaughter of millions, if the price they have to pay is to reflect for an hour, to look into their own hearts and ask to what extent they themselves have a share in and are responsible for the chaos and evil in the world. None of them are prepared to do this! And that's the reason things will go on as before. Day after day, thousands of people are eagerly engaged in preparations for the next war. Ever since I realized this, it has had a paralysing effect on me, reducing me to despair. I have no Fatherland left and no ideals, all that kind of thing is just window-dressing for the gentlemen who are preparing the next round of slaughter. There is no point in thinking, saying or writing anything humane; there is no point in turning over good thoughts in one's head because for every two or three people who do so there are, day in, day out, a thousand newspapers, magazines, speeches, public and secret meetings that are all striving to achieve the opposite, and succeeding too.'

Hermione had been listening sympathetically.

'Yes,' she now said, 'you're right, I agree. Of course there will be another war; you don't need to read the newspapers to know that. And of course it's something you can feel sad about. But it's not worth it. It's just the same as someone feeling sad about the fact that, whatever they do to combat it, they are despite all their efforts inevitably going to die one day. When you are fighting death, Harry, dear, the cause you are fighting for is always fine, noble, splendid and honourable, and the same is true of the fight against war. However, it's always hopeless too, like tilting at windmills.'

'That may be true,' I exclaimed heatedly, 'but by pointing to such truths as the fact that we are all bound to die before long and therefore nothing matters a jot you simply reduce the whole of life to something shallow and idiotic. So, what are we supposed to do? Just jettison everything, give up all our thought, all our striving, all our humanity, allow ambition and money to go on ruling us and wait over a glass of beer for the next mobilization to take place?'

The look Hermione now gave me was remarkable, full of amusement, full of mockery, mischievousness and comradely solidarity, yet at the same time so weighty, knowledgeable and immeasurably serious!

'That's not what I mean you should do,' she said, sounding just like a mother. 'And anyway, knowing that the fight is bound to fail doesn't make your life shallow and idiotic. Life is much shallower, Harry, if you are fighting for something good and ideal in the belief that you are bound to achieve it. Are ideals necessarily there to be achieved? Do we as human beings live only in order to abolish death? No, we live to fear death, then to love it again, and it's precisely because of death that the brief candle of our lives burns so beautifully for a while. You are a child, Harry. Now do what you're told to and come with me. We have a lot to do today. I'm not going to worry about the war and the press any more today. What about you?'

I was certainly in no mood to either.

We went together – it was our first walk with each other in town – to a music shop. There we looked at gramophones, opening and closing their lids, and getting the shopkeeper to play them for us. When we had found one that was perfectly suitable, nice, and cheap, I wanted to buy it, but Hermione was determined to take much longer over it. She held me back, insisting that I first visit a second shop with her, where I had to look at and listen to all systems and sizes from the dearest to the cheapest. Only then did she agree to go back to the first shop and buy the set we had found there.

'You see,' I said. 'We could have saved ourselves the trouble.'

'Do you think? And then tomorrow we might have seen the same gramophone on display in another shop window for twenty francs less. And anyway, it's fun to go shopping, and everything that is fun should be enjoyed to the full. You still have a lot to learn.'

With the help of a porter, we took our purchase to my lodgings.

Hermione inspected my living room closely, praising the stove and the couch, trying out the chairs, picking up some books and standing for quite some time in front of the photograph of my loved one. We had set down the gramophone between piles of books on a chest of drawers. And now my lessons began. Putting on a foxtrot, she demonstrated the first few steps for me, then, taking me by the hand, she started to lead me in the dance. I tried obediently to match her steps, but I kept bumping into chairs. I was listening to her commands but not understanding them, and since I was just as clumsy as I was keen to do what I was told, I kept treading on her toes. After the second dance she threw herself on to the couch, laughing like a child.

'My God, how stiff you are! Just take a few steps forwards as you do when going for a walk. There's absolutely no need to strain. I can hardly believe it, you've even worked up a sweat already! Come on, we'll take a rest for five minutes. Look here, once you can do it, dancing is just as easy as thinking. And it's much easier to learn. Perhaps now you won't get quite so impatient when people are reluctant to learn how to think, but instead call Herr Haller a traitor to his country and are willing to allow the next war to happen without lifting a finger against it.'

She left after an hour, telling me not to worry, I was sure to be better at it next time. This was not my view. I was very disappointed with my own stupidity and clumsiness. It seemed to me that I hadn't learned a thing during the last hour and I didn't believe a second attempt would be any better. No, dancing called for the sort of qualities I totally lacked: gaiety, innocence, nonchalance, verve. Ah well, wasn't that what I'd known all along?

But lo and behold, it was actually better the next time. I even began to enjoy it and, at the end of the lesson, Hermione claimed I could now do the foxtrot. However, when on that basis she said I must go dancing with her in a restaurant the next day, I took fright and protested vehemently. She coolly reminded me that I had vowed to obey her and asked me to meet her for tea next day in the Hotel Libra.

I spent that evening sitting at home, wanting to read but unable to do so. I was afraid of the next day. It horrified me to think that I, an old, shy and sensitive misfit, should not only visit one of those dreary modern tea-dance places where they played jazz, but also, without yet being able to do a thing, put in an appearance on the dance floor among strangers. And I confess to laughing at myself and feeling ashamed at my own behaviour when, alone in the silence of my study, after winding up the gramophone and setting it in motion, I quietly rehearsed the steps of my foxtrot in my stockinged feet.

The next day in the Hotel Libra there was a small band playing, and tea and whisky were being served. I tried to bribe Hermione by offering her cakes; I tried inviting her to share a bottle of fine wine, but she would not relent.

'You're not here to enjoy yourself today. It's a dancing lesson.'

I had to dance with her two or three times. In between dances she introduced me to the saxophonist, a swarthy, handsome young man of Spanish or South American origin who, so she said, could play every instrument and speak every language in the world. This señor seemed to know Hermione very well and to be great friends with her. Standing in front of him were two saxophones of different sizes, which he played alternately while attentively and happily running his fiery black eyes over the people dancing. To my own amazement I felt something akin to jealousy of this harmless, good-looking musician, not the jealousy of a lover, since there was absolutely no question of love between me and Hermione, but rather the jealousy that troubles the mind of a friend. It seemed to me that he was not really worthy of the interest in, indeed reverence for him that she showed by singling him out so conspicuously for special favour. Pretty strange people I'm being expected to mix with, I reflected sullenly.

Then Hermione was invited to dance time and again. I remained sitting on my own at the tea table, listening to the music, the sort of music I had until now been unable to stand. Good God, I thought, I'm now being initiated into and expected to feel at home in a place like this, a world that is so strange and abhorrent to me, a world that until now I've taken such care to avoid and so profoundly despised as a world of layabouts and pleasure-seekers, this sleek, typecast world of marble-top tables, jazz music, cocottes and commercial travellers! Feeling depressed, I gulped down my tea and stared at the semi-chic crowd on the dance floor. My eyes were drawn to two beautiful girls, both good dancers. Full of admiration and envy, I watched as they swept lithely and appealingly, gaily and confidently across the floor.

Then Hermione reappeared. She was dissatisfied with me. I wasn't here to pull faces like that, she said, telling me off, or to sit at the tea table without budging. Would I mind stirring myself, please, and going for a dance? What did I mean, I didn't know anyone? That was quite unnecessary. Weren't there any girls there at all that I liked?

I pointed out the more beautiful one of the two to her, who happened to be standing close to us. With her short, strong blonde hair and her full, womanly arms she looked enchanting in her pretty little velvet skirt. Hermione insisted I should go immediately and ask her for a dance. I desperately tried to resist.

'Don't you see, I can't!' I said sadly. 'Of course if I were a good-looking young chap, but a stiff old fogey like me who can't even dance, well she'd just laugh at me!'

Hermione looked at me contemptuously.

'And whether *I* laugh at you or not is, I suppose, all the same to you. What a coward you are! Anyone approaching a girl risks being laughed at, it's the stake you pay to enter the game. So take the risk, Harry, and if the worst comes to the worst simply get laughed at. Otherwise I'll lose all faith in your willingness to obey my commands.'

She didn't relent. Having apprehensively got to my feet, I was walking towards the beautiful girl just as the music began again.

'Actually, I'm not free,' she said, looking at me curiously with her big fresh eyes, 'but my partner seems to be caught up at the bar. All right, come on.'

Putting my arms around her, I danced the first few steps, still amazed that she hadn't sent me packing. Then, having noticed already what a hopeless beginner I was, she took over the lead. She danced wonderfully well, and I was swept along by her momentum. Forgetting for a few moments all the rules I'd been taught, I simply drifted with the tide. I could feel the taut hips, the swift, supple knees of my partner and, looking into her youthful, radiant face, I confessed that today was the first time I had danced in my life. She smiled and encouraged me, responding with marvellous suppleness to the looks of delight in my eyes and my flattering remarks, not with words but with gentle, enchanting movements that brought us all the more enticingly close together. Holding her tight by my right hand just above the waist, I joyfully and zealously followed the movements of her legs, her arms, her shoulders. To my amazement, I never once trod on her toes. When the music stopped we both stood there clapping until they played the dance once more and I, enamoured, again went through the ritual with zeal and devotion.

When the dance was over, all too soon, the beautiful girl in velvet withdrew and suddenly Hermione, who had been watching us, was standing next to me.

'Have you noticed something?' she asked, laughing appreciatively. 'Have you discovered that women's legs aren't table legs? Well, good for you! You can do the foxtrot now, thank God. Tomorrow we'll make a start on the Boston, then in three weeks' time there's a masked ball in the Globe Rooms.'

There was a break in the dancing now and we had returned to our seats. Señor Pablo, the good-looking young saxophonist, came over too and, after nodding to us, sat down next to Hermione. He seemed to be very good friends with her, but I must admit I didn't take to the man at all that first time we were together. He was handsome, undeniably so, both in looks and stature, but that apart I couldn't detect any great merit in him. Even his supposed multilingualism turned out to be no great achievement since he didn't really speak at all, just words like 'please', 'thanks', 'indeed', 'certainly', 'hello' and the like, though he did, it is true, know these in several languages. No, he didn't say a thing, our Señor Pablo, and he didn't exactly seem to think a great deal either, this handsome caballero. His business was playing the saxophone in the jazz band, and he seemed to fulfil his professional obligations with love and passion. When the band was playing he would sometimes clap his hands all of a sudden or indulge in other outbursts of enthusiasm, such as loudly breaking into song with words like 'oh oh oh oh, ha ha, hello!' Otherwise, however, he clearly lived only in order to appeal to women, to sport the latest fashions in collars and ties, and also to wear lots of rings on his fingers. In his case, conversation took the form of sitting at our table, smiling at us, looking at his wrist-watch and rolling cigarettes, at which he was highly skilled. Behind his dark, handsome, half-cast eyes and under his black locks there lurked no secret romance, no problems, no thoughts. When observed at close quarters, this good-looking exotic demi-god turned out to be nothing more than a happy and somewhat spoiled boy who was agreeably well mannered. I talked to him about his instrument and about tone colours in jazz. He must have realized that in matters musical I was an old hand, appreciative and knowledgeable, but he didn't respond. While I, out of politeness to him or actually to Hermione, embarked on a sort of theoretical justification of jazz on musical grounds, he just smiled his harmless smile as if oblivious to me and the effort I was making. I suppose he was totally ignorant of the fact that there had been other kinds of music before jazz and apart from it. He was nice, nice and well behaved, his large, vacant eyes smiling sweetly, but there seemed to be nothing that he and I had in common. Nothing that might be important or sacred to him could also be so to me; we came from opposite ends of the earth; there wasn't a word in our respective languages that we shared. (Subsequently, however, Hermione told me something remarkable. She said that after this conversation Pablo had asked her, whatever she did, to take real care in her dealings with 'that chap' because he was, as he put it, so very unhappy. And when she asked what made him think this he had said: 'Poor, poor chap. Look at his eyes! Can't laugh, he can't.')

When black-eyed Pablo had taken leave of us and the music started up again, Hermione got to her feet. 'You could dance with me again now, Harry. Or have you had enough?'

Now, when dancing with her too, I was lighter, freer on my feet and more cheerful, though not as carefree and unselfcon-scious as with the other girl. Hermione got me to lead and, as light and gentle as a petal, adjusted her movements to suit mine. With her too I now discovered and experienced all those beautiful sensations, as her body from time to time closed on me, from time to time retreated. She too had the scent of woman and love about her; her dance too was a gentle, intimate song, the sweetly alluring song of sex, yet I was unable to respond to all this freely and serenely, could not totally forget myself and surrender. I was far too close to Hermione. She was a companion to me, a sister, a kindred spirit. She was like me and like my boyhood friend Hermann, the dreamer and poet who had so enthusiastically shared in my intellectual and spiritual pursuits and escapades.

'I know,' she said afterwards when I spoke of this. 'You don't need to tell me. I do mean to make you fall in love with me one day, but there is no rush. For the time being we will remain companions. We are two people hoping to become close friends because we have recognized each other for what we are. Let's now learn from one another, play with one another. I'll show you my little theatre, I'll teach you to dance, to experience a bit of happiness and foolishness, and you'll reveal your ideas to me and some of your knowledge.'

'Ah, Hermione, there's not much to reveal. It's clear you know far more than me. What a remarkable person you are, lass. There's nothing about me you don't understand, you're a step ahead of me in every respect. Can I possibly mean anything to you? Surely you must find me boring?'

Her eyes darkening, she looked down at the ground.

'I don't like to hear you talk like that. Think of the evening when you first came across me and I became your companion. You had been living a tormented life, isolated from others; you were washed up, desperate. Why do you think I was able to understand you then, to recognize you for what you were?'

'Why, Hermione? Tell me.'

'Because I am like you. Because I'm just as lonely as you and just as incapable as you are of loving and taking life, my fellow human beings or myself seriously. There are always a few people like this, as you know, who make the highest possible demands on life and have a hard time coming to terms with the stupidity and coarseness of it.'

'You, you!' I cried, deeply amazed. 'I understand you, my friend, I understand you as no one else does. And yet you are a mystery to me. You haven't the slightest difficulty in coping with life; you have this admirable reverence for the little things, the minor enjoyments it offers; you have mastered the art of living to such a degree. How can you suffer at the hands of life? How can you despair?'

'I don't despair, Harry. But, suffering at the hands of life, oh yes, that's something I'm experienced at. You are amazed that I'm not happy since I can, after all, dance and am well versed in the superficial aspects of life. And I, dear friend, am amazed that you are so disappointed with life since you, after all, feel at home with precisely the things that life at its finest and most profound has to offer: things of the mind, the arts, ideas. That's why we attracted one another, that's why we are kindred spirits. I'm going to teach you to dance, to play, to smile and still not to be satisfied. And I'm going to learn from you how to think and know things, and still not be satisfied. Don't you know that we are both children of the devil?'

'So we are, yes. The devil – that's our intellectual faculty, our mind – and we are its unfortunate children. We have fallen away from nature and are now left dangling in the void. But now I'm reminded that in the Steppenwolf tract that I told you about there is a passage explaining that it is only a figment of Harry's imagination when he thinks he possesses two souls or consists of two personalities. Every human being, it says there, is made up of ten, of a hundred, of a thousand souls.'

'I like that very much,' Hermione exclaimed. 'In you, for

instance, the intellectual faculty is very highly developed, but on the other hand, when it comes to all sorts of little skills needed in life, you are backward. Harry the thinker is a hundred years old, but Harry the dancer is barely half a day old as yet. He is the one we now need to foster, and all his tiny little brothers who are just as small, stupid and ungrown-up as he is.'

She looked at me with a smile on her face, then, in a changed tone of voice, quietly asked:

'And how did you like Maria, then?'

'Maria? Who is that?'

'She's the one you were dancing with, a beautiful girl, a very beautiful girl. As far as I could tell you fell for her a bit.'

'Do you know her, then?'

'Oh yes, we know each other really well. Do you care that much about her?'

'I liked her, and I was glad that she showed so much consideration for my attempts at dancing.'

'Well, if that's all there is to it! You ought to court her a bit, Harry. She is very pretty, and such a good dancer. And you have fallen for her too, haven't you? I think you'll be successful.'

'Oh, I've no ambitions in that direction.'

'Now there you are telling a bit of a lie. I know, of course, that somewhere or other in this wide world you've got a lover. You see her once every six months, and then only to fall out with her. It's very sweet of you, wanting to remain faithful to this strange girlfriend, but forgive me if I can't take the whole affair quite so seriously. And anyway, I have my suspicions that you treat love in general as a terribly serious matter. You may do that, for all I care, go on loving in your idealized fashion as much as you like, it's your business. My business is to see to it that you learn to master life's little, simple skills and games a bit better. In that sphere I am your teacher, and I'll be a better teacher for you than your ideal beloved was, you can depend on that! What you're desperately in need of after all this time, Steppenwolf, is to sleep with a good-looking girl again.'

'Hermione,' I exclaimed in a pained voice. 'Just look at me. I'm an old man!'

'No you're not, you're a little boy. And just as you were too idle to learn to dance until it was almost too late, so you've been too idle to learn how to make love. You're certainly capable of an excellent performance as a lover in the ideal, tragic mode, I've no doubt of that, my friend, and all credit to you. But now you're also going to learn to love a bit in a normal human way. You see, we've already made a start. Pretty soon we'll be able to let you loose at a ball, but you need to learn the Boston first. We'll begin on that tomorrow. I'll come at three o'clock. How did you like the music here, by the way?'

'It was excellent.'

'You see, you've made progress there too, learned something new. Until now you couldn't stand all this dance music and jazz; it wasn't serious or deep enough for you, but now you've realized that there is no need to take it seriously at all, though it can be very pleasant and delightful. Incidentally, the whole band would be nothing without Pablo. He's the one who gives them the lead, puts some spark into them.'

*

In the same way that the gramophone had a harmful effect on the ascetic, intellectual ambiance of my study, and the alien American dance tunes represented a disturbing, indeed destructive, intrusion into my refined musical world, so new, daunting, disruptive elements were forcing their way into my hitherto so sharply defined and so strictly secluded life. The doctrine of the thousand souls expounded in the Steppenwolf tract and endorsed by Hermione was correct. In addition to all the old ones, every day revealed a few new souls within me, all creating a fuss and making demands. Now I could see as clearly as daylight what a delusion my previous personality had been. The only things I had regarded as at all valid were the few skills and activities I happened to be strong in. I had painted the picture of a Harry and lived the life of a Harry who was in fact nothing but a very sensitively trained specialist in literature, music and philosophy. All the rest of myself, the whole remaining confused assemblage of skills, instincts and aspirations, I had felt to be a burden and had filed away under the label Steppenwolf.

Yet, far from being a pleasant and amusing adventure, my conversion to the truth, the dissolution of my personality, was on the contrary often bitterly painful, often almost unbearable. In the surroundings of my room, attuned to other frequencies, the gramophone often sounded truly devilish. And at times, when dancing my one-steps in some fashionable restaurant amid all the elegant playboys and confidence tricksters, it seemed to me I was a traitor to everything in life that had ever been honourable and sacred to me. If only Hermione had left me alone for a week I would have made a swift getaway from all these laborious and ludicrous experiments in living the high life. But Hermione was always there. I may not have seen her every day, but I was constantly seen by her, directed, supervised, assessed by her. She could even tell from the expressions on my face what angry thoughts of rebellion and escape were going through my mind, but she merely smiled in response.

As the destruction of what I used earlier to call my personality progressed I began to understand why, despite all my despair, I had been bound to fear death so terribly. I started to realize that this appalling and shameful dread of dying was also a part of my old, bourgeois, inauthentic existence. This previous Harry Haller, the gifted writer, the connoisseur of Goethe and Mozart, the author of critically acclaimed reflections on the metaphysics of art, on genius and tragedy, and on humanity, this melancholy hermit in his cell crammed full of books was now being exposed, step by step, to self-criticism, and found wanting on every count. True, this gifted and interesting Herr Haller had preached reason and humanity, had protested against the brutality of the war, but he had not, while the war was taking place, allowed himself to be lined up against a wall and shot, which would have been the logical outcome of his ideas. Instead, he had arrived at some sort of accommodation, needless to say an extremely respectable and noble accommodation, but when all is said and done a compromise nonetheless. What's more, though he had opposed power and exploitation, he had more than a few securities issued by industrial enterprises deposited at his bank, and he had no qualms whatsoever when spending the interest paid on them. And that is how things stood in every respect. Harry Haller may have succeeded wonderfully well in passing himself off as an idealist scornful of all worldly things, a nostalgic hermit and rancorous prophet, but at bottom he was a bourgeois who found the kind of life Hermione lived reprehensible, who fretted about the evenings he was wasting in the restaurant and the amount of cash he was squandering there. He had a bad conscience and, far from yearning to be liberated and fulfilled, was on the contrary dearly longing to return to those cosy days when all his intellectual dabbling still gave him pleasure and brought him fame. In this he was no different from the newspaper readers he so despised and derided who, because it was less painful than learning the harsh lesson of all they had endured, longed to return to those ideal times before the war. Ugh, he was enough to make you sick, this Herr Haller! And yet I still clung to him, or to what remained of the already crumbling mask he had worn, his flirtation with things intellectual, his bourgeois dread of all things random and contingent (of which death was an example too). And I scornfully and enviously drew comparisons between the new, developing Harry, the rather shy and comical dilettante of the dance halls, and the pseudo-ideal image of the earlier Harry, in which he, the new Harry, had now discovered all the embarrassing features that had so disturbed him at the time in the professor's Goethe engraving. He himself, the old Harry, had been just such a bourgeois-style idealized Goethe, an intellectual hero with a look in his eyes that was all too distinguished, radiating grandeur, high-mindedness and humanity as if his hair had been coated with brilliantine, and almost moved by his own nobility of soul. Damn me if that image hadn't now got some bad holes in it! The ideal Herr Haller had been reduced to a wretched state. He looked like some dignitary with his trousers in tatters after being robbed of his wealth in the street. And he would have been better advised to learn the part of the ragged-trousered wretch he now was instead of wearing his rags as if his medals were still pinned to them and tearfully persisting in laying claim to his lost dignity.

Again and again meeting up with the musician Pablo, I was obliged to revise my judgement of him, if only because Hermione was so fond of him and assiduously sought his company. In my memory I'd registered Pablo as a handsome nonentity, a little, rather vain dandy, a happy child without a care in the world who took great delight in blowing into the toy trumpet he'd won at the fair and could easily be made to toe the line if you gave him enough praise and chocolate. But Pablo was not interested in my judgements. He was as indifferent to them as he was to my musical theories. He would listen to me in a polite and friendly way, smiling the whole time, but never giving any real response. In spite of this, however, I did seem to have aroused his interest, since he clearly went to some trouble to please me and show me goodwill. Once when, during one of these fruitless conversations of ours, I became irritated almost to the point of rudeness, he gave me a look of dismay and sadness and, taking hold of my left hand and stroking it, invited me to take a sniff of something from a small gold-plated snuffbox. It would do me good, he said. I glanced inquiringly at Hermione, who nodded her approval, so I took a pinch and sniffed it. In no time at all I did indeed feel fresher and livelier, probably because there was some cocaine mixed in with the powder. Hermione told me Pablo had lots of substances like this, which he obtained by secret routes and occasionally offered to friends – to deaden pain, to help sleep, to produce beautiful dreams, to make you feel merry, to act as aphrodisiacs – and he was, she said, a past master when it came to mixing them and getting the dosage right.

Once, when I bumped into him in the street down by the river, he was perfectly happy to walk my way, and I finally managed to get a word out of him.

'Herr Pablo,' I said to him, as he toyed with a slender little ebony-and-silver cane, 'you are a friend of Hermione, which is why I am interested in you. But I have to say that you don't exactly make it easy for me to hold a conversation with you. I have tried several times to talk about music with you because it would have interested me to hear your opinion, your judgement or whatever counter-arguments you may have, but you never deigned to reply to me, even in the slightest way.'

Laughing at me heartily, he didn't fail to answer this time but calmly said: 'You see, in my opinion, talking about music is of no value. I never talk about music. I ask you, what should I have replied to your astute and accurate remarks? Everything you said was so right, you see. But listen, I'm a musician, not a scholar, and I don't believe that being right is of the slightest value where music is concerned. With music, it's not a matter of being right, or of taste and education and all that.'

'Fair enough. But what is it matter of, then?'

'It's a matter of making music, Herr Haller, making music as well, as much and as intensively as possible! That's the point,

Monsieur. I can have the complete works of Bach and Haydn in my head and be able to say extremely clever things about them, but that's of no use to anybody. However, when I pick up my horn and play a brisk shimmy, regardless of whether it's a good or a bad dance tune, it's going to bring joy to people by putting a spring in their step and getting into their bloodstream. That's the only thing that matters. Next time you are in a dance hall, just take a look at people's faces at the moment when the music starts up again after a longish break. You'll see their eyes beginning to sparkle, their legs starting to twitch, and their faces beaming brightly! *That's* the point of making music.'

'All very well, Herr Pablo, but music aimed at the senses isn't the only kind. There's music of the spirit and mind too. Nor is there only the music that people just happen to be playing at a given moment. There's also immortal music, music that lives on even though it's not currently being played. It's possible for people lying alone in bed to bring back to life a tune from the *Magic Flute* or the *Matthew Passion* in their heads. Then you have music taking place without a soul blowing on a flute or bowing a violin.'

'Certainly, Herr Haller. "Yearning" and "Valencia"* are also silently reproduced every night by lots of lonely and wistful people. Even the poorest of girls sitting typing in her office has the latest one-step going through her head and taps the keys to its rhythm. You are right, there are all these lonely people and as far as I'm concerned they are welcome to their silent music, whether it be "Yearning", the *Magic Flute* or "Valencia". But where do all these people get their solitary, silent music from? They get it from us musicians. It first has to have been played and heard

* The foxtrot 'Yearning', written by the Philadelphia-born composer Joseph A. (Joe) Burke (1884–1950), was very popular from 1925 onwards. 'Valencia', another foxtrot, written by the Spanish composer José Padilla (1889–1960), became a major hit for the Paul Whiteman Orchestra in 1926.

and has to have got into the bloodstream before anyone can think or dream of it in the privacy of their home.'

'Agreed,' I said coolly. 'Nevertheless, you can't go putting Mozart and the latest foxtrot on one and the same level. And it does make a difference whether the music you play to people is divine and ageless or the cheap variety that only lasts a day.'

Noticing from the sound of my voice how worked up I was, Pablo immediately put on his kindest expression, tenderly stroked my arm and adopted an incredibly gentle tone of voice.

'Ah, my dear man, what you say about different levels may well be right. I certainly don't mind you situating Mozart and Haydn and "Valencia" on any level that suits you. It's all the same to me. It's not for me to decide on levels, that's not something I'm asked to judge upon. People may still be playing Mozart in a hundred years' time, whereas in two years from now they will perhaps already have stopped playing "Valencia". I think that's something we can safely leave to the dear Lord to decide. He has control of all our lifespans, even those of every waltz and foxtrot, and, since he is just, he will surely do what is right. But we musicians have to do our bit by carrying out the duty assigned to us. That means we must play whatever people desire at the moment and must play it as well, as beautifully and as forcefully as we possibly can.'

With a sigh, I gave up. There was no getting the better of the man.

★

I was now often experiencing an odd mixture of the old and the new, of pain and pleasure, of fear and joy. One moment I was in heaven, the next in hell; mostly in both at once. Now the old Harry and the new would be living in bitter strife, now at peace with one another. Sometimes the old Harry seemed to be totally extinct, dead and buried, then suddenly he was on his feet again, giving orders, ruling the roost and behaving like a know-all. And the new, little, young Harry, feeling ashamed, allowed himself to be pushed into the background without a word of protest. At other times the young Harry would seize the old one by the throat and nearly throttle him. That would lead to a deal of groaning, much mortal combat and many thoughts of the dreaded razor.

Often, however, I felt engulfed by sorrow and happiness in a single wave. There was one such moment only a few days after my first attempt at dancing in public when, going into my bedroom at night, to my indescribable amazement, dismay, shock and delight I discovered the lovely Maria lying in my bed.

Of all the surprises Hermione had sprung on me so far this was the most powerful. You see, I didn't doubt for one moment that *she* had sent me this bird of paradise. For once I had not spent the evening with Hermione, but had instead gone to hear a good performance of early church music in the Minster. It had been a nice, wistful outing, a return to my former life, to the haunts of my youth, to the territory of the ideal Harry. In the high Gothic choir of the church, the beautiful net vaulting of which, brought to ghostly life by the few lights playing on it, seemed to be swaying back and forth, I had heard pieces by Buxtehude, Pachelbel, Bach and Haydn. Wandering once more down the much-loved paths of my past, I had again heard the glorious voice of a Bach singer, a woman I once counted my friend and in whose presence I had experienced many extraordinary performances. The voices in these old compositions, the music's infinite dignity and sanctity, had reawakened in me all the uplifting experiences of my youth, everything that had then enthused and delighted me. Feeling sad, but totally absorbed, I sat there in the lofty choir of the church, a guest for an hour or so in this noble, blessed world which had once been my home. During a Haydn duet I had suddenly been moved to tears and, not waiting for the concert to finish, had stolen out of the Minster, thus forgoing the opportunity to meet my singer friend again. Oh what marvellous evenings I'd spent together with the concert artists after such recitals in the old days! Now I had been walking till I was weary through the dark narrow streets in which here and there behind restaurant windows jazz bands were playing the melodies of my current existence. Oh what a dismal maze of error and confusion my life had become!

For a long time in the course of this nocturnal walk I had also been pondering my strange relationship to music. And, not for the first time, I had come to recognize that my own relationship to this art form, which was as unwholesome as it was touching, was a fate I shared with the German intelligentsia as a whole. To an extent never experienced by any other nation, the intellectual and spiritual life of Germany is dominated by the notion of matriarchy, of close ties to Mother Nature, and this finds expression in the hegemony of music. Instead of manfully resisting this by obeying the dictates of the mind, the Logos, the Word, and winning a hearing for them, we intellectuals all dream of a language without words, a language that will express things inexpressible, represent what cannot be given shape. German intellectuals, instead of sticking as faithfully and honestly as possible to the instrument they were born to play, have constantly engaged in hostilities against reason and the Word, and flirted with music. Neglecting most of their real responsibilities, they have overindulged in music, wallowing in wonderful, blissful tonal structures, in wonderful, lovely feelings and moods that they never felt the urge to translate into reality. We German intellectuals, all of us, were not at home in reality, were alien and hostile to it, and that is why we have played such a lamentable role in the real world of our country, in its history, its politics and its public opinion. Well, what of it? I'd often pursued this train of thought, not without feeling the occasional strong desire to play a part in shaping reality, to be seriously and responsibly active for once instead of always confining myself to aesthetics and the arts and crafts of the mind. Always, however, I ended up resigning myself to my lot. The generals and the captains of heavy industry were perfectly right to say that we 'intellectual types' were not up to much. Divorced from reality, we were an irresponsible bunch of clever chatterboxes that the nation could well do without. Ugh! Pass me the razor!

Thus I had finally returned home, my head full of thoughts and echoes of the music, my heart heavy with sadness and desperate longing for life, for reality, for meaning and for things irretrievably lost. I had climbed my stairs, put the light on in the living room and made a vain attempt to read a little. I had thought of the date I had made for the following evening, obliging me to go dancing and drinking whisky in the Cécil Bar, and had felt bitterly resentful, not only against myself, but also against Hermione. For all that her intentions might be sincere and good, and however wonderful a creature she might be, she ought at that time to have let me perish rather than dragging me down into this chaotic, alien, shimmering world of entertainment where it was clear I was bound to remain a stranger for ever and where, severely impoverished, my best qualities were going to seed.

And in this sad frame of mind I had put out the light, made my way sadly to my bedroom and begun sadly to undress, when I smelled something unusual that made me stop short. There was a slight scent of perfume and, looking round, I saw the beautiful Maria with her big blue eyes lying in my bed, smiling and rather anxious.

'Maria!' I said. Then the first thing that occurred to me was that my landlady would give me notice to quit if she knew.

'I've come to see you,' she said softly. 'Are you cross with me?'

'No, no. Hermione gave you the key, I know. Well, so be it.'

'Oh, you clearly are cross about it. I'll go again.'

'No, Maria, stay, beautiful one. Only, tonight of all nights, I am very sad. I can't be cheerful tonight, though tomorrow I may be able to be again.'

I had bent down a little towards her and she now took my head in her two large, firm hands, drew it down and gave me a long kiss. Then I sat down by her on the bed and, holding her hand, asked her to speak softly since we must not be heard. I looked down at her beautiful full face, a strange and wonderful sight, lying there on my pillow like a large flower. Drawing my hand slowly to her mouth, she then pulled it under the blanket and placed it on her warm, silently breathing chest.

'You don't have to feel cheerful, dear,' she said. 'I already know from Hermione that you are troubled in mind. Anyone can understand that. But tell me, do you still find me attractive? The other day, when we were dancing, you really fell for me, didn't you?'

I kissed her eyes, her mouth, her neck and her breasts. Only a moment ago, I had been bitterly blaming Hermione in my thoughts. Now, holding her gift to me in my hands, I felt grateful. Maria's caresses didn't in the least jar with the glorious music I had heard that evening. They were worthy of it, indeed complemented it. Slowly I removed the blanket from her beautiful body until I reached her feet with my kisses. And when I lay down beside her she gave me a kind smile, an all-knowing smile that lit up her floral face.

That night, lying beside Maria, I slept, though not for long, deeply and satisfyingly like a child. And between my bouts of sleep I drank my fill of her lovely serene youthfulness and, as we chatted softly, discovered a lot of things worth knowing about her life and Hermione's. I had scant knowledge of creatures and lives of this kind. Only occasionally, in the theatrical world, had I previously encountered similar existences, both women and men, half artists, half good-time girls or playboys. Not until now did I gain a little insight into these curious, strangely innocent yet strangely degenerate lives. All these young women, usually from poor backgrounds but too clever and too good-looking to spend their whole lives earning their living in one single, badly paid and joyless job or another, were dependent partly on casual work, partly on their charming looks for survival. From time to time they would spend a few months sitting at a typewriter; periodically they were the lovers of affluent playboys who rewarded them with pocket money and presents. At times they lived a life in furs, limousines and grand hotels; at others they just had a room in some attic. If offered a high enough sum, they could possibly be persuaded to marry, but generally speaking they were far from keen on the idea. Many of them were devoid of sexual desire, only reluctantly granting their favours, and then only for the highest price, arrived at after considerable haggling. Others, and Maria was one of them, were unusually gifted lovers with strong sexual needs. Most of these were also experienced in the arts of making love with both sexes. Living solely for sex, they constantly had other, thriving relationships on the go in addition to those with their official and paying partners. Restlessly busy, full of care yet careless, clever yet thoughtless, these butterflies lived their lives, which were as childlike as they were sophisticated, independently. They could not be bought by just anybody; they expected no more than their fair share of good fortune and good weather. In love with life, yet far less attached to it than conventional members of society, they were forever willing to follow some fairy-tale prince to his castle, forever half aware that they would surely come to a sad and difficult end.

In that first strange night and the following days Maria taught me a great deal, not only bewitching new games and sensual delights, but also fresh understanding, fresh insights, a new kind of love. The world of dance halls and nightclubs, cinemas, bars and hotel tea rooms, which I, as an aesthete and recluse, still considered somewhat common, taboo and beneath my dignity, was the only world that existed for Maria, Hermione and their female companions. It was neither good nor evil, neither desirable nor detestable. It was in this world that their brief lives full of yearning flourished. They were at home in it, experienced in its ways. They liked a glass of champagne or a chef's speciality in the grill room in just the same way that you or I might like a composer or writer, and they would lavish the same amount of enthusiasm and emotional involvement on a new hit dance tune or the sickly sentimental song of a jazz singer that people like you and me would on Nietzsche or Hamsun.* Chatting to me about Pablo, the good-looking saxophone player, Maria mentioned an American song he had occasionally sung to them. She talked of it as if spellbound, with a degree of admiration and love that gripped and moved me far more than the ecstasies any highly educated person might go into over pleasurable aesthetic experiences of an exquisitely cultivated kind. I was willing to share in her enthusiasm, no matter what the song was like, because Maria's fond words and the look of longing that lit up her face were opening up wide gaps in my aesthetic defences. Of course there were some things of beauty, some few exquisitely beautiful creations that in my view were beyond all criticism or dispute, first and foremost Mozart. But where should one draw the line? Hadn't all of us connoisseurs and critics in our youth fervently adored works of art and artists that seemed to us nowadays to be of doubtful quality or embarrassing? Wasn't this something we had experienced in the case of Liszt, Wagner, perhaps even Beethoven? Wasn't Maria's glowing, childlike emotional response to the popular song from America an

* Knut Hamsun (1859–1952), Norwegian writer, winner of the Nobel Prize in Literature in 1920. Like the philosopher Nietzsche, Hamsun influenced a whole generation of German writers, including Hesse.

aesthetic experience just as pure, just as fine as that of any senior schoolmaster spellbound by *Tristan and Isolde* or any orchestra conductor going into ecstasies over Beethoven's Ninth? And didn't this accord remarkably well with the opinions of our Herr Pablo, confirming that he was right?

That handsome Pablo! Maria, too, seemed to be extremely fond of him.

'He is a good-looking chap,' I said, 'and I too like him a lot. But, tell me, Maria, how can you, besides him, also be fond of a boring old chap who isn't good-looking, is even starting to go grey, and can neither play the saxophone nor sing love songs in English?'

'Don't say such ugly things!' she said, telling me off. 'Don't you see it's quite natural? I like you too. There's something attractive, loveable and special about you too. You mustn't try to be different from what you are. It's not right to go talking about things like this and demanding explanations of people. Look, when you kiss me on the neck or the ear, I can sense that you are fond of me and find me attractive. You have a way of kissing, a bit on the shy side, that tells me: "He's fond of you, he appreciates your good looks." I like that very much, very much. Yet with a different man, on the other hand, I may like exactly the opposite: the fact that I seem to count for nothing in his eyes, so that when he kisses me it's as if he is doing me a favour.'

Again we fell asleep. Again I woke to discover that I still had my arms around her, this beautiful, beautiful flower of mine.

And, strange to say, this beautiful flower nevertheless constantly remained the present bestowed on me by Hermione. The latter constantly interposed herself between me and Maria, masking her fully. And at one juncture I suddenly thought of Erika, my poor girlfriend, the woman I loved who was somewhere far away, and cross with me. She was scarcely less good-looking than Maria, though not in such full bloom, not as liberated, less gifted in those ingenious little touches Maria brought to the art of lovemaking. For a while I could picture her clearly and painfully, the object of my love, her fate deeply bound up with mine. Then her image faded away again into my sleep and was forgotten, far off, an absence only half lamented.

After being devoid and deprived of them for so long, I saw many images from my past surfacing before me in this way during that lovely night of tenderness. Released now by the magic of Eros, they welled up from the depths in all their abundance, making my heart momentarily stand still, so enchanted and at the same time saddened was I to realize how rich the picture gallery of my life had been, how full poor Steppenwolf's psychological firmament had been of eternal stars and constellations. I had a vision, gentle and blissful, of my childhood and mother, like some faraway mountain range, infinitely blue and remote. I heard the chorus of my friendships resound with brass-like clarity, beginning with the legendary Hermann, the psychological counterpart of Hermione. Fragrant and unearthly, like marine flora emerging moist from the water to display their blooms, the images of many women drifted into view; women I had loved, desired and celebrated in verse, and only a few of whom I had won or attempted to make my own. My wife appeared too, with whom I had lived for many a year, and who had taught me the values of companionship, conflict and resignation. In spite of all my dissatisfaction with our life together, the profound trust I placed in her had remained alive in me until the day when, deranged and sick, in an act of sudden desertion and wild rebellion, she abandoned me. And I realized how much I must have loved her, how deeply I must have trusted her for her breach of trust to have had such a grave and lifelong impact on me.

These images – there were hundreds of them, some I could put names to, some not – were all present again, having emerged young and fresh from the well of this night of love, and I realized again something I had long forgotten in my misery: that they constituted everything of value that my life possessed. Remaining indestructibly in existence, they were fixed for ever like the stars, experiences I could forget but not destroy. Their sequence represented the saga of my life, their bright starlight the indestructible worth of my existence. My life may have been arduous, wayward and unhappy, my experience of humankind's bitter fate causing me to renounce and reject a great deal, but it had been rich, proud and rich, a life – even its misery – fit for a king. No matter how pitifully I might waste what little time was left to me before finally going under, my life was essentially a noble one. It had a profile and pedigree. Not content with cheap rewards, I had aimed for the stars.

It is already some time ago, and a lot has happened and changed since that night so that I can only remember little of it in detail: odd words we exchanged, odd gestures and amorous acts of profound tenderness, bright, starlit moments when we awoke from the heavy sleep that followed our exhausting love-making. However, it was during that night, for the first time since my decline, that my own life looked back at me once again with relentlessly beaming eyes; that I was once again able to see fate at work in what I'd considered mere chance events and to recognize the ruined landscape of my existence as a small part of some divine plan. My soul could breathe again, my eyes see, and for a few moments I sensed intensely that all I needed to do in order to gain admittance to this world of images and become immortal was to gather up the scattered, fragmentary images of my life as Harry Haller alias Steppenwolf and raise them to the level of one rounded portrait. After all, was it not the point of every human life that it should be a determined attempt to reach such a goal?

The next morning, after she had shared my breakfast, I had to smuggle Maria out of the building, which I succeeded in doing.

That very same day I rented a small room for the two of us in a nearby part of the town, to be used solely for our meetings.

Dutifully putting in an appearance, my dancing teacher Hermione made me learn the Boston. Strict and unsparing, she wouldn't let me miss a lesson because it had been decided that I would attend the next masked ball with her. She had asked me for money to pay for her costume, but refused to give me any information as to what it would be. I was still forbidden to call on her or even to know where she was living.

This period leading up to the masked ball, a matter of some three weeks, was extraordinarily beautiful. It seemed to me that Maria was the first woman I had really loved. I had always demanded a degree of intellect and education from the women I loved, without ever fully noticing that even the most intellectual and relatively best-educated woman never responded to the Logos in me, but rather clashed with it. I used always to take my problems and ideas along with me to my rendezvous with women, and it would have seemed quite impossible for me to spend longer than an hour loving any woman who had scarcely read a book, hardly knowing what reading meant, or was unable to tell the difference between a Tchaikovsky and a Beethoven. Maria had no education. She had no need of such diversions or surrogate worlds because all her problems were directly sensuous in origin. Her art, her mission in life, consisted in striving to achieve as much sensual and sexual happiness as was humanly possible, in seeking and enticing from her partner in love – by means of the senses she had been endowed with, her exceptional figure, her colouring, her hair, her voice, her skin, her vivacity – a sympathetic response and a lively, gratifying counter-play to everything she was capable of, to every supple adjustment of her curves, every extremely delicate modulation of her body. This was something I had felt when dancing shyly with her on that first occasion. Even then I had picked up the clear scent of an ingenious, highly refined sensuality in her, and had been enchanted by it. And it was certainly no coincidence that Hermione, omniscient as she was, had put this girl Maria in touch with me, for she had the scent of summer, of roses about her. It was the hallmark of her whole being.

I was not fortunate enough to be Maria's sole or preferred lover. I was one of several. Often she found no time for me, sometimes one hour in the afternoon, on very few occasions a whole night. She refused to take money from me, which was probably Hermione's doing. However, she was happy to accept gifts and when, for instance, I gave her a dainty new purse made of shiny red leather she didn't object to the two or three gold coins it contained. That little red purse, by the way, prompted her to laugh right in my face because, charming though it was, it was long since out of fashion and no longer selling well. From Maria I learned a great deal about matters such as this, about which previously I had known and understood less than I did any Eskimo language. Above all I learned that these little playthings, fashionable accessories and luxuries are not just tawdry kitsch, invented by money-grabbing manufacturers and dealers, but quite legitimate, beautiful and diverse objects. They constitute a small, or rather large, world of things, all of them designed with the sole aim of serving Eros, refining the senses, breathing fresh life into the dead world we inhabit and magically endowing it with new sexual organs, from powder and perfume to dance shoes, from rings to cigarette cases, from belt buckles to hand-bags. These handbags were not handbags, the purses not purses, flowers not flowers, fans not fans – no, all of them were the visual and tangible material of Eros, of magic, of stimulation. They functioned as messengers, touts, weapons, battle cries.

I often wondered who it was Maria really loved. I think of all people she loved youthful Pablo the most, he of the saxophone, the dreamy black eyes and the long, pale, noble and melancholy hands. I would have judged Pablo to be a rather languid, spoiled and passive lover but Maria assured me that, though it took a long time, once aroused, he was rougher, more muscular, masculine and demanding than any boxer or horseman. In this way I got to know intimate details of this or that person: the jazz musician, the actor, women, girls, men from our milieu. I knew all sorts of secrets, had insight into alliances and enmities that lay beneath the surface, was slowly initiated into and became familiar with this world in which I had been a completely alien presence with no links whatsoever to anyone. About Hermione too I learned a great deal, but above all I was now in frequent contact with Herr Pablo, whom Maria loved very much. She also used his secret substances from time to time, occasionally procuring these delights for me too, and Pablo was always ready, indeed especially keen, to oblige me. Once he told me in no uncertain terms: 'You are unhappy so much of the time. Nobody should be like that, it's not good. I'm sorry for you. Try smoking a little opium.' My opinion of this cheerful, clever, childlike and yet unfathomable human being was constantly changing. We became friends, and not infrequently I accepted some of the drugs he had on offer. It was with a degree of amusement that he observed my infatuation with Maria. Once he organized a 'party' in his room up in the attic of a hotel in the suburbs. Since there was only one chair, Maria and I had to sit on the bed. To drink, he served us a mysterious, wonderful liqueur he had mixed from the contents of three small bottles. And, once I was feeling in a really good mood, he suggested, his eyes sparkling, that the three of us should have an orgy. Abruptly refusing, since for me that sort of thing was out of the question, I nevertheless cast a brief sidelong glance at Maria, wondering what her attitude might be. She did, like me, immediately say no, but I could sense from the glint in her eyes that this was an opportunity she was sorry to miss. Pablo was disappointed by my refusal, but he didn't take offence. 'Pity,' he said. 'Harry has too many moral scruples. It can't be helped, yet it would have been so beautiful, so very beautiful. However, I know something we can do instead.' Each of us now got to take a few pulls on a pipe Pablo had filled with opium. Sitting motionless, our eyes open, all three of us underwent the experience he had suggested, Maria trembling with delight. Afterwards, when I felt slightly unwell, Pablo laid me on the bed and gave me a few drops of medicine. And as I closed my eyes for a few minutes, I felt the briefest and faintest touch of lips on each eyelid. As if believing that the kisses came from Maria, I let it happen, but I knew full well they came from him.

And one evening he had an even greater surprise in store for me. Appearing in my flat, he told me he needed twenty francs. Could I let him have them? If so, he offered, I could take his place that night with Maria.

'Pablo,' I said, shocked, 'you don't know what you are saying. There's nothing we in this country consider more despicable, Pablo, than letting another man have the woman you love in exchange for money. I didn't hear what you just proposed.'

He gave me a pitying look. 'You refuse to do it, Herr Harry. Very well. You are always making things difficult for yourself. Still, if you prefer it that way, don't spend the night with Maria, just give me the money. You'll get it back. I need it urgently.'

'What for?'

'For Agostino, you know who I mean, the lad who plays second violin. He's been ill for a week now and no one's looking after him. He hasn't got a penny of his own, and now I've run out of money too.'

Mainly out of curiosity, but also by way of self-punishment, I went with him to the garret, a truly wretched garret, where Agostino lived. Pablo took him some milk and medicine, freshened up his bed for him, aired the room, and put a neat, skilfully fashioned compress round his fevered head. All this was swiftly and gently done, with the expertise of a good nurse. That same night I saw him playing until the early hours of the morning in the City Bar.

Often I would talk to Hermione at length and in a matter-of-fact way about Maria, about her hands, her shoulders, her hips, about the way she laughed, kissed and danced.

'Has she shown you this yet?' Hermione once asked me, going on to describe a particular trick of the tongue when kissing. I asked why she didn't demonstrate it to me herself, but she earnestly refused. 'That can wait till later,' she said. 'I'm not your lover yet.'

I asked her how she came to be familiar with Maria's kissing skills and many an intimate detail of her body that only a man making love to her could know.

'Oh,' she cried, 'after all, we are friends. Surely you don't think we keep things secret from one another? I should know, I've slept with her and played with her often enough. Believe me, you've got yourself a fine girl there, one who knows more than other girls do.'

'But, Hermione, I still think there must be some things even the two of you keep secret from one another. Or have you also told her everything you know about me?'

'No, that's a different matter. Those are things she wouldn't understand. Luckily for you, Maria is wonderful, but there are things private to the two of us of which she has no idea. Of course I told her a lot about you, a lot more than you would have wished at the time. After all, I had to seduce her for you. But as for understanding you, my friend, in the way I understand you, that's something Maria will never be capable of, or any other woman either. I've also found out quite a few new things about you from her, so I am well informed, at least as far as her knowledge of you goes. I know you almost as well as if we had often slept with one another.'

When I was next together with Maria it was strange and mysterious, knowing as I did that she had held Hermione close to her
like me, that she had fondled, kissed, tasted and examined her
limbs, hair and skin exactly as she had mine. Visions arose in me
of new, indirect, complicated relationships and connections, new
opportunities to experience life and love, which made me think
of the thousand souls mentioned in the Steppenwolf tract.

*

In that short period between getting to know Maria and the day
of the grand masked ball I was positively happy, yet I never felt
that I had found some kind of ultimate bliss or salvation. Instead,
I had a very clear sense that all this was merely a prologue and
preparation. There was a strong forward impulse to everything,
but the real thing was still to come.

By now I had learned enough in my dancing lessons to feel
that it would be feasible for me to attend the ball, which was
being talked about more and more with every day that went by.
Hermione's costume remained a secret. She was absolutely determined not to tell me what she would be going as. I was not to
worry, she said. I would recognize her, and failing that she would
help me out, but I was not allowed to know anything in advance.
Nor, for this reason, was she the least bit curious about what I
was planning to wear, so I decided not to dress up at all. Maria,
when I wanted to invite her to the ball, explained that she already
had a partner for the occasion. And since she did indeed have a
ticket already, I realized to my disappointment that I would have
to attend the ball on my own. The most exclusive of all the city's
masked balls, it was put on annually in the Globe Rooms by the
Society of Artists.

I saw little of Hermione during this time, but on the eve of
the ball she visited me to collect the ticket that I had ordered for

her. Sitting peacefully in my room, she began a – to my mind – strange conversation that made a profound impression on me.

'You are really well now, in fact. Dancing suits you. Anyone seeing you for the first time in four weeks would scarcely know you.'

'True,' I conceded. 'I've not been this well for years. It's all your doing, Hermione.'

'Oh really? Not your lovely Maria's?'

'No. She was your gift to me as well, as you know. She's wonderful.'

'She's the lover you needed, Steppenwolf, good-looking, young, cheerful, very good in bed and not always available. If you didn't have to share her with others, if she were ever more than just a fleeting guest, things wouldn't be as good.'

It was true. I had to concede that she was right about that too.

'You've got everything you need now, then?'

'No, Hermione, that's not the case. What I have is something very beautiful, something that delights me, brings me great joy and welcome comfort. I am positively happy . . .'

'There you are, then! What more can you want?'

'I do want something more. I'm not content to be happy, that's not what I'm cut out to be, not what fate intended for me. I'm destined to be the very opposite.'

'To be unhappy, you mean? Well, you had more than your fair share of unhappiness that time when you couldn't bring yourself to go home for fear of the razor waiting there.'

'No, Hermione. Don't you see, I mean something else. I was very unhappy then, I grant you, but my unhappiness was stupid, barren.'

'Why was that?'

'Because if I wanted to die, and I did, I ought not to have been so afraid of death. The unhappiness I'm in need of and longing for is different. It's of a kind that will make me hunger for suffering and lust for death. That's the sort of unhappiness, or happiness, I am waiting for.'

'I can understand you. We are like sister and brother in that respect. But what is wrong with the happiness you have now found with Maria? Why are you not satisfied?'

'There is nothing wrong with this happiness. On the contrary, I love it, feel grateful for it. It's as beautiful as a sunny day in a summer of rain. But I sense that it can't last, so it is barren too, this happiness. It is satisfying, but satisfaction is not the nourishment I need. It's enough to fill Steppenwolf's stomach and send him to sleep, but it's not the kind of happiness to die for.'

'So dying is of the essence, is it, Steppenwolf?'

'I think so, yes. I am very satisfied with my happiness. It's something I can live with for quite a while yet, but if it occasionally deserts me for an hour or so, allowing me to wake from my sleep and experience a longing for something, what I long for with all my being is not this happiness, not that it should last for ever. Rather, I long to experience suffering again, only more exquisitely, more richly this time. What I yearn for are the kinds of suffering that will make me ready and willing to die.'

Tenderly Hermione gazed into my eyes, her own eyes suddenly darkening in the way they could: splendid, fearsome eyes! Slowly, searching for her words one by one and piecing them together, she said – so quietly that I had to strain to hear her:

'Today I want to tell you something, something I have known for a long time. You too already know what it is, but it may be that you have not yet said it to yourself in so many terms. I'm now going to tell you what I know about me and you and our destiny. You, Harry, were an artist and thinker, someone full of joy and faith, always on the trail of great and eternal ideas, never content with minor attractions. However, the more life brought you to your senses and turned your attention to yourself, the more acute your situation became and the more profound your suffering, anxiety and desperation until you were up to your neck in them. Then all the beautiful and sacred things you knew, loved and revered, all your earlier faith in human beings and the high achievements they were destined for were of no avail, worthless, shattered to pieces. Your faith had no air left in which to get its breath. And suffocating is a hard way to die. Is that right, Harry? Is that what fate decreed for you?'

I nodded, nodded, nodded.

'You had an image of life in your head, a faith, a challenge. You were prepared to do great things, to suffer, to make sacrifices – and then bit by bit you noticed that the world wasn't demanding great deeds, sacrifices and the like from you at all; that life wasn't an epic poem with heroic roles and that kind of thing, but more like the parlour of a conventional household where the inhabitants are perfectly content to eat, drink coffee, knit stockings, play cards and listen to music on the radio. And anyone wanting the other heroic and noble life, and having it in them, anyone venerating great writers or venerating the saints, is a fool and a Don Quixote. Good. And my experience, my friend, was exactly the same! I was a gifted girl, destined to live according to high ideals, to make high demands on myself and to carry out worthy tasks. I had the ability to take on great responsibilities, to be the wife of a king, the lover of a revolutionary, the sister of a genius, the mother of a martyr. But all that life allowed me to become was a courtesan of reasonably good taste, and even that was made difficult enough for me! That is how I fared. For quite a while I was disconsolate, for a long time I sought to blame myself. Surely, I thought, when all's said and done, life must always be right. If life treated my beautiful dreams with derision, my dreams must simply have been stupid and wrong, I thought. But that was of no help at all. And since I had good eyes and ears, and a rather inquisitive nature, I took a really close look at so-called life, at people I knew and my neighbours, fifty or more individuals and their fates. And what did I see, Harry? That my dreams had been right, a thousand times right, just as yours were, whereas life, reality, was wrong. That a woman of my kind should have no alternative but to grow old sitting at a typewriter, working pointlessly and for a pittance in the service of someone well paid, or to marry someone like that for the sake of his money, or else to become a kind of whore – all that seemed just as wrong as someone lonely, shy and in despair like you being forced to reach for his razor. The misery I went through was perhaps more financial and moral, yours more intellectual and spiritual, but our journeys were the same. Do you think I'm incapable of understanding your fear of the foxtrot, your distaste for bars and dance floors, your resistance to jazz music and all that sort of stuff? I understand it all only too well, just as I do your disgust with politics, your sadness at the way the parties and the press ramble on and kick up a fuss about things, your despair over wars, the one there has just been and those still to come, and about modern habits of thinking, reading, building, making music, celebrating things and providing education! You are right, Steppenwolf, a thousand times right, and yet you must perish. You are far too demanding, too hungry for today's straightforward, cosy world, satisfied as it is with so little. You have one dimension too many for its liking, so it will spit you out. It is impossible for anyone wishing to live and enjoy life in today's world to be like you or me. It is no home, this fine world, for people like us who, instead of nonsensical noise, demand music; instead of pleasure, joy; instead of money, soul; instead of industrial production, genuine labour; instead of frivolity, genuine passion . . .'

She looked down at the ground, deep in thought.

'Hermione!' I exclaimed lovingly. 'How well you see things, dear sister! And yet you taught me the foxtrot! What do you mean, however, by saying that people like us, people with one dimension too many, are unable to live in this world? What is it that prevents them? Is it only true of the present day, or was it always the case?'

'I don't know. To be fair to the world I'd like to think that it is merely true of the present day, just a sickness, a temporary misfortune. The political leaders are resolutely and successfully working to bring about the next war while the rest of us are dancing the foxtrot, earning money and eating fancy chocolates. In an age like this the world is bound to look well and truly lousy. Let's hope other ages were better and will be better again, richer, broader, deeper. But all that's of little use to us. And perhaps it has always been like this . . .'

'Always like today? Always a world fit for politicians, conmen, waiters and playboys, a world where there is no air fit for human beings to breathe?'

'Who knows? I don't, nobody does. It makes no difference anyway. But now I'm wondering what it must have been like for your great favourite Mozart, whom you've told me about from time to time, even reading to me from his letters. How was it for him? Who was ruling the world in his day, creaming off the best, setting the tone, and considered important? Was it Mozart or the profit-seekers, Mozart or shallow, run-of-the-mill types? And how did he die? How did they bury him? And I think it has perhaps always been like that and always will be. And the subject they call "World History" in schools and the things you have to learn off by heart in them in order to be educated – all those heroes, geniuses, great deeds and senti-ments – is just a confidence trick devised by the schoolteachers for the purposes of education and to give the children some-thing to keep them occupied during the prescribed years of schooling. It has always been the case and always will be that time and the world, wealth and power belong to those who are petty and shallow, whereas the rest, the real human beings, have nothing. Nothing other than death.'

'Otherwise absolutely nothing?'

'No, they have eternity.'

'You mean they achieve fame, their names going down to posterity?'

'No, little wolf, not fame. Is fame of any value? Surely you don't think all really authentic and complete human beings have achieved fame and are known to posterity?'

'No, of course not.'

'So we are not talking about fame. Fame wouldn't exist if it weren't for education. It's only of concern to schoolteachers. Oh no, we are not talking about fame, but what I call eternity. Believers call it the kingdom of God. The way I see it, all of us more demanding people, those of us who long for something better and have that one dimension too many, would be incapable of living if, apart from this world's atmosphere, there weren't another air to breathe; if, apart from time, eternity didn't also exist, the kingdom of authentic life. Mozart's music is a part of it, as are the poems of your great writers. So too are the saints who performed miracles, died as martyrs and set a great example to people. But the image of every authentic act, the strength of every authentic emotion, are just as much a part of eternity, even if nobody knows about them, witnesses them, writes them down and preserves them for posterity. There is no such thing as posterity in eternity, only contemporaneity.'

'You are right,' I said.

'True believers,' she continued, deep in thought, 'of course knew more than anyone about this. That's why they established the saints and what they call the communion of saints. The saints, they are the authentic human beings, the Saviour's younger brethren. Our lives are one long journey towards them; our every good deed, every bold thought, every act of love is a stage along that road. In times gone by painters portrayed the communion of saints in the setting of a golden heaven where all was radiant, beautiful and full of peace, which is precisely what I earlier called "eternity". It is the realm beyond time and appearances. That is where we belong, it is the home we are striving with all our heart to reach, Steppenwolf, and that's why we long for death. It is where you will rediscover your Goethe, your Novalis and Mozart, and I my saints, St Christopher, St Philip Neri and all the rest. There are lots of saints who were bad sinners to begin with. Sin too can be a pathway to sanctity, sin and vice. Don't laugh, but I often think even my friend Pablo might be a secret saint. Sadly, Harry, we have to grope our way through so much filth and rubbish in order to reach home! And we have no one to show us the way. Homesickness is our only guide.'

As she uttered these final words her voice had become quite quiet again, and now all was peacefully silent in my room. The gilt lettering on the spines of the many books that made up my library was gleaming in the rays of the setting sun. Taking Hermione's head in my hands, I kissed her forehead, then rested her cheek against mine, as a brother might his sister's. We remained like this for a moment. I would have much preferred to stay close to her in this way and not to venture out again that day, but Maria had promised to spend the night with me, the last one before the Grand Ball.

On the way to meet her, however, I wasn't thinking of Maria but only about what Hermione had said. All those thoughts, it seemed to me, were not hers but perhaps my own which she, perceptive as she was, had read and digested and was now returning to me, having shaped them in such a way that they struck me as fresh. I was particularly thankful to her for having put into words during that hour together the idea of eternity. It was vital to me since I could not live without it, or die either. That day, at the hands of my friend and dancing teacher, my faith in a sacred afterlife, a timeless realm, a world of everlasting value and divine substance, had been restored. I could not help thinking of my

Goethe dream, of the image of the wise old man laughing his non-human laughter and amusing his immortal self at my expense. Only now did I understand that laughter of Goethe, the laughter of the Immortals. It had no object, this laughter. It was pure light, pure brightness; it was what remains when an authentic human being has lived through humankind's sufferings, vices, errors, passions and misunderstandings and managed to break through into the realm of eternity, into outer space. And 'eternity' was none other than the redemption of time, so to speak, its restoration to a state of innocence, its retransformation into space.

I looked for Maria in the place where we used to eat on our evenings together, but she had not yet arrived. Waiting in that quiet pub in the suburbs, sitting at the table that was already laid, my thoughts were still of the conversation with Hermione. All the ideas that had arisen in it seemed so deeply familiar, so well known to me for such a long time, it was as if they had been drawn from the well of my own most private imagery and mythology! The Immortals, remote icons now, living in timeless space, immersed in crystalline eternity like ether, and the cool clarity, starlike in its radiance, of this extraterrestrial world – how come all of this seemed so familiar to me? On reflection, what occurred to me were passages from Mozart's *Cassations* and Bach's *Well-Tempered Clavier* and it seemed to me that this music was permeated with the same cool, bright, starry radiance and the same vibrant, ethereal clarity. Yes, that was it. This music was rather like time frozen to become space, and it was suffused with a never-ending, superhuman serenity, a laughter that was eternal and divine. Oh yes, and this was where the aged Goethe of my dream fitted in perfectly! All at once I could hear this fathomless laughter all around me, could hear the Immortals laughing. I sat there spellbound. Spellbound, I felt for the pencil in my waistcoat pocket and, looking around for some paper, saw the wine list in front of me on the table. Turning it over, I started to write on the reverse, lines of poetry that I rediscovered in my pocket only the next day. They read like this:

The Immortals

Time and again we spot the rising fumes,
Products of high-pressure life on earth;
All its drunken excess, its misery and dearth,
Bloodstained smoke from countless hearty meals
For those condemned to die; fits of carnal lust;
Hands that murder, make money and pray;
Teeming masses, whipped up by fear and greed,
All emitting a rank, stuffy, warm and acrid dust,
The breath of bliss and rampant lechery;
Devouring their own flesh and spitting it out,
Devising future wars and pleasing forms of art,
Painting the brothel red even as it burns,
Gorging, stuffing, whoring their infantile way
Through the gaudy, tawdry fairground array
That's born afresh for each of them in turn,
But one day will for each to dust return.

Unlike you we've found ourselves a home
Up in the starry ether, bright and cold.
Oblivious to the passing hours and days,
We're neither male nor female, young nor old.
To us your murderous and lecherous ways,
Your fears, your ecstasies and sins
Are merely a show like the circling suns,
And every day is as long as the last.
While you fret and fidget we quietly slumber,
Inhaling the icy cold of outer space,

Or quietly gaze at stars without number
And the heavenly dragon, our friend.
Our life is eternal, cool and unchanging;
Cool and star-bright, our laughter knows no end.

Then Maria arrived and, after a cheerful meal together, I went with her to our small rented room. That evening, Maria was more beautiful, warmer and more intimate than ever before, and I savoured the caresses and love-play she lavished on me, thinking them the ultimate in passionate abandon.

'Maria,' I said, 'only a goddess is as extravagant with her favours as you are tonight. Don't go wearing us both out, after all it's the masked ball tomorrow. What kind of partner are you going with? I fear he may be a fairy-tale prince and you'll be seduced by him, my little flower, never more to return to me. Tonight you are making love to me almost as devoted lovers do for the last time when they are about to part.' Pressing her lips right inside my ear, she whispered:

'Don't say a word, Harry. Any time may be the last time. When Hermione takes you, you'll never return to me. Perhaps she will take you tomorrow.'

I never experienced the characteristic feeling of those days, their strangely bitter-sweet alternating mood, more powerfully than in the night before the ball. Happiness was what I experienced as a result of Maria's beauty and her winning ways; the opportunity to relish, feel and breathe countless sensual delights that I, as someone getting on in years, had never known until now; a chance to splash around like a child, rocked by gentle waves of pleasure. And yet this was only on the surface. Inside me, everything was laden with meaning, tension and destiny. While amorously and tenderly engaged in the touching sweet nothings of lovemaking, seemingly afloat in a warm bath of pure happiness, in my heart I could feel my destiny propelling me forwards at a headlong pace, whisking me along at a gallop like a frightened steed towards the abyss into which I would plunge, filled with fear and longing, in total surrender to death. In much the same way that only a little while ago I had still been shyly and timidly resisting the agreeable frivolity of exclusively sensual lovemaking and feeling afraid of Maria's radiant beauty, all the benefits of which she was willing to lavish upon me, so now I was feeling afraid of death. However, I knew that this fear I was experiencing would soon turn to willing and liberating surrender.

While we were silently absorbed in the energetic play of our lovemaking, more intimately at one with each other than ever, my soul was already taking leave of Maria and everything that she had meant to me. Before the final curtain, she had taught me childlike trust once more in the surface play of things, how to find joy in the most transient of experiences, how to be both child and animal in the innocence of sexual intercourse, a condition I had known only on rare and exceptional occasions in my earlier life. The reason was that sexuality and the life of the senses almost always had a slightly bitter taste of guilt about them for me, alongside the sweet but worrying taste of forbidden fruit, something anyone with an intellectual bent needs to guard against. Hermione and Maria had now shown me this garden in all its innocence and I had been grateful to be their guest in it, but it was too beautiful, too warm, and the time was fast approaching for me to move on. To go on pursuing the crown of life, to continue to atone for the infinite guilt of life, was what I was destined for. An easy life, an easy love, an easy death were out of the question for me.

From things the girls had hinted at, I gathered that quite special delights and sensual excesses were being planned for the next day's ball, or immediately after it. Perhaps this was the finish, perhaps Maria was right in sensing that we were lying together for the last time tonight. Tomorrow, perhaps, my fate was to take a new turn. Full of ardent yearning, full of suffocating dread, I clung desperately to Maria, fitfully and hungrily exploring once again every path and all the undergrowth in her garden, once again sinking my teeth into the sweet fruit of the tree of paradise.

*

The next day I made up for the sleep I had lost that night. In the morning I went to the public baths, before going home totally exhausted. There, having shut out the daylight from my bedroom, I discovered in my pocket, as I was undressing, my poem. Forgetting it again, I immediately lay down and slept right through the day. Maria, Hermione and the masked ball were forgotten too. Waking up in the evening, it was only when having a shave that I realized the ball was already due to start in an hour and I needed to look among my things for a dress shirt. I finished dressing in good spirits and went out for a meal before things began.

This was to be the first masked ball I had participated in, for although I had now and again attended such festivities in earlier years, sometimes even finding them fun, I had not joined in the dancing but merely been an onlooker. And it had always struck me as strange that other people should talk about them and look forward to them so enthusiastically. Today's ball was now a special event for me too and I was looking forward to it, if somewhat nervously, with eager anticipation. I decided, since I had no partner to take with me, to leave it late before going, which is what Hermione had also recommended.

In recent times I had seldom been to the Steel Helmet, my former refuge where disillusioned men sat whiling away their evenings, supping their wine and playing at being bachelors. It no longer suited the style of life I was now leading. That evening, however, I was drawn to it willy-nilly. My current mood, a mixture of nervousness and gaiety resulting from the sense that my fate was about to be decided and the time had come to say my farewells, meant that all the stations of my life, all the places steeped in memory, were once again bathed in that painfully beautiful light that attaches to things past. And this was the case with the small, smoke-filled pub where, not long ago, I had still been a regular; where, not long ago, that crude narcotic, a bottle of country wine, was all I needed to get through one more night in my lonely bed and make life bearable for one more day. Since then I had been sampling other substances, stronger stimulants, and savouring poisons that were sweeter. It was with a smile on my face that I now entered the old place to a welcome greeting from the landlady and nods all round from the taciturn regulars. The roast chicken I had been recommended arrived and my rustic tumbler was filled to the brim with crystal-clear young wine from Alsace. The scrubbed white wooden tables and the old yellow panelling had a familiar, friendly look about them. And as I ate and drank I had the increasingly strong sensation of time running out, of formally taking my leave of things and scenes with which my previous life had been inextricably entwined. Never having managed to tear myself away from them fully, I now felt the time was almost ripe for me to make the break, and the feeling was at once sweet and painfully intense. So-called 'modern' individuals call this sentimentality. They are no longer fond of inanimate things, even those most sacred to them, their cars, which they hope to exchange for a better model as soon as possible. These modern individuals are well drilled, efficient, healthy, cool and muscular. They will give a splendid account of themselves in the next war. I had no desire to emulate them. Neither modern nor old-fashioned, I had dropped out of time and was drifting along close to death, and willing to die. I had nothing against sentimental feelings; I was pleased and thankful that this burned-out heart of mine could still experience feelings of any kind. So I luxuriated in my memories of the old pub, my fondness for its clumsy old chairs, its smell of smoke and wine, the warm glow of familiarity and something akin to homeliness that all these things brought to me. It is beautiful to take leave of things. It puts you in a gentle frame of mind. I felt a fondness for the hard chair I was sitting on and for my rustic tumbler, a fondness for the cool, fruity taste of the wine from Alsace, a fondness for each and everyone known to me in that room, for the faces of the drinkers perched dreamily on the bar stools, those disillusioned figures I had long thought of as my brothers. What I was experiencing here were the sentimental feelings of a typical bourgeois, given just a touch of added spice by an old-fashioned, romantic attachment to the atmosphere of pubs that stemmed from my boyhood, when such establishments with their wines and cigars were still forbidden things, strange and glorious. Yet no Steppenwolf reared up and bared his teeth, threatening to tear my sentimental feelings to shreds. I went on sitting there peacefully, basking in the glow of the past, in the now feeble rays of a sun that had already set.

A street trader came in, selling roast chestnuts, and I bought a handful from him. Then an old woman came with flowers and I bought a few carnations for the landlady from her. Only when I was about to pay and reached in vain for my usual coat pocket did I again become aware that I was in evening dress. Masked ball! Hermione!

However, I couldn't bring myself to go to the Globe Rooms just yet. There was still ample time. And besides, I felt reluctant to go, held back by misgivings of one sort or another, as had been the case recently every time I had been facing such an evening's entertainment. I had a horror of entering vast, overcrowded and noisy rooms, for instance, and still felt as intimidated as a school-boy by the strange atmosphere in this world of the playboy, and by the prospect of having to dance.

Sauntering along, I happened to pass by a cinema with its bright lights and gigantic coloured posters. I walked on a few steps but then turned back and went in, thinking that I could sit there nice and quietly in the dark until about eleven o'clock. Following the boy-usher with his torch, I stumbled through the curtains into the dark of the auditorium where, having found a seat, I was suddenly immersed in the Old Testament. It was one of those films produced at great expense and with considerable sophistication, allegedly not for profit, but with noble and sacred intentions, so that even schoolchildren were taken to see them in the afternoon by the teachers responsible for their religious instruction. This one, enacting the story of Moses and the Israelites in Egypt, involved an enormous contingent of people, horses and camels in addition to the splendour of the ruling Pharaoh's palaces and scenes of Jewish hardship in the hot desert sands. I saw old Moses, a splendidly theatrical Moses, his hairstyle loosely modelled on Walt Whitman's, striding through the desert with a long staff, looking grim and fiery like some Wotan at the head of the Jews. I saw him praying to God by the Red Sea, saw the Red Sea parting to form a passageway, a sunken track between mountainous masses of water dammed back. (Quite how the production team had contrived to stage this was an issue that might be debated for hours by the members of confirmation classes taken by their ministers to see the film.) Then I saw the Prophet and his fearful people striding across, while behind them the Pharaoh's war chariots came into view. I saw the Egyptians hesitating at the sea's edge and shrinking back before plucking up their courage and daring to wade in. Then I saw the mountainous masses of water closing over the Pharaoh, resplendent in his golden armour, and over all his chariots and warriors. I couldn't help thinking at this point of a wonderful duet for two basses by Handel, a glorious musical setting of this event. In addition I saw old Moses climbing Mount Sinai, a sombre-looking hero in a sombre wilderness of rocks, and there I watched Jehovah communicating the Ten Commandments to him by means of storm clouds, thunder and lightning, while at the foot of the mountain his good-for-nothing people were erecting the golden calf and indulging in pretty uproarious merry-making. To sit there and witness all this was such a bizarre and incredible experience for me, seeing the sacred stories with their heroes and miracles which, long ago in our childhood days, had conjured up a first, dim awareness of another world beyond the merely human, now being enacted in exchange for a modest admission fee in front of a grateful cinema audience which was sitting there quietly munching the sandwiches they had brought with them to eat. The whole thing was a fine vignette of our times with their vast junk culture on sale at knock-down prices to the masses. My God, to avoid an obscenity like this, it would have been better if at that time, in addition to the Egyptians, the Jews and indeed all other human beings had immediately perished too, meeting a violent but respectable end instead of dying the kind of dreadful, unreal, lukewarm death we were nowadays. Ah well, what was the point?

The film and the issues raised by it had done nothing to reduce the secret qualms I had about the masked ball or my undisclosed reluctance to attend it. On the contrary, it had had the unpleasant effect of increasing them, and, with Hermione in mind, I had to jolt myself into finally making my way to the Globe Rooms and venturing in. By now it was late, and the ball had been in full swing for some time. Sober as I was, and shy, I was caught up in a milling throng of costumed figures even before I had a chance to hand in my coat. I was nudged and jostled as if I were a close acquaintance; girls invited me to accompany them to the champagne parlours, and clowns clapped me heartily on the shoulder, addressing me with the familiar 'du', but I was having none of it. With some difficulty I squeezed my way through the overcrowded premises to the cloakroom and when I had been given my numbered token I made sure I put it carefully in my pocket, thinking I might need it again soon if the general hubbub became too much for me.

The revels extended to every part of the large building. There was dancing in all the main rooms, even down in the basement, and every corridor and flight of stairs was inundated with dancers in fancy dress, the sound of music and the laughter of groups scurrying to and fro. I sneaked apprehensively through the throng, moving from the Negro band to the homespun rustic musicians, from the vast, brightly lit main hall to the corridors and stairways, the bars, buffet restaurants and champagne parlours. Bizarre, zany paintings could be seen hanging on most of the walls, the work of the latest artists. The ball had attracted everyone: artists, journalists, academics, businessmen and also, of course, all the local fun-loving men and women about town. In one of the bands I saw Mr Pablo blowing enthusiastically on his curved horn, and when he spotted me he called out a loud greeting. Carried along by the crowd, I ended up in one room or another, going up one staircase and down the next. In one passage down in the basement the artists had created a make-believe hell in which a gang of musical devils were drumming away like madmen. I gradually started to keep an eye out for Hermione or Maria. Setting off in search of them, I made several efforts to get through to the main hall, but each time I either lost my way or had to give up because of the surge of people moving in the opposite direction to mine. By midnight I still hadn't found anyone. Feeling hot and dizzy already, although I hadn't danced, I threw myself in the nearest chair I could find, and ordered some wine, surrounded by people who were all total strangers to me. Noisy festivities of this sort, I concluded, were not the thing for an old man like me. Drinking my glass of wine in a resigned frame of mind, I stared at the naked arms and backs of the womenfolk, eyed the many grotesque costumed figures wafting by me, and had to put up with their constant nudging and pushing. The few girls who asked to sit on my lap or wanted to dance with me were sent on their way without so much as a word. 'Sulky old so-and-so,' one of them cried, and she was right. I decided to raise my spirits and give myself some Dutch courage by carrying on drinking, but even the wine didn't taste good and I scarcely managed to down a second glass. And bit by bit I became aware of Steppenwolf standing behind me and sticking out his tongue. I was out of place here, a forlorn, lifeless figure. There was no doubt I had come with the best of intentions, but I just couldn't get into the right party mood. The deafening roars of enjoyment, the laughter, all the high jinks going on around me struck me as stupid and forced.

The upshot was that at one o'clock, feeling disappointed and cross, I stole back to the cloakroom to put on my coat and leave. This was a defeat, a relapse into wolfishness on my part, something Hermione would scarcely forgive me for. But there was nothing else for it. While laboriously making my way through the crowds as far as the cloakroom, I had again taken a good look around to see whether I could spot either of my girlfriends. But to no avail. Now I was standing at the counter, and the polite man behind it was already holding out his hand to take my token, when I reached into my waistcoat pocket only to discover that it was gone! Oh hell, that was all I needed! Struggling to make up my mind whether I should leave, I had on several occasions felt in my pocket as I meandered sadly through the rooms or sat drinking my insipid wine, and I had always found the round, flat token in place there. And now it had gone. Everything was conspiring against me.

'Lost your number?' asked a shrill voice, that of a small devil standing next to me dressed in red and yellow. 'Here, you can have mine, chum,' he added, already offering it to me in his outstretched hand. I automatically took it with my fingers and by the time I had given it a twirl the nimble little chap had already vanished.

However, when I raised the little round cardboard token to my eyes to identify the number on it, all I saw was the scrawl of some tiny handwriting, and no number at all. Asking the cloak-room attendant to wait a while, I moved under the nearest chandelier and tried to read. There was something scribbled on it in tiny wobbly block letters that were hard to decipher:

TONIGHT FROM 4 AM ONWARDS MAGIC THEATRE
– FOR MAD PEOPLE ONLY –
PAY AT THE DOOR WITH YOUR MIND.
NOT FOR EVERYBODY. HERMIONE IS IN HELL

Just as a marionette, when the puppeteer has momentarily let slip its wire, comes back to life after a brief spell of stiff lifeless-ness and apathy, is again part of the play, dancing and acting, so I, at the sudden pull of the magic wire, rushed back lithely, youth-fully and eagerly to join the hustle and bustle that I had just fled from, feeling tired, unenthusiastic and old. Never has a sinner been in more of a hurry to get to hell. Only a moment ago my patent-leather shoes had been pinching, I'd been nauseated by the perfume-laden air and wilting in the heat. Now I was hurtling spring-heeled towards hell, crossing all the rooms to the rhythm of a one-step. The air felt full of magic spells, I was cradled and carried along by the warmth, by all the blaring music, the riot of colour, the scent of women's shoulders, the intoxication of the partying hundreds, the laughing, the dance rhythms, the glint in all the inflamed eyes. A girl dressed as a Spanish dancer flew into my arms, cheekily ordering me to dance with her. 'Not possible,' I said, 'I have to go to hell. But I don't mind taking a kiss from you along with me.' Her red lips under the mask came closer, but it was only when they met mine in a kiss that I recognized Maria. I put my arms tight around her. Her full lips were like a summer rose in full bloom. And now we were indeed dancing already, our lips still touching, dancing past Pablo too, who was bending over his softly wailing reed instrument, in love with its sound. His beautiful, animal-like, gleaming eyes took us in, though his mind seemed to be half elsewhere. Before we had danced twenty steps, however, the music stopped, and reluctantly I released Maria from my arms.

'I would have loved one more dance with you,' I said, thrilled by her warmth. 'Walk with me a little way, will you, Maria? I'm so enamoured of your beautiful arm I'd like to hold on to it for a moment longer. But Hermione has summoned me, you see. She's in hell.'

'I thought as much. Farewell, Harry, you'll always have a place in my heart.' These were her parting words. Parting, autumn, destiny: all these had been evoked for me by the full, ripe fragrance of this late rose of summer.

On I went, along the corridors milling with flirting couples, down the stairs to hell. There, on the pitch-black walls, infernally harsh lights were burning and the musical devils were feverishly playing away. A handsome youth without a mask was sitting on a tall bar stool in evening dress. With an air of disdain he briefly looked me up and down. Getting on for twenty couples were dancing in the very cramped space and I was forced up against the wall by the whirling crush. Avidly and nervously I observed all the women. Most of them were still wearing their masks; a few laughed at me; but none of them was Hermione. The handsome youth, perched on his bar stool, was looking scornfully across at me. The next time there was a break in the dancing Hermione would call out to me, I thought. But the dancing finished and nobody came.

I went over to the bar, which was wedged into one corner of

the low-ceilinged room. Joining the queue by the youth's stool, I ordered myself a whisky. As I was drinking it I could see the young man's profile. It looked as familiar and charming as a picture from the remote past, made precious by the still veil of dust cast upon it over the years. Then all of a sudden it clicked. Yes, of course, that's who it was. Hermann, my best friend when I was a boy!

'Hermann!' I said tentatively.

He smiled. 'Harry? Have you found me?'

It was Hermione, only with a slightly different hairstyle and a touch of make-up. Pale and distinctive, her intelligent face gazed out at me from the fashionable stand-up collar of her dress shirt. Her hands, protruding from the shirt's white cuffs and the wide black sleeves of her dinner jacket, looked strangely small, her feet strangely dainty in the black-and-white men's silk socks emerging from her long black trousers.

'Is it dressed up like this you intend to make me fall in love with you, Hermione?'

Nodding, she said: 'So far I have only succeeded in making a few ladies fall in love. But now it's your turn. Let's drink a glass of champagne first.'

This we did, squatting on our tall bar stools, while right next to us people went on dancing to the increasingly heated and violent sound of the strings in the band. And very soon I had fallen for Hermione, apparently without her going to the least trouble to make me do so. Since she was wearing men's clothes I couldn't dance with her, couldn't permit myself any show of affection or make any advances, yet while she seemed remote and neutral in her masculine disguise she was enveloping me in all her feminine charms by means of looks, words and gestures. Without so much as even touching her I succumbed to her spell, a spell which, consistent with the role she was playing, was herm-aphrodisiac. For what she talked to me about was Hermann and childhood, my childhood and hers, those years before puberty when our youthful capacity for love extends not only to both sexes but to everything under the sun, things intellectual and spiritual as well as sensual, casting its spell over them all and endowing them with that fairy-tale aptitude for transformation that only poets and a chosen few occasionally regain even in the later stages of life. She was playing the role of a young man, no question, smoking cigarettes, indulging in witty, light-hearted chat, frequently seizing the opportunity to poke a little fun, but her every word and gesture had an erotic charge, transforming it, en route to my senses, into an agent of sweet seduction.

There had I been thinking I knew everything there was to know about Hermione, yet that night she appeared to me in a totally new light! She tightened the desired net around me so gently that I hardly noticed it, toyed with me like a mermaid as she passed me the sweet poison to drink.

We sat chatting and drinking champagne. We sauntered through the ballrooms, observing the goings-on like adventurous explorers, eavesdropping on the lovemaking of couples we had singled out. Pointing out women she wanted me to dance with, Hermione gave me tips as to how I might best win over this one or that. We acted as rivals, both on the trail of the same woman for a while, both dancing with her in turn, both attempting to win her. Yet all this was just a masquerade, a game between the two of us, binding us more closely together, kindling the fire of our passion for one another. It was all a fairy-tale experience, made richer by an additional dimension, deeper by an additional layer of meaning. Everything was make-believe, symbolic. We saw a very beautiful young woman who looked slightly ailing and out of sorts. 'Hermann' danced with her, restoring some colour to her cheeks, after which the two of them disappeared into an alcove where sparkling wine was on offer. She told me afterwards that she had conquered her as a woman by the magic charms of Lesbos, not as a man. For me, on the other hand, the whole building, ringing with music and full of rooms echoing to the sound of dancing by intoxicated crowds of masked revellers, was gradually turning into a wonderland, the paradise of my dreams. Blossom upon blossom lured me with its fragrance, my fingers reached out tentatively to fondle fruit upon fruit, serpents eyed me seductively from the shade of green foliage, lotus blossom drifted eerily across a black swamp, magic birds were singing their enticing songs in the branches of the trees. Yet all of this was leading the way to one destination, making my heart heavy with fresh yearning for the one and only woman I desired. At one point I was dancing passionately with a girl I didn't know, making a play for her, sweeping her along in a heady whirl when all at once, as we were floating on a cloud of unreality, she burst out laughing and said: 'You've changed out of all recognition! Earlier tonight you were such a stupid bore.' Then I recognized her as the one who, hours ago, had called me a 'sulky old so-and-so'. Now she thought I was hers, but come the next dance it was another I was holding passionately close. I danced for two hours or more without letting up, each and every dance, even those I hadn't learned. Again and again Hermann, the smiling youth, would pop up near to me and give me a nod before disappearing from view in the milling crowd.

That night of the ball I experienced a sensation which, though familiar to any teenage girl or student, I had not known the like of in all my fifty years. I mean the thrill of a party, the exhilaration that comes from celebrating with others, the mystery of losing one's identity in the crowd, the *unio mystica* of joy. I had often heard people talk about it, there wasn't a servant girl who hadn't experienced it, and I had frequently seen the gleam in the eyes of those describing it. My response had always been a half supercilious, half envious smile. In the course of my life I must have witnessed that gleam a hundred times: in the eyes of people deep in drunken reverie or freed from all self-restraint; in the semi-deranged smile of someone utterly carried away, absorbed in the euphoric mood of a crowd. I had seen both noble and ignoble instances of it: on the faces of drunken recruits and naval ratings, for example, just as much as those of great artists, say, enthusiastically taking part in performances at a festival, and not less on those of young soldiers going to war. Even very recently I had admired, adored, mocked and envied such a gleam in the eyes and faraway smile on the face of my friend Pablo when, blissfully carried away by the excitement of playing in the band, he was bending over his saxophone or watching the conductor, the drummer or the banjo player with rapt and ecstatic attention. There were times when I had thought it possible only for really young people or nations which didn't permit individuals to stand out strongly from the tribe to produce smiles like this, childlike, beaming faces of this sort. Yet on this blissful night, here was I myself, I, Harry alias Steppenwolf, with just such a smile on my beaming face. I myself was afloat in this deep, childlike, fairy-tale pool of happiness, breathing this sweet, dreamlike, intoxicating atmosphere composed of communal revelry, music, rhythm, wine and sexual desire. To think that in the past I had so often listened with a disdainful and woefully superior attitude when some student or other, reporting on a ball, was singing the praises of all these things! I was no longer myself. In the heady atmosphere of the festivities my personality had dissolved like salt in water. I was dancing with this or that particular woman, but she was not the only one in my arms, not the only one whose hair brushed against me or whose perfume I inhaled. No, they were all mine, all the other women in the same room, afloat in the same dance as me and the same music, their beaming faces sailing by me like fantastically large flowers. And I was all theirs, we were all part of one another. The men too had a part in everything. They were no strangers to me, I felt part of them as well.

Their smiles were mine, the amorous advances they made were mine, and mine theirs.

That winter a new dance tune, a foxtrot entitled 'Yearning' was taking the world by storm. There were constant requests for it at the ball and it was played time and again. It was in all our heads, we were carried away by it, all of us humming along to its tune. I kept on dancing without a break, with every woman who happened to come my way, with very young girls, women in the full flush of youth, women in the summer of their lives, women beginning wistfully to fade. Delighted by them all, I was beaming, laughing, happy. When he saw me in such a radiant mood, Pablo, who had always considered me a poor devil who was greatly to be pitied, gave me a joyful look, his eyes flashing. Then, rising enthusiastically from his seat in the band and playing a powerful flourish on his horn, he climbed on his chair and, standing up there, puffed out his cheeks, blowing for all he was worth and blissfully rocking himself and his instrument in time to 'Yearning'. My partner and I blew kisses to him, singing along loudly to the dance tune. Ah well, I was thinking to myself meanwhile, whatever might happen to me, for once in my life I too have been happy, beaming, liberated from my self, a brother of Pablo, a child.

I had lost all sense of time. I don't know how many hours or moments this euphoric happiness of mine lasted. It also escaped my notice that the festivities, the more feverish they became, were concentrated in an ever-more confined area of the building. Most of the guests had already left, the corridors were now silent, and many of the lights had gone out. The staircase to the first floor was deserted, in the upper rooms one band after another had ceased playing and departed. Only in the main dance hall and down in hell were the frantic drunken revels still going on, and their fever was rising steadily. Since I could not dance with Hermione in her young man's clothes, we had only briefly encountered and greeted each other during breaks between dances and in the end she had vanished completely, not just from my sight, but also from my thoughts. I no longer had any thoughts. I was beside myself, floating along in the drunken throng of dancers; affected by scents, colours, sights and snatches of conversation; in receipt of welcoming and inspiriting looks from strangers, surrounded by strange faces, lips, cheeks, arms, breasts and knees; flung backwards and forwards like a wave to the rhythm of the music.

Half emerging from my reverie for a moment, I suddenly spotted among the remaining guests, who were now crammed into one of the small rooms, the last one where music was being played, a dark-haired Pierrette, her face painted white. She was a beautiful, fresh-looking girl, the only one wearing a mask, a delightful creature that I had not once set eyes on during the whole night. Whereas you could tell just how late it was from the appearance of everyone else, their ruddy faces, their crumpled costumes, their limp collars and ruffs, the dark-haired Pierrette, her white face covered by a mask, was standing there looking as fresh as a daisy. There wasn't a crease in her costume, her ruff was immaculate, her lace cuffs shone, and not a hair on her head was out of place. Irresistibly attracted to her, I took her in my arms and drew her on to the dance floor. Her sweet-smelling ruff tickling my chin, her hair brushing my cheek, with her taut young body she responded to my movements more delicately and intimately than any other partner I had danced with that night, now ducking away from me, now playfully luring me into continually renewed physical contact. And all of a sudden, when bending down and seeking her lips with mine as we danced, I saw those lips break into a superior smile, familiar to me of old. Now I recognized the firm chin, rejoiced to recognize the shoulders, the elbows, the hands. It wasn't Hermann any more, but Hermione, in a change of clothes, refreshed by a hint of perfume and a touch of face powder. Our lips met in a passionate kiss, and in a momentary gesture of longing and surrender, she pressed her whole body up against me, as far down as her knees, before withdrawing her lips and retreating to dance at a greater distance. When the music stopped we stood there, still in an embrace, and all the flushed couples around us clapped, stamped their feet and shouted out, goading the exhausted band to play an encore of 'Yearning'. And now, suddenly feeling the approach of dawn, seeing its pale light behind the curtains, and sensing that our enjoyment was coming to an end, soon to be replaced by tiredness, we all threw ourselves blindly into one last desperate dance, laughing out loud as we entered the swell of music and light. It was a romp. We strode along to the beat, couple upon couple tightly pressed together, all feeling the great wave of blissful happiness breaking over us again. During this dance Hermione abandoned her air of superiority and cool disdain, knowing that no further effort was required to make me fall in love with her. I was hers, and this showed in the way she danced, the look in her eyes, the smile on her face, and her kisses, all of which were unrestrained. All the women of that fervid night, all those who had aroused my passion, all those I had made a play for or lusted after from afar, had now merged into just one, and she was bursting into flower in my arms.

This nuptial dance went on for a long, long time. On two or three occasions the music faltered, the wind and brass sections lowering their instruments, the pianist getting up from his stool at the grand, the first violinist shaking his head in refusal. And each time, their enthusiasm rekindled by the frenzied pleas of the remaining dancers, they started playing again, playing faster and more animatedly. Then all at once, as we were still standing in each other's arms, catching our breath after the latest eager exertions on the floor, we heard the loud bang of the piano lid being shut and our arms drooped wearily to our sides, as did those of the musicians in the wind and string sections of the band. His eyes blinking, the flautist packed his instrument away in its case, doors opened and cold air came flooding in. Attendants appeared with our coats and the barman switched off the lights. Everyone rapidly dispersed in eerie, ghostlike fashion. The dancers, only moments ago still aflame, were shivering as they hurriedly slipped into their overcoats and turned up their collars. Hermione was standing there, looking pale but smiling. As she slowly raised her arms to brush her hair back, the light caught one of her armpits and I could see a thin, infinitely delicate line of shadow running from there to her hidden breast. It seemed to me that all her charm, all her beautiful body's potential for love-play was concentrated in that tiny dark thread, hovering there like a smile.

We stood looking at one another, the last people in the room, the last in the whole building. Somewhere down below I heard a door bang, a glass being dashed to pieces, the dying sound of people giggling, all intermingled with the harsh, urgent noise of cars being cranked up. Somewhere else, at an indeterminable distance and altitude, I heard laughter ring out, an extraordinarily bright and cheerful kind of laughter that was nevertheless eerie and alien too. As if made of crystal and ice, it was clear and radiant, but cold and inexorable. How come this strange laughter sounded so familiar to me? I couldn't put my finger on it.

The two of us stood looking at one another. Momentarily I regained consciousness, sobering up. Overcome by a sudden attack of great weariness from the rear, I could feel the sweat-drenched clothes clinging to my body, disgustingly damp and tepid, and could see my red hands, covered in swollen veins, poking out from my crumpled, sweaty cuffs. But this awareness was gone again in a flash, nullified by one look from Hermione. Before her gaze, which seemed like the mirror of my own soul, all reality disintegrated, even the reality of my sensual desire for her. We were looking at one another spellbound; my poor little soul was looking at me spellbound.

'Are you ready?' Hermione asked, her smile vanishing, just as the shadow above her breast had vanished. Far away and high up, in regions unknown, the strange laughter died away.

I nodded. I was ready, no doubt about it.

Now Pablo, the musician, appeared in the doorway, his cheerful eyes gleaming at us, eyes that were essentially those of an animal, although an animal's eyes are always serious, whereas his were forever laughing, which made them human. With all the cordial friendliness typical of the man he signalled to us to follow him. He had put on a casual jacket of brightly coloured silk. Above its red lapels his soft, floppy shirt collar and his pale, worn-out face combined to make him look faded and wan, but this impression was nullified by his radiant dark eyes. They too were capable of nullifying reality, they too could work magic.

As invited, we joined him in the doorway, where he said to me in a whisper: 'Harry, brother, there's a little entertainment I'd like to invite you to. Only mad people admitted. You pay at the door with your mind. Are you ready?' Again I nodded.

The dear chap! Linking arms with us, Hermione on his right and me on his left, he led us with tender loving care up a flight of stairs into a small, round room. Lit by a bluish light from above, it was almost completely empty save for a small, round table and three armchairs, in which we sat down.

Where were we? Was I sleeping? Was I at home? Was I sitting in a car, going somewhere? No, I was sitting in the blue light of a round room, where the air was thin and reality too, having lost much of its density, was just a thin veneer. Why was Hermione so pale? Why was Pablo doing so much talking? Could it be that I was making him talk? Was it my own voice emerging from him? Was it not my own soul, that frightened, lost bird, I could see mirrored in his dark eyes, just as I had in the grey eyes of Hermione?

Our friend Pablo, looking at us with all that good-natured and slightly formal kindness of his, talked and talked at length, and about many things. This man, whom I had never heard string two sentences together, who showed no interest in debating any topic or statement, whom I would scarcely have considered capable of thinking about anything, was now talking, indeed speaking fluently in that kind, warm voice of his, and without a slip of the tongue.

'Friends, I have invited you to an entertainment that Harry has long been dreaming of and wishing to attend. It is rather late, and like as not we are all slightly tired, so let us rest a while here first and take a little something to fortify us.'

From a niche in the wall he took down three small glasses and a quaint little bottle, also a tiny, exotic-looking box made of varie-gated wood. He poured three full glasses from the bottle, then took three long, thin, yellow cigarettes from the box and, produc-ing a lighter from his silk jacket, offered it to us in turn. Now, leaning back in our armchairs, we all slowly smoked the cigar-ettes, which gave off fumes as dense as incense, and, sip by tiny sip, slowly drank the unfamiliar, bitter-sweet liquid with its curi-ously alien taste. The drink really did have the effect of putting new life into us and making us feel extremely happy. It was as if we were being filled with gas and becoming weightless. There we sat, taking short puffs on our cigarettes, relaxing, sipping from our glasses, able to feel ourselves becoming lighter and merrier. And as we did so, the muffled sound of Pablo's warm voice could be heard, saying:

'It gives me great pleasure, dear Harry, to be allowed to play host to you in a small way tonight. You have often been sick to death of life, haven't you, longing to see the back of it? You are yearning to leave this world behind, the time and reality we live in, and to exchange them for a different reality more suited to you, a world that is timeless. Well, do so, dear friend, I'm offering you the possibility. You know, of course, where this other world lies hidden, know that the world you are seeking is that of your own soul, and that the different reality you are longing for is only to be found deep in your own self. I can give you nothing that doesn't already exist in you. I can open the doors to no picture gallery other than that of your mind. All I can give you is the opportunity, the stimulus, the key. I am going to help you make your own world visible, that is all.'

Again feeling in the pocket of his brightly coloured jacket, he took out a round pocket mirror.

'Take a look. This is how you have perceived yourself until now!'

As he held the little looking glass in front of my eyes I couldn't help thinking 'mirror, mirror in the hand', a variation on the familiar line from my childhood. What I now saw was rather blurred and hazy, a disturbingly agitated image, full of inner turmoil and ferment. It was of me myself, Harry Haller, and inside Harry was Steppenwolf, a timid, handsome, apparently stray wolf, looking around nervously with a glint in its eyes that was now furious, now sad. Incessantly on the move, the image of the wolf was flowing through Harry just as a tributary of a different colour can be seen merging with a major river, churning and clouding its waters. The two were locked in painful combat, eating away at one another, each longing to assert a fully formed identity, but in vain. The fluid, half-formed wolf was gazing at me sadly, ever so sadly, with its handsome, timid eyes.

'This is how you have perceived yourself,' Pablo repeated softly, putting the mirror back in his pocket. I was thankful to close my eyes and take another sip of the strange elixir.

'Now we've had a good rest, a fortifying drink and a bit of a chat, I'd like to take you to my peep show, if you are no longer feeling tired, and show you my little theatre. Agreed?'

We stood up and Pablo, smiling, led the way. Opening a door, he pulled a curtain to one side and we found ourselves standing exactly in the middle of the rounded, horseshoe-shaped corridor of a theatre. This corridor curved away on both sides past a large number, an incredibly large number, of narrow doorways to the theatre's boxes.

'This is our theatre,' Pablo explained, 'an entertaining theatre, in which I trust you will find a whole variety of things to make you laugh.' As he said this, he himself suddenly laughed out loud, shaking me to the core, even though his laughter lasted no more than a few notes. It was the same clear, alien-sounding laughter I had already heard earlier coming from on high.

'My little theatre has doors leading to however many boxes you wish, ten or a hundred or a thousand, and behind each door you will find the very things you are seeking waiting there for you. It is a fine cabinet of curiosities, my dear friend, but you would not benefit from it in the least if you were to do the rounds of it as you are now constituted, for you would be inhibited and blinded by what you are accustomed to term your personality. I have no doubt you guessed long ago that the terms you use to character-ize what you are longing for – "overcoming time" or "finding release from reality" or whatever – have no other significance than your desire to rid yourself of your so-called personality. It is the prison you are doing time in. And if you were to enter the theatre as you are, you would see everything through Harry's eyes, perceive everything through Steppenwolf's old pair of spectacles. You are therefore invited to take off the said spectacles and to kindly divest yourself of your dear personality, leaving it here at the cloakroom, where you may reclaim it any time you wish. The wonderful evening you have spent at the ball, your reading of the Steppenwolf tract and lastly the little stimulant we have just consumed will in all likelihood have prepared you adequately. Once you have divested yourself of your esteemed personality, Harry, you will have the left-hand side of the theatre at your disposal, Hermione the portion to the right, and you can meet up again on the inside as and when you wish. Hermione, I would like you to please go behind the curtain while I take Harry in first.'

Hermione disappeared to the right, past a gigantic mirror that covered the rear wall from the floor right up to the vaulted ceiling.

'Now then, Harry, come along and cheer up, do. The whole point of the exercise is to cheer you up and teach you how to laugh, and I hope you will make my task an easy one. You do feel well, don't you? Yes? You are not anxious, by any chance? That's good then, very good. You are now about to enter our make-believe world, not anxiously at all, but with genuine pleasure, and you will be introduced to it, as is customary, by means of a little make-believe act of suicide.'

Taking out his little pocket mirror again, he held it in front of my face. Once more I could see the blurred, confused image of Harry, fused with the wrestling figure of the wolf. To tell the truth, this familiar image was not at all congenial to me, so putting an end to it was unlikely to worry me at all.

'My dear friend, all that's required of you is to obliterate this now redundant mirror image. If you can bring yourself to laugh heartily when you contemplate it, that will be enough. This is a school of humour that you are in, designed to teach you how to laugh. You see, the first requirement of our advanced humour course is to stop taking yourself seriously.'

Taking a steady look in the 'mirror, mirror in the hand', I saw the hybrid Harry-Wolf going through his painful convulsions. Momentarily I felt a slight but painful twinge in my innards too, something akin to memory, homesickness, remorse. Then this slight anxiety gave way to a feeling similar to the one you have when a bad tooth is extracted from your cocaine-numbed jaw and you sigh, not just with relief, but also amazement at the fact that it hasn't hurt at all. And this feeling was accompanied by a fresh sense of joviality, an urge to laugh that I could not resist. Indeed, I burst out laughing, which was a great release.

The little cloudy image in the looking glass flared up briefly, then vanished, leaving the small round surface of the mirror looking suddenly grey, rough and opaque, as if it had been scorched. With a laugh, Pablo threw the fragment of glass away and it rolled out of sight along the floor of the endless corridor.

'What a good laugh that was, Harry!' Pablo exclaimed. 'Well done! One of these days you'll be able to laugh like the Immortals. At last you've managed to kill off Steppenwolf, which it's impossible to do with a razor. Just make sure he stays dead. In a short while you will be able to leave stupid reality behind you. You are more likeable today than you've ever been, my dear chap. We must drink to our close friendship the next time we get the opportunity. Then we can say 'du' to one another and, if it still matters to you, we can talk philosophy and argue with one another, discussing music, Mozart and Gluck, Plato and Goethe to your heart's content. You will understand now why such things were impossible before. – I hope you have succeeded in ridding yourself of Steppenwolf for the day, because of course your suicide is not final. We are not dealing with reality here, but mere images. By choosing beautiful and cheerful images you can demonstrate that you aren't in fact still in love with your questionable personality. Should you nonetheless feel the urge to have it restored, you need only look into the mirror I am now about to show you. However, I take it you are familiar with the old wise saying "A mirror in the hand is better than two on the wall". Ha! Ha!' (Again that fine, terrible laughter of his rang out.) 'So there, and now we just need to perform one little amusing ritual. Now that you have cast off the spectacles of your personality, come and take a look in a proper mirror. You'll find it fun.'

Laughing as he did so, and giving me the odd little friendly pat and stroke, he turned me round to face the gigantic mirror on the wall. In this one I could see myself.

For just the briefest of moments I saw the Harry I knew, except that the look on his face was unusually good-humoured, bright and radiant. However, scarcely had I time to recognize him when he disintegrated, a second figure detaching itself from him, then a third, a tenth and a twentieth until the whole gigantic mirror was full of nothing but Harrys or fragments of Harrys, innumerable Harrys, each of which I only managed to glimpse and recognize for a fleeting instant. Some of these many Harrys were as old as me, some older, some really aged, whereas others were very young, young men, lads, schoolboys, little rascals, children. Fifty-year-old and twenty-year-old Harrys were running and jumping all over the place. There were thirty-year-olds and five-year-olds; serious and funny, dignified and comical Harrys. Some were well dressed, some in rags, some totally naked even, while some were bald and others had long hair. Yet all of them were me, and they were all only glimpsed and recognized in a flash before vanishing again. They were dispersing in all directions, to the left, to the right, into the depths of the mirror or right out of it. One of them, an elegant young chap, leaped into Pablo's arms with a laugh, pressed him to his breast and ran off with him. And another one that I particularly liked, a charming, handsome lad of sixteen or seventeen, darted off along the corridor, eagerly reading the inscriptions on all the doors. Following him, I saw him stop outside one door, on which I read:

> ALL GIRLS ARE YOURS
> INSERT 1 MARK PIECE

With one jump the dear boy shot up head first, threw himself into the slot and vanished behind the door.

Pablo too had vanished, as had the mirror, so it seemed, and with it all the numerous Harry figures. Sensing that I was now left to my own devices and that the theatre was mine to explore, I walked from door to door, full of curiosity. On each one I read an inscription, an enticing message, a promise.

★

Attracted by the inscription

> TALLY-HO! A-HUNTING WE WILL GO
> HIGH SEASON FOR MOTOR CARS

I opened the narrow door and went in.

I was whisked away into a world of loud noise and turbulence. Cars, some of them armour-plated, were tearing along the streets, hunting down pedestrians, running them over and reducing them to pulp, squashing them to bits against the walls of the buildings. Immediately I understood that the war between human beings and machines, long prepared, long expected and long feared, had now finally broken out. Everywhere there were dead and mutilated bodies lying around; everywhere too there were the buckled and half-burned-out wrecks of cars that had skidded out of control. Aeroplanes were circling above this utterly chaotic scene, and people with rifles and machine guns were shooting at them too from many windows and rooftops. On all the walls there were garish, splendidly provocative posters. In gigantic letters, flaring up like torches, the nation was being called upon to finally take up arms on behalf of humanity against machines; to finally exterminate the fat, handsomely dressed, perfumed plutocrats who, with the help of machines, were living off the fat of others. Also to put an end to their huge, coughing, evilly snarling and devilishly humming motor cars; to finally set fire to the factories and go some way towards clearing out and depopulating the desecrated earth so that grass might grow again and the dust-filled concrete jungle might give way to things such as woods, meadows, heaths, streams and marshland. From other posters, in contrast, splendidly stylized and beautifully painted in gentler, less childish colours, came stirring warnings, composed with extraordinary subtlety and wit, about the chaos and anarchy that were threatening all prudent property owners. In truly gripping terms these posters pictured the blessings of law and order, hard work, property and culture, and they praised machines as human beings' latest and greatest invention, with the aid of which they would be transformed into gods. As I read them, deep in thought, I could not help admiring the posters, the red ones as well as the green. Both their fiery eloquence and their compelling logic made an enormous impression on me. They were right, I thought, as I stood there profoundly convinced, now in front of one poster, now in front of another, albeit perceptibly disturbed by the fairly hefty shooting match going on all around me. Well, there was a war being fought, that was the main thing: a vehement, spirited war that was highly congenial because it wasn't a matter of the Kaiser, the Republic or national frontiers, or of flags and battle colours and such things of a more decorative and theatrical kind – all essentially shabby issues. No, this was a war in which all those who felt stifled, all those for whom life had acquired a nasty taste, were giving full vent to their grievances and trying their hardest to set in train a process leading to the general destruction of the shoddy world of civilization. All their eyes were shining so brightly with a genuine, burning desire to destroy and kill that I felt the same passions burning just as fiercely in me, flourishing unchecked like tall, rank, blood-red flowers. I was more than happy to join in the fighting.

However, the nicest thing of all was the sudden appearance at my side of my former classmate Gustav, whom I had completely lost touch with decades ago. Of all my early-childhood friends he had once been the wildest and strongest, the one with the greatest appetite for life. My heart leaped to see his bright blue eyes winking at me once again, and when he beckoned to me I was at once delighted to follow him.

'Good Lord, Gustav!' I exclaimed happily. 'I never expected to see you again! What have you been doing with yourself all these years, then?'

Annoyed, he burst out laughing, just as he used to as a boy.

'Stupid fool! Do we really have to begin right away with tittle-tattle and questions like that? If you must know, I became a theology professor. There you have it, but luckily there's a war on now, my lad, and no call for theology. Come on, what are you waiting for?'

Just then a small motor-truck came puffing its way towards us. Shooting down the driver, Gustav leaped up in the cab with all the agility of a monkey and brought the vehicle to a stop. He got me to climb up alongside him and we drove off at one hell of a pace, past upturned vehicles and through a hail of rifle bullets, making our way out of the town and its suburbs.

'Are you on the side of the factory owners?' I asked my friend.

'Don't ask me, it's just a matter of taste. We can worry about that once we're out of town. But no, hang on. If anything, I think we should opt for the other side, even though it basically makes no difference, of course. I'm a theologian, and since my predecessor Luther in his day came to the aid of the rich and the princes against the peasants, I think we ought now to redress the balance a little. This vehicle's no good. Let's hope it holds out for another few kilometres!'

As fast as the wind, the heaven-born wind, we rattled along, entering a peaceful green stretch of land many miles wide; then on through a vast plain before slowly climbing into a huge mountain range. Here we came to a halt on a smooth, shimmering road that boldly wound its way upwards between sheer walls of rock and a low protecting wall, high above a bright blue lake.

'Lovely area,' I said.

'Very pretty. We can call it Axle Road, Harry my boy, since various axles are about to come to grief on it. Just you watch.'

There was a large pine tree by the roadside, and high up in it we could see something like a hut made of planks, a raised stand with a lookout. Smiling brightly, Gustav gave me a sly wink with those blue eyes of his and we both hurriedly got out of our truck. Clambering up the trunk of the pine, we hid ourselves, gasping for breath, in the lookout. It was an ideal spot. We found shotguns, pistols and boxes of cartridges there. And we scarcely had time to cool off and settle down in this shooting box before we heard the hoarse, domineering sound of a car's horn as it approached the nearest bend. It was a huge limousine, its engine humming as it drove at high speed along the smooth mountain road. We already had hold of the shotguns. The excitement was wonderful.

'Aim at the chauffeur,' Gustav ordered swiftly, just as the heavy vehicle was racing by beneath us. And, before I knew it, I was taking aim at the blue cap of the man at the steering wheel and pulling the trigger. The man slumped at the wheel. The car careered on, smashed into the cliff wall and rebounded, only to crash heavily against the low protecting wall like a great fat bumble bee in a rage. Then it overturned and there was a short, soft thud as it jumped the wall and plummeted into the depths.

'That's one done for,' Gustav said with a laugh. 'The next one's mine.'

And no sooner had he said it than another car came racing by, the three or four people in it looking very small in their upholstered seats. I could see part of a woman's veil, blown back in a stiff, horizontal line from her head. It was a light blue veil, and I actually felt sorry about it because, for all we knew, it might be concealing the shining face of the most beautiful of women. Good Lord, I thought, if we really must act the bold robber we might have done better to take our cue from those great model outlaws of the past who, for all their bloodlust, drew the line at killing members of the fair sex. However, Gustav had already fired. With a jerk the driver slumped down in his seat, the car mounted the vertical rock face, tipped over and, its wheels uppermost, landed back down on the road with a loud crash. We waited, but nothing moved. As if caught in a trap, the car's occupants remained silently lying under their vehicle. It was still humming and throbbing, its wheels turning comically in the air. All at once, however, there was a terrifying explosion and the car was engulfed in bright flames.

'It was a Ford,' Gustav said. 'We need to go down now and clear the road.'

Climbing down, we took a look at the flaming heap. By the time the wreck had fully burned out, which was not long, we had cut some young branches which we used to lever it aside and tip it over the road's edge into the abyss. For quite a while we could still hear it crashing down through the undergrowth. Two of the dead occupants, having fallen out of the car when it overturned, were lying there on the road, their clothes partly burned. The coat of one of them was still fairly intact, so I went through the pockets in the hope of finding out who he was. I discovered a leather wallet with visiting cards in it. Taking one out, I read on it the words: 'Tat tvam asi.'*

---

* A Sanskrit saying, literally meaning 'You are that' where 'Tat' ('that') is the fundamental principle underlying all cosmic reality, and 'tvam' ('you') denotes an individual's innermost self. To recognize that the two are identical, as this pronouncement of Vedantic Hinduism teaches, is to achieve salvation or liberation.

'Very amusing,' Gustav said, 'though in fact it makes no difference what the people we are killing are called. They're poor devils like us; their names are immaterial. This world has to be destroyed, and all of us with it. The least painful solution would be to flood it with water for ten minutes. Come on, back to work.'

We threw the dead bodies after the car. Another was already on its way, tooting its horn. We shot this one to pieces right there on the road. It spun on for a stretch, reeling like a drunk, before sagging and chugging to a halt. One occupant remained motionless inside but another, a pretty young girl, got out unscathed, even though she looked pale and was trembling violently. Greeting her in a friendly manner, we asked what we could do to help. For quite a while she just stared at us like one deranged, far too shocked to be able to speak.

'Come on, we might as well check on the old gentleman first,' Gustav said, turning towards the passenger who was still stuck there in his seat behind the dead chauffeur. He had short grey hair and intelligent, light-grey eyes that were open, even though, to judge from the blood flowing from his mouth and the worryingly stiff and crooked look of his neck, he seemed to be very badly injured.

'Allow me to introduce myself, Sir, my name is Gustav,' said my companion, addressing the old gentleman. 'We've taken the liberty of shooting your chauffeur. May I ask with whom we have the pleasure of speaking?'

The old man's small grey eyes gazed coolly and sadly at us.

'I am Senior Public Prosecutor Loering,' he said slowly. 'You have not only killed my poor chauffeur, but me too, for I can feel my end is near. Tell me, why did you shoot at us?'

'Because you were driving too fast.'

'We were driving at the normal speed.'

'It may have been normal yesterday, Your Honour, but it isn't normal today. Today we are of the opinion that any speed a car is driven at is too high. We have now taken to wrecking cars, all of them, and the rest of the machines too.'

'Even your shotguns?'

'Their turn will come too, if we have time. By tomorrow or the day after we'll presumably all be wiped out. As you know, our continent was terribly overpopulated. So the idea now is to clear the air.'

'Are you shooting indiscriminately at everyone?'

'Certainly. It's a shame to kill some of them, no doubt. I would have been sorry, for instance, to see the pretty young lady die. I suppose she's your daughter.'

'No, she is my typist.'

'So much the better. And now get out of the car, please, or let us pull you out, because it's going to be destroyed.'

'I prefer to be destroyed with it.'

'As you wish, but let me ask you one more thing, if I may. You are a public prosecutor. I've never been able to understand how anyone can bring themselves to make a living from prosecuting others, the majority of them poor devils, and then sentencing them. But that's what you did, isn't it?'

'It is. I did my duty. It was my office, just as it was the office of the executioner to take the lives of those I sentenced to death. Now you yourselves have taken on the same role, haven't you? You too are taking lives.'

'Correct. Only we are not killing because it is our duty to. We are killing for pleasure, or rather out of displeasure, out of despair at the way the world is going. That's why we take a certain delight in killing. Did it never delight you?'

'You are starting to bore me. Be so kind as to finish your task. If duty means nothing to you . . .'

He fell silent, tightening his lips as if intending to spit, but all that emerged from his mouth was a trickle of blood that stuck on his chin.

'Wait,' Gustav said politely. 'It is true the concept of duty means nothing to me, not now at any rate, but it once concerned me a great deal in my official capacity as a professor of theology. What's more, I was a soldier, serving in the war. Yet what I considered my duty, and all the things I was ordered to do, whether by figures in authority or my superior officers, was anything but good. In every case I would have preferred to do the opposite. However, even if duty has no meaning for me now, I do recognize the concept of guilt. Perhaps they amount to the same thing. By being born of a mother I am guilty, condemned to live, obliged to belong to a state, to serve it as a soldier, to kill, to pay taxes in support of armaments. And now, at this moment in time, the guilt that attaches to living has again led me, as it once did in the war, to the point where I have to kill. But this time I don't find killing repugnant. I have totally accepted the burden of guilt because I have no objection to this stupid, congested world being blown to smithereens. I'm happy to lend a hand, and to perish myself in the process.'

In spite of the blood sticking to his lips, the public prosecutor made a great effort to produce a bit of a smile. The result was not marvellous, but his good intentions were clear for all to see.

'Fair enough,' he said. 'In that case we are colleagues. Now please do your duty, Colleague.'

In the meantime the pretty girl, having sat down at the edge of the road, had fainted.

At that moment yet another car could be heard tooting its horn as it approached at full speed. Pulling the girl to one side a little, we pressed ourselves up against the rocks and allowed the oncoming car to crash into the wreckage of the other one. It braked sharply and reared upwards, but managed to come to rest undamaged. Quickly picking up our guns, we trained them on the newcomers.

'Out you get!' Gustav ordered. 'Hands up!'

Three men emerged from the car, their hands in the air.

'Is any one of you a doctor?' Gustav asked.

The answer was no.

'Then please be so good as to release this gentleman carefully from his car seat. He is badly injured. Then you can take him with you in your vehicle to the next town. Come on! Get a hold of him!'

The old gentleman was soon bedded down in the other car and they all drove off at Gustav's command.

Meanwhile our typist, having come to again, had been watching the proceedings. I was glad to see that our actions had brought us such handsome spoils.

'You have lost your employer, Fräulein,' Gustav said. I hope the old gentleman's relationship with you went no further than that. Now I'm taking you on. Make sure you do a good job for us. There, and now we need to get a bit of a move on. Things will soon get uncomfortable here. Can you climb, Fräulein? Yes? Then let's be off. Best go up between us, that way we can give you a hand.'

We all three of us now clambered up into our tree house as fast as we possibly could. Once we were up there the young lady started to feel unwell, but we gave her some brandy and she had soon recovered sufficiently to be able to appreciate the splendid view we had over the lake and the mountains, and to tell us her name was Dora.

Immediately afterwards, yet another car had arrived below us. Without stopping, it cautiously rounded the wrecked vehicle, then accelerated at once.

'Cowardly shirker!' Gustav exclaimed with a laugh as he shot down the driver. The car hopped and skipped a little before lunging at the wall and smashing it in. It ended up hanging diagonally over the abyss.

'Are you used to handling guns, Dora?' I asked.

She wasn't, but we taught her how to load a rifle. She did it clumsily at first, howling with pain when one of her fingers got caught, and demanding a plaster to stop the bleeding. However, when Gustav pointed out that this was war and asked her to please show us what a good, brave lass she was, she managed well.

'But what's to become of us?' she then asked.

'I don't know,' Gustav said. 'My pal Harry likes good-looking women, he'll be a friend to you.'

'But they'll come after us with policemen and troops and kill us.'

'There is no police force any more, or anything of that kind. The choice is ours, Dora. Either we don't worry and simply stay up here, shooting to bits every car that goes by, or we ourselves take a car, drive off in it and get fired on by others. It's all the same whichever side we take. I'm for staying here.'

Down below there was another car. We could hear the clear sound of its horn. In no time we had put paid to it, and it lay there on the road, its wheels uppermost.

'Strange,' I said, 'that there is so much fun to be had from shooting. To think I used to be an opponent of war!'

Gustav smiled. 'Indeed. The thing is, there are far too many people in the world. It wasn't so noticeable before. However, now that everyone not only wants their share of fresh air but also a car of their own, you simply can't help noticing the problem. Of course what we are doing isn't rational. It's puerile, just as the war too was puerile, enormously so. At some stage in the future humankind is going to have to learn to keep its growth in check by rational means. For the time being we are reacting to an intolerable state of affairs in a pretty irrational manner, but by reducing our numbers we are basically doing the right thing.'

'Yes,' I said, 'what we are doing is probably mad, but it is probably good and necessary nonetheless. When human beings push common sense too far, attempting with the aid of reason to order things that are not accessible to reason, it is not good. It gives rise to ideals like those of the Americans or those of the Bolsheviks, both of which are extraordinarily rational but nevertheless violate and impoverish life terribly because they simplify it in a way that is so utterly naive. The image of humankind, once a lofty ideal, is currently turning into a cliché. Perhaps mad people like us will be the ones to restore its nobility.'

Laughing, Gustav responded: 'What a splendidly clever way with words you have, old boy. You're such a fount of wisdom it's a joy to listen to you, and instructive too. Besides, there may even be a grain of truth in what you say. But now reload your gun, there's a good chap, you're a bit too dreamy for my liking. A few plump little roebuck may come running by again any moment now, and we can't shoot them with philosophy. Our gun-barrels are no good without bullets in them, after all.'

A car arrived and immediately fell victim to our fire, blocking the road. The one survivor, a fat, red-haired man, stood by the wreckage, gesticulating wildly and looking up and down, his eyes gaping. When he discovered our hideaway he ran over with a roar and fired several shots up at us with his revolver.

'Be off with you now, or I'll shoot,' Gustav shouted down to him. The man took aim at him and fired again. We then mowed him down, with two salvos.

Two more cars came, both of which we finished off. Afterwards the road remained empty and quiet. Word had apparently spread that it was a dangerous route to take. We had time to contemplate the beautiful view. Beyond the lake was a small town in the plain. Smoke was rising from it, and soon we saw roof after roof catching fire. We could hear shooting too. Dora wept a little and I stroked her damp cheeks.

'Must we all die?' she asked. Neither of us answered. In the meantime a pedestrian came along beneath us. On seeing the wrecked cars lying there, he started nosing around them. Leaning over into one, he fished out a brightly coloured parasol, a ladies' leather bag and a wine bottle. He then sat down peacefully on the wall, took a drink from the bottle and ate something wrapped in silver paper from the bag, before polishing off the rest of the wine and contentedly resuming his walk, clutching the parasol under his arm. He went on his way so peacefully that I said to Gustav: 'Could you possibly bring yourself to fire on that nice chap and shoot a hole in his head? The Lord knows I couldn't.'

'Nobody is asking you to,' my friend muttered. But deep down he too had begun to feel uncomfortable with what we were doing. Scarcely had we set eyes on a human being who was still behaving in a harmless, peaceful, childlike manner, still living in a state of innocence, when all our praiseworthy, necessary activity suddenly struck us as stupid and disgusting. Ugh, all that blood! We were ashamed of ourselves. But then even generals, so they say, occasionally felt ashamed during the war.

'Let's not stay up here any longer,' said Dora plaintively. 'Let's go down. We're sure to find something to eat in the cars, or aren't you Bolsheviks the least bit hungry?'

Down there in the town where fire was raging the bells started furiously and fearsomely ringing. We set about climbing down. As I was helping Dora clamber over the wooden surround of the hut, I kissed her on the knee. She gave a bright laugh, but at that moment the supporting struts gave way, and we both plunged into the void . . .

*

I found myself back in the theatre's round corridor, feeling animated by the hunting venture. And all around me I could see the alluring inscriptions on the innumerable doors:

MUTABOR
CHANGE INTO ANY ANIMAL OR PLANT YOU LIKE

KAMASUTRA
INSTRUCTION IN THE INDIAN ARTS OF LOVE
BEGINNERS COURSE: 42 DIFFERENT WAYS
TO PRACTISE SEXUAL INTERCOURSE

HIGHLY ENJOYABLE SUICIDE
YOU'LL DIE LAUGHING

IS THE SPIRITUAL LIFE THE THING FOR YOU?
ORIENTAL WISDOM

O FOR A THOUSAND
TONGUES!
FOR GENTLEMEN ONLY

DECLINE OF THE WEST
PRICES REDUCED. STILL UNSURPASSED

> THE ESSENCE OF ART
> TIME TRANSFORMED INTO
> SPACE
> BY MEANS OF MUSIC

> LAUGHING TILL YOU WEEP
> CABINET OF HUMOUR

> PLAYING THE HERMIT
> THE PERFECT SUBSTITUTE FOR ALL SOCIABILITY

The series of inscriptions was endless. One of them read:

> GUIDE TO RECONSTRUCTING ONE'S PERSONALITY
> SUCCESS GUARANTEED

I went in through this door, thinking it worth a try.

The room I found myself in was dimly lit and quiet. There was a man sitting on the floor, oriental fashion, with what looked like a large chessboard in front of him. For a moment I thought it was our friend Pablo. At any rate he was wearing a similar brightly coloured silk jacket and had the same darkly gleaming eyes.

'It's not Pablo, is it?' I asked.

'I'm nobody,' he explained in a friendly manner. 'We don't have names here; none of us here is a real person. I'm a chess player. Do you want me to teach you how to reconstruct your personality?'

'Yes please.'

'Then be so kind as to hand over a few dozen of your pieces.'

'My pieces . . .?'

'The pieces you saw your so-called personality disintegrate into. I can't play without pieces, you know.'

He held a mirror up in front of me and in it I again saw my unified self disintegrate into many separate figures. There seemed to be an even larger number of them now, but they were very small, roughly as big as handy-sized chessmen. Picking up a few dozen of them with his calm, steady fingers, the chess player placed them on the floor next to his board. As he did so, he said in a monotonous voice, like someone repeating a speech or a lesson he has frequently given before:

'You are familiar with the mistaken and harmful notion that human beings constitute lasting, unified wholes. You are also aware that they are made up of a multiplicity of souls, of very many selves. To split up the ostensible unity of the person into all these different pieces is considered mad. Science has coined the term schizophrenia for it. Of course, in as much as it is impossible to bring any large number of things under control without leadership or a degree of combination and categorization, science is right to do so. On the other hand, scientists are wrong in believing that the only possible combination of our many sub-selves is a once-and-for-all thing, a binding arrangement valid for the whole of our lives. This error on the part of scientists has many unpleasant consequences. All that can be said in its favour is that it simplifies the task of those appointed by the state to teach and educate, sparing them the trouble of thinking and experimenting. As a result of this error, many human beings are considered "normal", indeed of great value to society, who are incurably mad. Conversely, there are quite a lot of people regarded as mad who are geniuses. What we here term the art of reconstruction is a way of filling in the gaps in science's inadequate view of human psychology. To those people who have experienced the disintegration of their selves, we demonstrate that they can reassemble the pieces in a new order of their own choosing whenever they like. They are thus in a position to master the infinite variety of moves in life's game. Just as writers create a drama from a handful of characters, we are forever able to regroup the separate pieces of our dismantled selves and thus offer them new roles to play, new excitements, situations that are constantly fresh. Look what I mean!'

With his calm, steady fingers he took hold of my figures, all the old men, youths, children and women, all the cheerful and sad, strong and gentle, agile and clumsy figures, and swiftly arranged them on his board in preparation for a game. Immediately the game started, they reconstituted themselves as a world in miniature, forming groups and families, playing and fighting with each other, making friends and enemies. To my delight, he set this lively but orderly small-scale world in motion for a while before my very eyes. I watched the figures play and fight, form alliances and engage in battles, saw them court one another, marry and multiply. It was indeed a drama, a lively and exciting one with a large cast.

Then, with one serene sweep of his hand across the board, he gently knocked over all the pieces and pushed them together in a heap. With all the thoughtful care and fastidiousness of an artist, he now proceeded to construct a new game from the same pieces, grouping them differently, altering their relationships and interconnections. This second game was not unrelated to the first. It was the same world he was constructing and its materials were the same, but it was a composition in a different key. The tempo had changed, the motifs were given fresh emphasis and the situations were set up differently.

And thus this artist adept at reconstruction assembled one game after another from the figures that were all part of my self.

They all bore a distant resemblance to one another, all recognizably belonged to the same world and shared the same origin, yet each game was totally new.

'This is the art of living,' he said, as if lecturing me. 'In future, you yourself may play out your life's game in this way, reshaping and enlivening it, making it richer and more complex as you wish. It's up to you. Just as madness in a higher sense is the beginning of wisdom, schizophrenia is the beginning of all art, all fantasy. Even scholars have already half acknowledged this, as you can tell by reading that delightful book *The Prince's Magic Horn*,* in which the painstaking, assiduous research of a scholar is lent nobility by the brilliant works of a large number of deranged artists who collaborated with him while confined in institutions. – Here, why not take your little chessmen with you? You'll often have the opportunity to enjoy a game in future. Then the figure that spoiled things for you today by his monstrously intolerable behaviour can be demoted to a minor role. And you can turn the poor, dear little figure that for a while seemed ill starred, dogged by sheer bad luck, into a princess in the next game. Sir, I wish you the greatest of pleasure.'

Expressing my gratitude to this talented chess player with a deep bow, I pocketed the little figures and made my exit through the narrow doorway.

I had actually intended to sit down at once on the floor of the corridor and play with my chess pieces for hours, for an eternity even, but no sooner was I standing there again in that brightly

---

* Hesse's invention, this work alludes to the famous collection of German folksongs *Des Knaben Wunderhorn* (*The Boy's Magic Horn*), which the Romantic writers Achim von Arnim and Clemens Brentano assembled in the years 1806–8. By slightly changing the title, however, Hesse is also alluding to the German psychiatrist and art historian Hans Prinzhorn (1886–1933), specifically to his 1922 study *Bildnerei der Geisteskranken* (*Artistry of the Mentally Ill*), which contained many illustrations of artworks produced by patients in the psychiatric hospital of Heidelberg University.

illuminated passage round the theatre than I was carried away by fresh currents that were stronger than me. My eyes suddenly lit on a garish poster with the wording:

THE TAMING OF STEPPENWOLF
AMAZING SCENES!

This inscription aroused a lot of different emotions in me. My heart ached as all kinds of anxieties and pressures from my past life, from the reality I had left behind, closed in on me again. With a trembling hand, I opened the door to find myself in a fairground booth. Once inside, I noticed that an iron grating had been installed between me and the makeshift stage. However, I could see an animal-tamer standing up there, a rather vociferous, self-important gentleman who, despite a large moustache, bulging muscles on his upper arms and a clown-like circus costume, resembled me in a manner that I found malicious and truly repulsive. This strongman was strutting around – what a sight for sore eyes! – with a wolf on a lead as if it were a dog: a huge, handsome, but terribly emaciated wolf with a timid, slavish look in its eyes. And to now watch the brutal tamer forcing this noble but so ignominiously compliant beast to perform a series of tricks and act out sensational scenes was an experience I found as disgusting as it was thrilling, as horrific as it was nonetheless secretly enjoyable.

I have to say that he had done a tremendous job, this damned distorted mirror image of me. The wolf alertly obeyed his every command, reacting slavishly to his every call or crack of the whip. It sank to its knees, played dead, sat up and begged. It obediently fetched a loaf of bread, an egg, a piece of meat, a basket, carrying them all in its mouth like a well-trained dog. It even had to pick up the whip dropped by the tamer and, holding it in its

mouth, follow him while wagging its tail in so abject a fashion
that it was unbearable to watch. A rabbit was presented to the
wolf, then a white lamb, but although it bared its teeth and sali-
vated over them, trembling with desire, it didn't touch either of
them. Instead, when ordered to, it leaped with one elegant bound
over the two animals that cowered there shuddering with fright.
Indeed, it lay down between the rabbit and the lamb, embracing
each of them with its front paws and forming a moving family
group. What is more, it ate a bar of chocolate from the man's
hand. The degree to which this wolf had learned to deny its
natural instincts was just fantastic, and it was agonizing to witness.
As I did so, my hair was standing on end.

In the second part of the performance, however, the enraged
spectator, and the wolf itself as well, were compensated for this
agony. You see, once that sophisticated demonstration of obedience had run its course, and after the tamer, smiling sweetly, had
taken a triumphal bow over the group with the lamb and the
wolf, the roles were reversed. All of a sudden, the Harry-like
animal tamer, bowing low to the wolf, laid his whip at its feet
and began to tremble and cower down, looking just as wretched
as the animal had done before. The wolf, on the other hand,
licked its lips and smiled, abandoning all its earlier forced and
false airs. Its eyes beamed and every sinew in its body tightened
as its savage self began to thrive again.

Now it was the wolf's turn to command, and the human being
had to obey. When ordered to, the tamer sank to his knees and
played the part of the wolf, letting his tongue hang out and using
his teeth, which were full of fillings, to tear the clothes from his
body. Depending on what the 'human-tamer' commanded, he
walked upright or crawled on all fours, sat up and begged, played
dead, let the wolf ride on him, fetched him his whip. He proved
a very gifted dog, highly imaginative in his willingness to submit
to every humiliation and perversion. A beautiful girl came on to

the stage and, going up to the tamed man, stroked his chin and rubbed her cheek against his. He, however, stayed on all fours, still an animal. Shaking his head, he began baring his teeth at the good-looking girl, eventually causing her to take flight, so menacing and wolf-like was his behaviour. When offered some chocolate he sniffed at it contemptuously and pushed it away. Finally, the white lamb and the plump, spotted rabbit were brought on again and the man showed what a willing pupil he was by playing the wolf to the hilt. His performance was breathtaking. Seizing on the screaming little creatures with his fingers and teeth, he tore scraps of skin and flesh from them, grinning as he ate them alive, and closing his eyes in drunken ecstasy as, beside himself, he quaffed their warm blood.

Horrified, I fled, out through the door. I could see that this Magic Theatre was no unalloyed paradise. Under its attractive surface there were all manner of hidden hells. Dear God, was there no salvation to be found here either?

I walked anxiously to and fro, my mouth tasting of blood and chocolate, the one just as nasty as the other. Longing to escape these troubled waters, I struggled inwardly with all my might to conjure up more tolerable, more congenial images. The line 'O friends, not these tones!'* resounded in my head, and I remembered with horror those appalling photographs taken at the front that one had occasionally glimpsed during the war, those piles of tangled corpses, their faces transformed into devilish gargoyles by their gasmasks. As a humanitarian opponent of war, I had been horrified by such images then. How stupid and naive I still

---

*'O Freunde, nicht diese Töne', the beginning of an introductory passage that precedes the singing of Schiller's 'Ode to Joy' in the last movement of Beethoven's Ninth Symphony. Hesse had already used the line as the title of a newspaper article he wrote in November 1914, a condemnation of the stridently nationalistic tones then universally to be heard in the first year of the First World War.

was! Today I knew better. No animal-tamer, no government minister, no general, no madman was capable of hatching up ideas and images in his head that didn't already exist within me, and mine were every bit as appalling, as savage and evil, as coarse and stupid as theirs.

With a sigh of relief I recalled the inscription that, when the theatre performance began, I had seen the handsome youth respond to with such enthusiasm:

> ## ALL GIRLS ARE YOURS

All things considered, there actually seemed to be nothing more desirable on offer than this. Pleased to be able to escape the damnable world of the wolf once more, I entered.

Here, strange to say, what greeted me was the sweet fragrance of my youth, the atmosphere of my boyhood and adolescence, and I felt the young blood of those days flowing through my veins. So unbelievable was it and yet at the same time deeply familiar, it sent shivers down my spine. All the things I had done, thought and been only a short time ago sank into oblivion, and I was young once more. Only an hour, only moments ago, I had thought I knew perfectly well what love, what desire, what longing was, but that had been the love and longing of an old man. Now I was young again, and all that I was feeling inside me, this red-hot lava, this powerful tug of yearning, this passion melting the ice like a warm March wind, was young, fresh and genuine. Oh, how the forgotten fires were suddenly rekindled; how the sounds of yesteryear came swelling darkly back! What fresh life was quivering in my pulse, what cries and songs were filling my soul! I was a boy of fifteen or sixteen, my head was full of Latin and Greek, and beautiful lines of poetry. Effort and ambition dominated my thinking, the dream of becoming an artist my imagination. But what was burning and flickering at a much deeper level than all these smouldering fires was the flame of love, sexual hunger, an all-consuming premonition of lust.

I was standing on one of the rocky outcrops above my small home town. The scents of a warm spring breeze and the first violets filled the air, and down there in the town I could see the river and the windows of my father's house glinting in the sun. Everything looked, sounded and smelled so abundant, so bursting with the freshness of creation; everything glowed with such rich colours; the spring breeze made everything it touched seem transfigured and hyperreal. The world was just as I had seen it long ago in the richest, most poetic hours of my first youth. I stood there on the hill, the wind ruffling my long hair. Lost in a daydream and filled with erotic longing, I unconsciously stretched out a hand and tore a half-opened bud from a shrub that was just coming into leaf. Holding it in front of my eyes, I sniffed at it, and its scent alone was enough to rekindle the memories of that time. Then I took this tiny green object playfully between my lips, lips that had yet to kiss a girl, and began to chew it. The tangy, aromatic, bitter taste of it at once brought home to me what I was experiencing. Everything fell into place again. What I was reliving was a moment from my last year as a schoolboy. One Sunday afternoon in the first days of spring when out walking alone, I had come across Rosa Kreisler, shyly said hello, and fallen head over heels in love.

At the time, I had been full of anxious anticipation as I watched the beautiful young girl, who had not yet spotted me, coming up the hill towards me, alone and deep in reverie. Although she wore her hair tied up in thick plaits, I had still glimpsed some loose strands of it blowing and waving in the breeze on either side of her cheeks. For the first time in my life, I had seen the beauty of the girl, the beautiful and dreamlike effect of the wind playing in her delicate hair, the beautiful and arousing cut of her thin blue dress as it hung down over her young limbs. And just as the spicy, bitter taste of the bud I was chewing on had imbued me with all the alarmingly sweet joy and anxiety of spring, the sight of the girl now filled me with a deadly premonition of sexual passion, a foretaste of femininity, a deeply shocking presentiment of all the enormous opportunities it promised, all the nameless delights, the unimaginable entanglements, anxieties and sorrows, the heights of fulfilment and the depths of guilt. Oh, how I could feel the bitter taste of spring burning on my tongue! Oh, how the wind was playing in the loose hair dangling by her red cheeks! Then, arriving close by, she had looked up and recognized me. Blushing slightly for a moment, she had looked away. Then I greeted her, raising the new hat I'd worn at that day's confirmation service. Her composure soon regained, she lifted her head in a faintly ladylike fashion and greeted me back with a smile before slowly walking on with an air of confidence and superiority. A host of amorous wishes, demands and tributes that I sent after her surrounded her like a nimbus.

That is how it had been one Sunday thirty-five years ago, and it had all come back to me at this moment: hill and town, March wind and scent of buds, Rosa and her brown hair, tumescent desire and sweet, suffocating anxiety. It was all as before, and it seemed to me that in all my life I had never again loved anyone in the way that I loved Rosa. This time, however, I was given the opportunity to welcome her differently. I saw her blush on recognizing me, saw her effort to disguise the fact, and knew at once that she liked me, that this encounter meant as much to her as it did to me. And this time, despite feeling anxious and inhibited, instead of raising my hat and holding it ceremoniously above my head as I stood there waiting until she passed by, I did as my pulsating heart commanded and cried: 'Rosa! Thank God you've come, you lovely lovely lass. I'm so very fond of you.' It may not have been the cleverest way of putting it, but this was no time for being clever, and it was perfectly adequate. Rosa gave me no ladylike look, stopped rather than going on her way, looked at me, blushing even more than before, and said: 'Hello, Harry. Are you really fond of me?' As she spoke her brown eyes beamed at me from her vibrant face and I felt that my whole past life and loves had been wrong, confused and full of misfortune since the moment when I allowed Rosa to walk away from me on that Sunday. But now I had put right my mistake and everything was changing, taking a turn for the better.

Clasping hands, we walked slowly on, both happy beyond words. We were very embarrassed, so unsure what to say or do that in our embarrassment we started to walk faster, breaking into a trot and ending up out of breath and having to stop, though still holding hands. Both children still, we were at a loss to know how to initiate things. That Sunday we didn't even get as far as a first kiss, but we were enormously happy. We stood there gasping for breath, then sat down on the grass. I stroked her hand, she shyly ran the other hand over my hair, then we stood up again and tried to measure which one of us was the taller. I was actually taller by the breadth of a finger, but instead of conceding the fact I insisted that we were exactly the same height. God had destined us for one another, I said, and one day we would marry. Then Rosa said she could smell violets and we kneeled down on the short grass of springtime to look for them. Each finding a few with tiny short stems, we made a present of them to one another. When it grew cooler and the sunlight was already falling at a sharp angle across the rocks Rosa said she must be getting back home. Since it was out of the question for me to accompany her we both felt sad, but we now had a secret we could share, and that was our most precious possession. Remaining up there among the rocks, I smelled Rosa's violets and lay face down on the ground overlooking a steep drop. I gazed down at the town, keeping watch until I spotted her sweet little figure appearing deep below me as she walked by the well and across the bridge. Now I knew she was back home in her father's house and passing through its cosy rooms while I was lying far away from her up here. But there was a bond uniting us, a current running from me to her, a secret carried on the air that separated us.

Throughout that spring, we saw each other again, here and there, up in the rocks, by garden fences, and when the lilac began to blossom we gave each other our first timid kiss. What we children were capable of giving one another wasn't much. Our kiss lacked passion and plenitude, and I only dared give the hair that curled around her ears the gentlest of caresses. Yet all that we were capable of in the way of love and joy was ours, and with every shy touch, with every immature expression of affection, with every anxious moment spent waiting for one another, we were discovering fresh happiness, climbing one small rung on the ladder of love.

In this way, starting with Rosa and the violets, I was able to relive my whole love life under happier auspices. Rosa was lost sight of and Irmgard appeared. The sun grew hotter, the stars giddier, but neither Rosa nor Irmgard became mine. I had to climb the ladder rung by rung, had to experience and learn a great deal, had to lose Irmgard, and after her Anna. Every girl I had loved once upon a time in my youth I was now permitted to love again, but this time I was able to inspire love in them, to give something to each one of them and to receive something in return. Wishes, dreams and possibilities that had once existed solely in my imagination were now made lived realities. Oh, Ida and Lore and all you other beautiful flowers that I once loved for a whole summer, for a month or just for a day!

Realizing that I was now that handsome, passionate little youth that I had earlier seen running so eagerly towards love's doorway, I understood that I was presently living to the full this part of my being and life, only a tenth – no, a thousandth of which had previously achieved fulfilment. It was now being allowed to flourish, unhampered by all the other figures that constituted my self, neither disturbed by the thinker, plagued by Steppenwolf, nor restricted in scope by the writer, the dreamer, the moralist in me. On the contrary, I was now the lover and nothing but the lover. Love was the sole air I breathed, in happiness and in sorrow. I had already learned to dance with Irmgard, to kiss with Ida, before, one autumn evening under the wind-blown leaves of an elm, Emma, the most beautiful of them all, became the first to let me kiss her brownish breasts and invite me to drink from the cup of desire.

I experienced a great deal in Pablo's little theatre, a thousand things more than can be put into words. All the girls I had ever loved were now mine. Each gave me what was hers alone to give and I gave to each of them what only she knew how to take from me. I got to sample much love, much happiness, much lust, and a great deal of confusion and sorrow too. In the space of this one dreamlike hour, all the love I had missed out on during my life returned magically to fill my garden with a variety of blooms: flowers that were chaste and delicate, garish flowers blazing with colour, dark flowers that swiftly faded. I ran the gamut of flickering desire, intense reverie, feverish melancholy, the anguish of death and the joyful radiance of rebirth. I found women who could only be won in haste, taken by storm; others it was a joy to woo at length and with utmost solicitude. Light was cast on every dim corner of my life in which I had once, if only for a minute, heard the voice of sex calling me, a look from a woman had aroused me, or I had been attracted by the glimpse of a girl's shimmering white skin. And now every previously missed opportunity was made up for, every woman becoming mine, each in her own way. There was the woman with the remarkably deep brown eyes under her flaxen hair that I had once stood next to for a quarter of an hour by the window in the corridor of an express train and who had later appeared to me several times in dreams. She didn't utter a word, but she taught me some things about lovemaking I never imagined existed, frightening, deadly arts. And then there was that sleek, calm Chinese woman from the dockside in Marseille with her glassy smile, smooth jet-black hair and swimming eyes. She too knew some outrageous things. Each of them had her secrets, each the perfume of her homeland. All of them kissed and laughed differently; all were bashful – and shameless too – in their own distinctive ways. The women came and went with the current. Either it bore them to me or I was washed towards them, then away again. To float like this on a wave of sexuality was like a childhood game, full of charm, full of danger, full of surprise. And I was amazed to discover how rich my ostensibly barren and loveless Steppenwolf existence had been in episodes of infatuation, sexual opportunities and temptations. I had let almost all of them slip by or had run away from them. Stumbling upon them, I had forgotten them as fast as I could, but here they were all stored up in their hundreds, every single one of them. Now I could see them, surrender to them, open myself to them and descend into the rosy half-light of their underworld. Even the orgy Pablo had once tempted me to indulge in recurred, along with other, earlier proposals I hadn't even understood at the time, to join in fantastic threesomes and foursomes. Now I was welcomed into such revels with a smile. Lots of things took place, lots of games were played, all of them unmentionable.

From this unending current of temptations, vices and entanglements I resurfaced calmly and silently. I was now well equipped, full of knowledge, wise, deeply experienced, ripe for Hermione. For it was she, Hermione, who emerged as the final figure in my mythical cast of a thousand. In the endless series of names, hers was the last to appear, and its appearance coincided with my return to consciousness. It also marked the end of my erotic fairy tale, because I had no desire to encounter her here in the half-light of a magic mirror. Only the whole Harry would suffice for her, and I was now oh so determined to reconfigure all my chess pieces solely with her and her fulfilment in mind.

The current had washed me up on dry land. I was again standing in the silent corridor behind the theatre's boxes. What now? I felt for the little chessmen in my pocket, but the urge to rearrange them had already lost its force. All around me I was confronted by this inexhaustible world of doors, inscriptions and magic mirrors. Mechanically my eyes lit on the next notice and I shuddered to see that it read:

> ## HOW TO KILL THE ONE YOU LOVE

I had a rapid flash of memory, lasting no more than a second. It was of Hermione at a restaurant table. Looking frighteningly serious, the food and wine forgotten, she was absorbed in profound conversation, telling me that she would make me fall in love with her only so that she could die by my hand. I felt a heavy wave of fear and gloom surge across my heart. Everything was suddenly confronting me again. Suddenly, deep down inside me, I could again sense fate pressing in on me. In my despair I felt for the figures in my pocket, meaning to take them out and work a little magic by rearranging them on my chessboard. But the figures had gone. Instead, what I took from my pocket was a knife. Frightened to death, I ran along the corridor, past all the doors, and suddenly found myself in front of the gigantic mirror. Looking into it, I saw a huge, handsome wolf, as tall as me. It was standing there motionless, its nervous, restless eyes flashing. Then, one eye glinting, it winked at me and laughed a little, its lips parting for an instant to reveal a red tongue.

Where was Pablo? Where was Hermione? What had become

of that clever chap with all his fine talk of reconstructing one's personality?

I took another look in the mirror. I must have been mad. There was no wolf there rolling its tongue in its mouth behind the tall looking glass. What I saw in the mirror was me, Harry, my face ashen now, showing no trace of all those games I'd been playing. I looked terribly pale, exhausted by all the vices I'd indulged in, but at least I was a human being, someone you could talk to.

'Harry,' I said, 'what are you doing there?'

'Nothing,' said the figure in the mirror. 'I'm just waiting. I'm waiting for death.'

'Where is death, then?' I asked.

'It is coming,' the other one said. And from the empty chambers in the interior of the theatre I heard some beautiful, terrible music ring out, the passage from *Don Giovanni* that accompanies the appearance of the Stone Guest. Arriving from the beyond, the world of the Immortals, the icy sounds of it echoed spine-chillingly throughout the haunted building.

'Mozart!' I thought, conjuring up the most noble and best-loved images of my inner life.

Behind me I now heard the sound of laughter, bright and ice-cold laughter, a product of the gods' sense of humour, originating from another world unheard of by human beings, a world beyond experienced suffering. I turned round, chilled to the bone yet delighted by this laughter, and there was Mozart walking towards me. Laughing, he passed by me and, strolling nonchalantly towards one of the theatre's boxes, opened the door and went in. Eagerly I followed him, the God of my youth, the object of my love and veneration throughout my life. The music continued to ring out. Mozart was standing at the front rail of the box, but nothing could be seen of the theatre. In the immeasurable space beyond him all was darkness.

'You see,' Mozart said, 'the effect music can achieve even without a saxophone. Mind you, I certainly wouldn't want to be standing too close to that splendid instrument either.'

'Where are we?' I asked.

'We are in the last act of *Don Giovanni*. Leporello is already down on his knees. An excellent scene, and the music's not bad either, come to think of it. It may still possess all sorts of qualities that are very human, but there's no denying that you can already hear traces of the world beyond in it, in the laughter – don't you agree?'

'It's the last great piece of music to have been written,' I said solemnly, like a schoolmaster. 'True, Schubert was still to follow, then Hugo Wolf came along, and I mustn't leave out poor magnificent Chopin either. Now you're frowning, Maestro. Oh, yes, there is also Beethoven, he too is marvellous. Yet, however beautiful all of that is, there is something piecemeal about it, a sense of things fragmenting. No human being has again produced a composition that is so perfectly integrated a whole as *Don Giovanni*.'

'Take it easy,' Mozart said, with a laugh that was terribly scornful. 'I suppose you're a musician yourself. Well, I've given up the job, gone into retirement. If from time to time I take a look at what's still going on in the profession, it's just for fun.'

He raised his hands as if conducting an orchestra and somewhere or other I saw a moon or some equally pale heavenly body rising. I was gazing out over the edge of the box into immeasurable depths of space. Mists and clouds were swirling in it; mountain ranges and coastlines came dimly into view; and beneath us stretched a desert-like plain as wide as the earth. On this plain we could see a venerable-looking old gentleman with a long beard who was walking mournful-faced at the head of an enormously long procession of tens of thousands of men dressed in black. He looked dejected and desperate, and Mozart said:

'Look, that's Brahms. He is doing his utmost to achieve salvation, but he's still got a long way to go.'

He told me that the black-clad thousands were the people who had sung or played all the notes in Brahms's scores that had been judged superfluous by the gods.

'All too densely orchestrated, you see, waste of material,' said Mozart with a nod.

And immediately after this we saw Richard Wagner marching at the head of an army just as large. He had the look of a martyr as he trudged along wearily, and we could sense what a heavy burden on him the thousands in his wake were.

'In my youth,' I remarked sadly, 'these two composers were regarded as the greatest opposites imaginable.'

Mozart laughed.

'Yes, that's always the case, but viewed from a certain distance, opposites like that tend to look more and more like one another. It wasn't, incidentally, a personal fault of either Wagner or Brahms to go in for such dense orchestration, it was a fault of the age they lived in.'

'What? And they now have to pay so dearly for it?' I exclaimed indignantly.

'Naturally. The law must take its course. Only when they have discharged the debt of their age will it become clear whether enough still remains that is personal to them to make a reassessment of their value worthwhile.'

'But surely neither of them is responsible for it?'

'Of course not, any more than you are responsible for the fact that Adam ate the apple, but you still have to pay for it.'

'But that's terrible.'

'Certainly. Life is always terrible. We are not responsible for things, yet we have to answer for them. Just by virtue of being born we are guilty. You must have enjoyed a strange kind of religious education if you didn't know that.'

By now I was feeling well and truly miserable. I had a vision of myself trudging dog-tired through that desert plain in the beyond, bearing the burden of the countless superfluous books I had written, all the essays and journalistic pieces too, and following in my train the host of those obliged to work on them as typesetters or to swallow the whole lot as readers. My God! And then there was Adam and the apple, and all the rest of that original sin business into the bargain! So all of that had to be atoned for, endless purgatory endured, before it would even be possible to consider whether there was still something of personal, individual value left behind, or whether all my activities and their consequences had been mere foam on the waves, a performance signifying nothing in the overall current of events.

When he saw my long face Mozart started to laugh. He laughed so much he turned somersaults in the air and played trills with his feet. And in doing so he shouted at me: 'Hey, my lad, you look so sad, are things that bad? Worried about your readers, the greedy bleeders? Printers' devils, rabble-rousers, sabre-rattlers? Laugh? My sides I've split, you stupid twit, I've nearly shit myself! You're so naive, prone to believe and constantly grieve, I'll sing a psalm on your behalf, but just for a laugh. What waffle and piffle, what melodramatic monkeying around! Come, wiggle and waggle your tail, don't shilly-shally or dilly-dally on the way! To hell with you and your scribble and scrawl, you deserve to be lynched for all that you pinched from Goethe and Nietzsche et al.'

This was simply too much to take. There was no time to dwell on my former melancholy now. I was so angry that I seized Mozart by his pigtail, which grew longer and longer like the tail of a comet as he hurtled off into space with me whirling along behind. God, it was cold out there! What a glacial, rarefied atmosphere these Immortals were able to survive in! Yet it put you in a cheerful mood, this ice-cold air; as I was just able to appreciate for a brief moment before falling unconscious. It was a bitterly sharp, icy cheerfulness that I felt penetrating my being like cold steel, and it made me want to laugh in just as bright, uninhibited and unearthly a manner as Mozart had done. But then, before I had chance to, I stopped breathing and lost consciousness.

*

When I came to again I was battered and bewildered. The white light of the corridor was reflected in its shiny floor. I was not in the realm of the Immortals, not yet. No, I was still in this world, the world of mystery and suffering, of Steppenwolf figures and agonizingly complex entanglements. It was not a good place to be, not a place I could abide for any length of time. I had to put an end to this existence.

Harry was facing me in the large mirror on the wall. He did not look well. He looked much the same as on that night after his visit to the professor's and the dance in the Black Eagle. But that was in the distant past, years, centuries ago. Harry was older now, he had learned to dance, visited the Magic Theatre, heard Mozart laugh. He was no longer frightened of dances, women or knives. Even a moderately talented person matures if he has raced his way through a few centuries. I took a long look at Harry in the mirror. I could still recognize him all right. He still looked a tiny bit like the fifteen-year-old Harry who had encountered Rosa one Sunday in March up in the rocks and, fresh from his confirmation, had raised his hat to her. Yet since then he had grown a good few hundred years older, had studied music and philosophy to the point were he was fed up with both, had drunk his fill of Alsace wine in the Steel Helmet, had taken part in debates on the God Krishna with reputable scholars, had loved

Erika and Maria, made friends with Hermione, shot down passing cars and slept with that sleek Chinese woman in Marseille.
In meetings with Goethe and Mozart he had also managed to
tear various holes in the mesh of time and pseudo-reality in which
he remained trapped. And even though he had lost his precious
chessmen, he still had a trusty knife in his pocket. Onwards,
Harry, old man, weary old chap!

Ugh! How bitter life tasted! I spat at the Harry in the mirror,
I kicked out at him, shattering him to pieces. Slowly I walked
along the echoing corridor, examining the doors of the Magic
Theatre that had promised so many wonderful things, but now
there wasn't an inscription to be seen on any of them. I paced
by all hundred of them slowly, as if inspecting troops. Hadn't
I been to a masked ball earlier today? Since then a hundred years
had gone by. Soon there won't be any more years. Something
still needed to be done. Hermione was still waiting. Ours would
be a strange wedding. These were troubled waters I was drifting
in, pulled along by a murky current, a slave, a Steppenwolf.
Ugh!

I stopped by the last of the doors, drawn to it by the murky
current. O Rosa, O my distant youth, O Goethe and Mozart!

Opening the door, I was witness to a scene that was simple
and beautiful. I discovered two naked people lying side by side
on rugs on the floor: beautiful Hermione and handsome Pablo.
They were fast asleep, utterly exhausted by lovemaking, one's
appetite for which, though seemingly insatiable, is nonetheless
rapidly satiated. Beautiful, beautiful people, splendid images,
wonderful bodies. Under Hermione's left breast there was a fresh,
round, richly dark mark, a love bite from Pablo's beautiful gleaming teeth. It was there that I plunged my knife in, as far as the
blade would go. Blood flowed over Hermione's tender white skin.
If the whole situation had been slightly different, if things had
turned out a little differently, I would have kissed the blood away.

As it was, I didn't. I just watched the blood flowing and saw the look of agony and utter astonishment in her eyes as they briefly opened. Why is she astonished? I thought. Then it occurred to me that I ought to close her eyes, but they closed again of their own accord. The deed was done. She just turned on her side a little. As she did so I saw a fine, delicate shadow playing between her armpit and her breast. It reminded me strongly of something or other, but annoyingly I could not remember what. Then she lay still.

I looked at her for a long time. Eventually, as if waking from sleep, I started with fright and made to leave. At that moment I saw Pablo open his eyes and stretch his arms and legs. Then he bent down over Hermione's dead body and smiled. He will never learn to take anything seriously, I thought. Whatever happens just makes the chap smile. Carefully turning up one corner of the rug, Pablo covered Hermione with it as far as her breast so that the wound was no longer visible. Then he silently left the theatre box. Where was he going? Were they all leaving me here alone? I stayed there, alone with the half-shrouded body of the dead woman that I loved and envied. Her boyish curl was hanging down over her pale forehead, her slightly open mouth stood out bright red from the extreme pallor of her face, her delicately perfumed hair allowed just a glimpse of her small, finely sculpted ear.

Her wish was now fulfilled. I had killed the woman I loved even before she had fully become mine. I had done this unimaginable deed and now I was kneeling there and staring into space, not knowing what it meant, unsure even as to whether it had been the right and proper thing to do, or the opposite. What would that shrewd chess player, what would Pablo have to say about it? I knew nothing. I was incapable of thinking. As the colour drained from Hermione's face the red glow of her lipstick became more and more intense. My whole life had been just like that. What little happiness and love I had experienced was like this rigid mouth of hers – a touch of red on the face of a corpse.

And the dead face, the dead white shoulders, the dead white arms exuded a breath of cold air that slowly crept up on me, making me shudder. In this atmosphere of wintry desolation and isolation, this slowly, very slowly increasing chill, my hands and lips started to freeze. Had I extinguished the sun? Had I killed the heart of all life? Was this the deathly cold of outer space I could feel invading?

Shuddering, I stared at Hermione's petrified forehead, at her stiff curl of hair, at her coolly shimmering, pale, shell-shaped ear. The chilling cold they exuded was lethal, but beautiful nevertheless. It had a wonderful ring to it, splendid vibrations. It was music!

Had I not already shuddered with cold like this once before, much earlier, and at the same time experienced something akin to happiness? Had I not heard this music once before? Yes, in Mozart's presence, in the presence of the Immortals.

Some lines of poetry came into my head. I had found them somewhere or other once long ago:

> Unlike you we've found ourselves a home
> Up in the starry ether, bright and cold.
> Oblivious to the passing hours and days,
> We're neither male nor female, young nor old . . .
> Our life is eternal, cool and unchanging;
> Cool and star-bright, our laughter knows no end . . .

*

Then the door to the box opened and in came Mozart. I had to look twice before recognizing him because he was in modern dress, without his knee breeches and buckled shoes, and without his pigtail. He sat down by me, so close that I almost tried to hold him back, lest the blood from Hermione's breast that had run on to the floor should dirty his clothes. He sat down and started working in a really detailed fashion on some gadgets and bits of apparatus that lay to hand on the floor. He was taking it very seriously, adjusting this and that and screwing parts together with those admirably skilful and agile fingers of his which I would have dearly loved to have seen playing the piano. I watched him deep in thought, or rather I was not so much thinking as dreaming, absorbed by the sight of his fine, clever hands, heartened but also somewhat unnerved to feel him so close. I paid no attention at all to whatever it was he was actually up to with the screwdriver and the gadgetry he was fiddling around with.

However, it turned out that what he had been assembling and getting to work was a wireless set. Switching on the loudspeaker, he now said: 'It's a broadcast from Munich: Handel's Concerto Grosso in F Major.'

And in fact, to my indescribable astonishment and horror, what the satanic metal horn of a loudspeaker now immediately spewed out was just that mixture of bronchial slime and chewed-up rubber which owners of gramophones and wireless subscribers have agreed to call music. Yet, just as a thick crust of dirt can conceal an exquisite old-master painting, behind all the murky slime and crackling noise you could indeed recognize the noble structure of this divine music, its princely composition, the cool, ample air it breathed, the full, rich sonority produced by the strings.

'My God,' I cried in disgust. 'What do you think you are doing, Mozart? Do you seriously want to subject yourself and me to such filth, to let this abominable gadget loose on the two of us, this triumphal invention of our times, the latest successful weapon in their campaign to destroy art? Is this really necessary?'

Oh, how he laughed now, this uncanny man! His laughter was cold, ghostly, noiseless, yet it was devastating, destructive of everything. Taking intense pleasure in tormenting me, he went on adjusting the damned screws of his wireless set and repositioning the metal horn speaker, thus ensuring that the distorted, lifeless, adulterated music went on seeping into the room. And he laughed as he did so, just as he laughed when answering me.

'Spare me your pomposities, if you please, neighbour! Incidentally, did you notice that ritardando just now? What a brilliant idea, don't you think? You impatient soul, why not let the thinking behind that ritardando influence you for once? Can you hear the basses? They are striding along like gods, another wonderful idea that old man Handel hit on. Just open up your restless heart to it, and it will bring you peace. I realize that this ridiculous apparatus casts a hopelessly idiotic veil over the distant form of the divine music, but just listen to it striding by, little man, and let us have no pathos or scorn. Pay attention, you can learn something from it. Notice how, thanks to this crazy sound system, the most idiotic, useless and forbidden feat on earth is made possible. It takes some random piece of music that is being played somewhere or other and hurls it in a stupid, crude and terribly distorted form into a room where it doesn't belong. Yet it cannot destroy the music's original spirit. Inevitably, all it can do is use the music as a vehicle to demonstrate its own tireless technology and mindless creation of commotion. Listen closely, little man, you need to. Come on, prick up your ears! That's right. What you are hearing now, you see, is not just Handel as violated by the radio, a Handel who even in this most abysmal of guises remains divine – no, what you are hearing and seeing, Sir, is at one and the same time an excellent metaphor of all life. When listening to the radio you are hearing and seeing the age-old conflict between ideas and appearances, between eternity and time, between things divine and things human. For you see, my dear friend, just as the radio randomly flings ten minutes' worth of the most magnificent music on earth into totally inappropriate spaces like middle-class drawing rooms and the garrets of the poor, filling the ears of its subscribers with it as they chatter, feed, yawn and sleep; just as it robs this music of all its sensuous beauty, ruins it, reducing it to mere mucus and crackling sounds, yet still failing to kill its entire spirit, so does life or so-called reality send the world's splendid repertoire of images hurling all over the place. It will follow Handel up with a talk on the techniques medium-sized firms use to doctor their balance sheets. It will transform magical orchestral harmonies into an unpalatable porridge of notes. With its technology, its frantic activity, its unrestrained expediency and vanity it will intrude everywhere between idea and reality, between the orchestra and the ear. The whole of life is like that, young man, and we have no choice but to accept the fact and – if we have any sense – laugh about it. People like you have absolutely no right to go criticizing either the radio or life. You ought rather to learn how to listen first, to take seriously what is worth taking seriously, and to laugh about the rest. Or have you yourself by any chance found a better, nobler, more intelligent and tasteful way of living? No, you have not, Monsieur Harry! You have managed to make your life one long appalling story of sickness. You have turned your talents into one great disaster. And it is clear that here you could think of nothing better to do with a girl as good-looking and charming as this than to destroy her by sticking a knife in her body. Surely you don't think that was right?'

'Right? Oh no!' I cried in despair. 'My God, Mozart, it's all so wrong, of course, so diabolically stupid and bad! I'm a beast, Mozart, a stupid, evil beast. I'm sick and depraved, you're right about that, a thousand times right. – But as far as this girl is concerned, I can only say that she herself wanted it that way. I merely fulfilled her own wish.'

Mozart laughed that silent laugh of his, but this time did at least do me the great favour of switching off the wireless.

Suddenly my defence sounded really foolish to me, even though I had still sincerely believed what I was saying only a moment ago. Now, all at once, I recalled that occasion when Hermione had been speaking of time and eternity. Then, I had immediately been willing to regard her thoughts as a reflection of my own. Yet I had taken for granted that getting me to kill her was entirely her own idea and wish, uninfluenced by me in the least. But if so, why had I not only accepted and believed a notion as horrific and strange as that at the time, but even guessed it in advance? Perhaps because it was my own idea after all? And why, of all times, had I killed Hermione when I found her naked in the arms of someone else? Mozart's silent laughter seemed all-knowing and full of scorn.

'Harry,' he said, 'you must be joking. Do you really expect me to believe that this beautiful girl wanted nothing from you other than to be stabbed in the breast with a knife? Pull the other one! Well, you did at least make a thorough job of it. The poor child is as dead as a doornail. Perhaps now would be a good time for you to accept the consequences of your gallantry towards this fair lady. Or could it be that you want to escape the consequences?'

'No,' I cried. 'Don't you understand a thing? Escape the consequences, me! There is nothing I desire more than to pay for what I've done, pay for it, pay for it, put my head under the executioner's axe, take my punishment and be exterminated.'

The look of scorn Mozart gave me was unbearable.

'Always the same pompous verbiage! But don't worry, Harry, you'll learn what humour is one of these days. Humour is always gallows humour, and if need be the gallows is just the place for you to learn about it. Are you ready to do it? Yes? Right, then go to the public prosecutor's office and subject yourself to the whole humourless paraphernalia of the Law, right down to the last stage in the prison yard when they coolly chop off your head at the break of day. You are ready to do it, then?'

Suddenly an inscription flashed up before my eyes:

HARRY'S EXECUTION

---

and I nodded to show willing. An austere courtyard enclosed by four walls with small barred windows, a guillotine prepared to perfection, a dozen gentlemen clad in black robes and frock coats – and there was I, standing in their midst, shivering in the chill, grey, early-morning air, so pitifully afraid that my blood ran cold, but ready and willing. I stepped forward when ordered to, kneeled down when ordered to. Taking off his cap, the public prosecutor cleared his throat, as did all the other gentlemen. Unfolding an official document and holding it up to his eyes, he then read aloud:

'Gentlemen, before you stands one Harry Haller, charged with wilfully abusing our Magic Theatre and found guilty as charged. Not only did Haller cause offence to fine art by confusing our beautiful picture gallery with so-called reality and stabbing to death the mirror image of a girl with the mirror image of a knife, but in addition he showed that he was intent upon using our theatre quite humourlessly as a mechanism for committing suicide. We therefore sentence Haller to eternal life while also withdrawing his entry permit to our theatre for a period of twelve hours. Nor can we spare the accused the further penalty of being laughed out of court. So let me hear it from you, gentlemen, after me: One – two – three!'

And every single one present came in precisely on the call of three, producing a chorus of high-pitched laughter, a terrible laughter from the beyond that human ears could scarcely bear.

When I came to again, Mozart was sitting by me as before.

Tapping me on the shoulder, he said: 'You have heard your sentence. So you see, you'll have to get used to going on listening to the radio music of life. It will do you good. You are uncommonly lacking in talent, my dear stupid chap, but by now I suppose even you have gradually realized what is being asked of you. You are to learn to laugh, that's what is being asked of you. You are to understand life's humour, the gallows humour of this life. But of course you are prepared to do anything on earth other than what is asked of you. You are prepared to stab girls to death; you are prepared to have yourself solemnly executed; you would no doubt also be prepared to spend a hundred years mortifying your flesh and scourging yourself. Or am I wrong?'

'No! With all my heart I'd be prepared to do so,' I cried in my despair.

'Naturally! There isn't a single stupid and humourless activity, anything pompous, serious and devoid of wit, that doesn't appeal to you! But, you see, nothing of that sort appeals to me. I don't give a fig for all your romantic desire to do penance. You must be berserk, wanting to be executed and have your head chopped off! You'd commit another ten murders to achieve this stupid ideal of yours. You want to die, you coward, but not to live. But to go on living, damn it, is precisely what you will have to do. It would serve you right if you were sentenced to the severest penalty there is.'

'Oh, and what sort of penalty might that be?'

'We could, for instance, bring the girl back to life and marry you to her.'

'No, I wouldn't be prepared to go along with that. It would end in misfortune.'

'As if what you did hasn't already caused misfortune enough! But it's now time to put a stop to all your posturing and killing. Can't you finally see sense? You are to live, and you are to learn to laugh. You must learn to listen to life's damned radio music, to respect the spirit that lies behind it while laughing at all the dross it contains. That's all. Nothing more is being asked of you.'

Gritting my teeth, I asked in a soft voice: 'And what if I refuse? What if I deny you, Herr Mozart, the right to intervene in Steppenwolf's fate and tell him what to do?'

'That being the case,' Mozart said peacefully, 'I would suggest you smoke another of my lovely cigarettes.' And as he said this, producing a cigarette from his waistcoat pocket like a conjuror and offering it to me, he suddenly ceased to be Mozart. Instead, he was my friend Pablo, gazing warmly at me with his exotic dark eyes. He also looked like the twin brother of the man who had taught me to play chess with the tiny figures.

'Pablo!' I exclaimed with a start. 'Pablo, where are we?'

Passing me the cigarette, Pablo gave me a light.

'We're in my Magic Theatre,' he said with a smile. 'And should you wish to learn the tango, become a general, or have a conversation with Alexander the Great, all of that can be arranged when you next visit. However, I'm bound to say I'm a little disappointed in you, Harry. Losing all control of yourself, you violated the humour of my little theatre by wielding a knife and committing a foul deed like that. You sullied the fine images of our magic realm with the stains of reality. That wasn't nice of you. I hope at least you did it because you were jealous when you saw Hermione lying there with me. Unfortunately you didn't know how to handle that figure. I thought you had learned to play the game better. Never mind, it can be put right.'

Taking hold of Hermione, who immediately shrank to the size of a chess piece, he put her in the very same pocket of his waistcoat that he had previously taken the cigarette from.

The sweet, heavy smoke from the cigarette had a pleasant smell. I felt as if hollowed out, fit to sleep for a year.

Oh, now I understood everything, understood Pablo, understood Mozart, whose terrible laughter I could hear somewhere or other behind me. I knew that the pieces of life's game were there in my pocket, all hundred thousand of them. Though shocked to the core, I had a sense of what the game meant, and I was willing to start playing it again, to sample its torments once more, once more to shudder at the nonsense it entailed, again to journey through my personal hell, a journey I would often have to repeat.

One day I would play the game of many figures better. One day I would learn to laugh. Pablo was waiting for me. Mozart was waiting for me.

The End

Author's Postscript (1941)

Works of literature may be understood and misunderstood in many a different way. In most cases the author of a work of literature is not the best-placed arbiter when it comes to deciding where the readers' understanding comes to an end and their misunderstanding begins. Indeed many authors have found readers to whom their work was more transparent than it was to themselves. Besides, it is of course possible for misunderstandings to be fruitful.

That said, of all my works *Steppenwolf* seems to me to be the one that has been more frequently and more drastically misunderstood than any other. And of all people it was often the affirmative, indeed the enthusiastic readers, and not those rejecting the book, whose comments took me aback. In part, but only in part, the frequency of such cases can be explained by the fact that this book, written by a fifty-year-old man and dealing with the problems associated with that particular age, very often fell into the hands of quite young people.

However, even among readers of my own age I often encountered some who, though impressed by the book, remained curiously blind to a good half of its contents. It seems to me that these readers, seeing themselves reflected in the figure of Steppenwolf, identified with him, suffered along with him, dreamed his dreams and in the process totally overlooked the fact that the book speaks and knows of other things than just Harry Haller and his difficulties. They failed to see that a second, higher, time-less realm exists above Steppenwolf and his problematic life or that the 'Tract' and all the other passages in the book concerning things intellectual, spiritual, artistic and the 'Immortals' evoke a positive, serene, supra-personal, timeless world of faith that contrasts markedly with Steppenwolf's world of suffering. These readers were thus incapable of appreciating that the book, though it does constitute a record of suffering and misery, is by no means the book of man despairing of life, but of one who believes.

Of course I cannot dictate to readers how they should under-stand my tale, and I have no desire to. May everyone make of it whatever strikes a chord in them and suits their needs. I would nevertheless be pleased if many readers could recognize that although Steppenwolf's story is one of sickness and crisis, these do not end in death or destruction. On the contrary: they result in a cure.

Hermann Hesse

Translator's Afterword

Hermann Hesse and his novel *Steppenwolf*

The 1927 novel *Steppenwolf* – literally 'Wolf of the Steppes' – laid the foundations of Hermann Hesse's worldwide fame. Posthumously his reputation merged with pop culture when a 1960s Canadian-American rock band named itself 'Steppenwolf', clearly in reference to the dissatisfaction the novel's hero feels with the state of modern civilization (and characteristically, the group's greatest hit was 'Born to be Wild').

What gives Hesse's *Steppenwolf* lasting international appeal is its aura of twentieth-century modernity and its (unresolved) quest for individual authenticity. That quest, it has to be said – the search for 'oneness' between self, world and universe – is perhaps the central theme in all of the author's work.

Hesse is that rare phenomenon, a writer who enjoyed enormous success and instant fame with what was virtually his first novel, *Peter Camenzind*. Published in 1903–4, some 60,000 copies of it had been sold by the outbreak of the First World War. Its success allowed the twenty-six-year-old Hesse to give up his job in a Basel bookshop and from then until his death in 1962 he was able to live as a full-time writer.

The main appeal of *Peter Camenzind* lay in its glorification of the simple life lived close to nature as opposed to the experience of modern civilization, especially that of the big city, which is viewed with a strong degree of cultural pessimism. The novel enjoyed great popularity among the *Wandervogel* and other German youth movements of the time, noted for their neo-Romantic love of the outdoor life. Yet, as Hesse himself stressed, its eponymous hero was not suited to such collective activities, not one to join any kind of movement, but essentially an individualist with a strong mystical bent, concerned to find his own path in life. As such he is the first in a long line of outsider figures in the author's work.

Hesse's best-known novels, *Demian*, *Siddhartha*, *Steppenwolf*, *Narcissus and Goldmund* and *The Glass Bead Game*, were all published after the First World War, which formed a caesura in his writing. Before 1914, his works showed a sentimental attachment to the region, or 'Heimat', a sense that even problematic individuals were somehow anchored by their roots. Like many other writers of his generation, Hesse welcomed the outbreak of war as a way towards cultural renewal and collective identity. Yet he soon took a decisive pacifist turn, which earned him, a resident of Switzerland since 1912, the hostility of Germany's nationalist circles and right-wing press. The cosmopolitan humanism that characterized his writing after 1914 was a factor in his being awarded the Nobel Prize in Literature in November 1946.

As a new literary departure, then, Hesse published *Demian* in 1919 under the pseudonym Emil Sinclair. The first-person narrator learns to reject any external norms as he tries to follow 'what is urging outwards' from within himself. For a moment, the war seems to offer him and all self-searching, 'marked' individuals the possibility of giving themselves up to a destiny shared with thousands of others. But *Demian* concludes by presenting the wounded Sinclair's rather different vision of his inner self – far from having merged with a collective whole, he has become totally assimilated to his wise, dead friend, Demian. Hesse's outsider has thus found himself in his own, radically self-reliant alter ego. Paradoxically, once again, the novel's individualist message turned it into the bible of the various post-war German youth movements.

In *Siddhartha*, published in 1922, Hesse's cultural critique takes the form of an 'Indian Tale' set at the time of Buddha and partly inspired by the author's journey to Ceylon and Indonesia in 1911. The son of a Hindu priest or Brahmin, Siddhartha eventually absorbs the essence of Buddhism (significantly, without ever submitting himself to Buddha's doctrine) in a state of unteachable wisdom under the practical influence of an old man. Through the central character's unflinching spiritual individualism, Hesse combined his own blend of Eastern religions with a distinctly Western element.

By the time *Steppenwolf* was published in 1927, Hesse's well-established intellectual nonconformism had taken its toll. A feeling of having excluded himself irreversibly from a disgusting, laughable contemporary world was evident in his autobiographical notes published in 1924–5, recording his visits to the spa town of Baden near Zurich, and in 1927, reflecting on his tour of public readings in south Germany. The sense of irremediable loneliness and a suicidal repulsion by modern realities are depicted in the form of the midlife crisis experienced by the central character of *Steppenwolf*, Harry Haller. Unlike Sinclair/Demian or Siddhartha, Haller remains an outsider figure unable to achieve fulfilment within himself. Yet, as Hesse himself indicated, the character's unresolved crisis, appealing powerfully to most readers and forming the basis of the novel's global fame, constitutes only one narrative level. The solution to Haller's problems is implied in the novel's serenely positive 'higher world' of contemplations and reflections, not least the dialogue with sublime 'Immortals' such as Goethe and Mozart.

By comparison with *Steppenwolf*, arguably the author's outstanding modernist achievement in terms of content and form, the later works seem to mark a regression. In *Narcissus and Goldmund* (1929–30), removed from the increasingly threatening world of the interwar years not only by a medieval setting, Hesse explored the dualism between other-worldly wisdom and life-affirming sensuality in the eponymous pair of outsider characters. The 'wholeness' to which they both aspire cannot be attained by either of them individually; it is to be found in their relationship. *The Glass Bead Game* (published in 1943), Hesse's last big novel and the fruit of twelve years, presents the culmination of his ambitions as a writer. In opposition to the barbarism of Hitler's Germany and the Second World War, it depicts a utopian future republic of the spirit, an elitist province called 'Castalia'. Here an exclusively male order of intellectuals celebrates the highest achievements of human cultural history in an esoteric, self-sufficient game, the rules of which are watched over by a 'Magister Ludi'. The novel follows the rise of Joseph Knecht from gifted schoolboy to this highest office in the hierarchy. Although showing the intellectual gear of Hesse's central figures, Knecht does not fall into the category of self-searching 'outsider' as long as he finds himself in harmony with the existing order. But eventually, in a reversal of the strife that is typical of Hesse's earlier characters, Knecht leaves behind the artificial harmony of Castalia for an involvement with the 'real world'. That world, too, is conceivably remote from the conflicts of the twentieth century, which Hesse's future humanity is imagined to have overcome. This was a far cry from *Steppenwolf* in its engagement with the realities of the 1920s and the acute crisis Hesse was experiencing as an ageing intellectual author.

Steppenwolf as self-portrait

On his own admission Hermann Hesse was a peculiarly autobiographical writer. The central figures of most of his stories and novels were, he once declared, symbolic vehicles for his own experiences, thoughts and problems at particular stages of his life. Of all such characters, Harry Haller is the most striking example. He shares the author's initials H. H. and his age – Hesse was approaching his fiftieth birthday when completing the novel. Like Hesse, Haller looks back on a broken marriage after his wife's sudden mental illness. Like Hesse, he is pilloried in the right-wing press as a traitor to his German Fatherland because of articles of an internationalist and pacifist persuasion he has written during and since the First World War.

Beyond these broad biographical parallels, however, *Steppenwolf* deals in a concentrated way with a particular period of crisis in Hesse's life, which was at its most acute during the years 1922 to 1926. Suicide is an option referred to more than once in Hesse's letters of these years. Aged forty-eight in 1925, he writes to his friends Emmy and Hugo Ball of his despairing attitude to life, but claims that he has overcome the worst depression by allowing himself two years' respite until his fiftieth birthday. Only then will he have the right to hang himself, should he still feel that way inclined. This is, of course, exactly the stratagem adopted by the 'suicidal' Haller in the novel.

An important forerunner of *Steppenwolf* is a cycle of over forty poems that Hesse wrote in the winter of 1925/6, significantly entitled 'Crisis'. The whole cycle was not published until 1928, and then only in a limited edition, but a selection from it appeared in the November 1926 issue of the periodical *Neue Rundschau* under the title: 'Steppenwolf. Extracts from a Diary in Verse'. The cycle includes the very poem 'Steppenwolf' that Haller, in the novel, says he has written late one night, and which he describes as 'a self-portrait in crude rhyming doggerel'. Much the same could be said of most of the poems in the cycle, which have little aesthetic merit, as Hesse himself admitted in a letter of

October 1926 to the critic Heinrich Wiegand, before justifying them in the following terms:

Years ago I gave up all aesthetic ambition. I don't write literature now but simply confessions, just as a drowning man or a man dying of poisoning no longer worries about the state of his hair or the modulation of his voice, but instead simply lets out a scream.

The 'Crisis' collection also contains verbatim the poem 'The Immortals', which Haller in the novel scribbles on the back of the wine list while waiting for Maria in a pub in the suburbs. Otherwise, however, its poems are mainly raw, subjective expressions of the problems Hesse is experiencing and his attempts to find new distractions as he feels old age coming on. Much the same ground is covered in his correspondence of the period before the real-life experiences find their way, often only slightly adapted, into the novel he sometimes called the 'prose Steppenwolf'.

Hesse's depressed state of mind in these years relates, as has already been stressed, largely to the process of ageing. His correspondence is full of complaints about physical ailments, principally sciatica and gout, but also failing eyesight and severe headaches, especially behind the eyes. All of these are reflected in the novel, as are Hesse's own preferred means of coping with pain, whether by resorting to strong opiates or to heavy drinking. His excessive consumption of wine and brandy, in particular, is frequently mentioned in the 'Crisis' poems and letters of the period, and both drinks feature prominently in Harry Haller's visits to city pubs in the novel.

Perhaps more surprising is the extent to which one of Haller's other activities in the novel – his dancing lessons, the purchase of a gramophone, his attendance at the masked ball – is based on Hesse's own experience at that time. A letter of February 1926 records that he has just finished a course of six dance lessons and, as far as can be expected of 'an elderly man with gout', now feels reasonably competent at the foxtrot and one-step. And one Saturday in March, during the Carnival season, he went, for the first time in his life, to a masked ball in Zurich, commenting shortly afterwards: 'I have been a real fool* to spend 30 years of my life wrestling with the problems of humanity without ever knowing what a masked ball is.' In June of the same year he confides to a friend that he has bought himself a small gramophone in Zurich and taken it back with him to his country retreat in Montagnola above Lake Lugano. There he winds it up from time to time of an evening and listens to 'Valencia' or 'Yearning', popular dance tunes of the time.

Hesse had moved to Montagnola from Berne in 1919 and very much regarded his house and garden there as a rustic refuge from city life and the modern world in general. His early years in this retreat were characterized by a degree of asceticism – he lived frugally, becoming a vegetarian for a spell, and also practised meditation. He saw himself as a kind of hermit, enjoying the isolation that was fruitful for his writing as well as the new art form he had taken up: painting. However, the harsh winters in Montagnola became unbearable and from 1924 onwards he regularly moved back to the city during colder months, taking lodgings in Basel and later Zurich. The experience of meeting friends, of living in proximity to 'normal' people like his first landlady in Basel, from whom he rented two rooms in the attic just as Haller does from the 'aunt' in the novel, led him to question the value of his years of isolation and independence. It also led to regrets that he had spent so much of his younger years in the pursuit of some kind of higher wisdom, thus missing out on the simpler, unreflective enjoyments of life. In his own words, he was now

* Hesse puns on the word 'Trottel' ('fool') by coining the word 'Foxtrottel' here, which is impossible to render in translation.

attempting to live for once like an 'overgrown child'. Success was only partial, but it was pleasurable. It seems, in addition to the dancing and pub-crawling, also to have involved a degree of sexual liberation, certainly of renewed attraction to often younger women, though there is nothing as explicit in Hesse's letters of the time as the account of Harry Haller's erotic education at the hands of the prostitute Maria.

The winter months Hesse spent in Basel and Zurich during these years were of course not wholly devoted to this life of dancing, drinking and erotic escapades. He himself writes of the need to pack his suitcases carefully before leaving Montagnola, ensuring that he has with him the books he requires, his watercolours and sketch pads, a few pictures and other objects with which to deck out his city lodgings. In the novel, Harry Haller arrives in the city with just this kind of intellectual and aesthetic 'baggage', and he fills his rented attic room with it, turning it into a sort of hermit's cell. His preferences correspond closely to Hesse's own. The picture of a Siamese Buddha that the landlady's nephew notices hanging on the wall, of course, reflects Hesse's interest in oriental religion and thought, its replacement by a portrait of Gandhi his pacifism. The near identity of author and character is even more strikingly apparent in Haller's reading. German Romanticism was an early and lasting influence on Hesse, and two of his favourite writers of that period, Jean Paul and Novalis, figure prominently in Haller's travel library. Heavily annotated volumes of Dostoevsky point to another preoccupation of Hesse. In 1920 he published three essays on the Russian novelist under the title 'Gazing into Chaos'. The presence of the complete works of Goethe in Haller's 'den' is of even greater significance in this respect. Hesse was a deep admirer of Germany's major poet, novelist and dramatist, though not uncritical of him, especially in his late 'Olympian' phase as the 'sage of Weimar', and both his admiration and his criticism are voiced by Haller in his dream encounter with Goethe in the novel. Goethe's influence on *Steppenwolf* and his role as a character in the novel, one of the so-called 'Immortals', indicate how firmly Hesse's imaginative autobiographical fiction is rooted in the German literary tradition.

Steppenwolf as a 'Bildungsroman'

A prominent genre in German literature is the 'Bildungsroman', or novel of education. In contrast to the broadly realist novel traditions of England, France and Russia it focuses on the development of a central character from inexperienced youth to eventual maturity. Wider social concerns, while by no means ignored, tend to play a subordinate role to this process of personal education, in which philosophical ideas also often have a big part to play. Hesse's *Steppenwolf* is a 'Bildungsroman', but with a difference in that Harry Haller is at the outset already a highly educated man, a published author and sophisticated connoisseur of literature and classical music. His is a very belated 'education', beginning in his late forties, and it follows a highly unusual curriculum. One of the key things he has to learn is to view himself differently. His image of himself as a hybrid creature, half human by virtue of his intellectual, spiritual and artistic qualities, half wolf by virtue of his instincts, appetites and urges, is dismissed as an instance of crude binary thinking in the Steppenwolf 'Tract', a pamphlet that comes into his hands after a night out drinking. 'Harry may be a highly educated human being, but he is acting like some savage, say, who is incapable of counting beyond two,' we are told there. Yet the Tract also points to an example of such thinking on the part of a literary character who is anything but a primitive man: the learned Doctor Faust of Goethe's drama and his famous declaration: 'Two souls, alas, dwell in my breast!' Such crude dualism is still central to Western thought, it is argued, despite the fact that Indian philosophy long ago exposed it as a delusion, since in reality human beings consist of multiple souls. Although he studies the Tract closely, there is little evidence that Haller – unlike perceptive readers of the novel – learns from it at this stage. Only in the 'Magic Theatre' sequence towards the end, when confronted by the image of his multiple selves, whether in the giant mirror on the wall or in the form of miniature figures on a chessboard, does he begin to appreciate the fact.

The form Harry Haller's dualistic self-image takes is a familiar one in Western philosophy, a dichotomy between mind/spirit on the one hand and body on the other, where things intellectual and spiritual are deemed positive while the instincts, appetites and carnal urges are regarded as inferior characteristics, shared with other animals and thus needing to be tamed. The 'editor' of Harry Haller's notebooks, his landlady's grammar-school-educated nephew, speculates that Haller's self-image has its origins in his upbringing by strict and piously Christian parents who, while encouraging him to love his neighbours, had taught him to hate himself. This puritanical background leads also to sexual inhibitions, since the self-hatred is directed at what Haller considers the wolf in himself. It is significant, for instance, that his first adolescent encounter with the opposite sex, when he does no more than raise his hat to the attractive Rosa Kreisler, takes place on the very Sunday in spring when he has just been confirmed. That the middle-aged Harry is still troubled by such inhibitions is evident from the dream he has about visiting the old Goethe in Weimar. For much of it he is irritated by the presence of a scorpion, associated in his subconscious with the beautiful lover Molly of August Bürger's poems and explicitly identified as 'a beautiful, dangerous heraldic creature representing femininity and sin'. In contrast, sexuality holds no such threat for Goethe. When asked whether Molly is there, he laughs out loud and takes from his desk a velvet-lined box containing a miniature female leg, which he dangles before Haller's face, taunting him. Reaching for the leg, Haller sees it twitch momentarily and, still suspecting it may be the scorpion, is torn between desire and fear.

Haller's belated 'education' in matters sexual comes from Maria, the beautiful young prostitute friend of Hermione during the three weeks leading up to the masked ball. It continues during the ball itself, first as he is made aware of the homoerotic component in his make-up when he encounters Hermione dressed as a young man, which evokes memories of his boyhood friend Hermann, then in the passionate 'nuptial dance' with her, now in the guise of a Pierrette. The new skills he has learned are then practised on the surreal level of the Magic Theatre when he enters the box promising 'ALL GIRLS ARE YOURS', in which he is allowed to relive all the sexual opportunities of his past life, this time not letting them slip by because of his inhibitions. When he leaves this box he feels he is ripe for Hermione, the one true woman of his dreams, but his new self-confidence proves misplaced. On subsequently discovering Hermione and Pablo lying exhausted together on a rug after making love, he stabs her to death. He later protests that he was only fulfilling her own wish, but the more plausible motive is jealousy, an indication that he has not yet learned to cope with sexuality in the sovereign, playful manner evinced by Goethe in the earlier dream sequence. This reading is borne out by Pablo's reaction towards the very end of the novel when, pointing to Hermione's corpse, he says to Haller: 'Unfortunately you didn't know how to handle that figure. I thought you had learned to play the game better.' As Pablo then picks up Hermione, her body shrinks instantaneously to the size of a toy, which he slips into his waistcoat pocket just as nonchalantly as Goethe had earlier returned the miniature woman's leg to its velvet box.

Inability to 'play the game of life' is something that characterizes Haller from the outset of the novel. On the occasion of their first visit to a restaurant together, Hermione tells him he still needs to learn the basic arts of living that most human beings practise as a matter of course, such as taking pleasure in eating food. And as early as their first encounter in the Black Eagle she claims he needs her if he is 'to learn how to dance, to learn how to laugh, to learn how to live'. She eventually succeeds in teaching him the first skill on this list, as we can see from his accomplishments at the masked ball, but the second one proves far more difficult, despite her constant playful mockery of him. It is claimed in the Tract that Steppenwolf shows signs of being blessed with the gift of humour, but Haller remains for the most part a character who takes both life and himself extremely seriously. Only momentarily does he burst out laughing and feel a great sense of release, and significantly that occurs in the Magic Theatre, which Pablo explicitly describes as a 'school of humour'. This is the moment when he is invited to carry out a 'make-believe act of suicide' by destroying his previous personality as seen in the pocket mirror Pablo holds up to him. In the end, however, he is the one on the receiving end of laughter when he is literally laughed out of court because, by insisting on his own execution for the murder of Hermione, he has used 'our theatre quite humourlessly as a mechanism for committing suicide'.

Ultimately, then, while he certainly learns to dance, Haller fails the test of laughter. Yet along the way he has been confronted with two figures who prove more than capable of both these 'skills', and might have served him as models. In his dream, watching Goethe prancing up and down, Haller has to grant that he can 'dance wonderfully well'. When asked about Molly, the aged writer's response is to laugh out loud, while at the end of the dream sequence he is described as 'chortling away to himself with the dark, inscrutable kind of humour typical of the very old'. In the Magic Theatre, Mozart, on seeing Haller's long face, starts turning somersaults and playing 'trills with his feet'. When he first appears, to the sound of the 'Stone Guest' music from *Don Giovanni*, the composer is laughing, and his laughter is 'bright and ice-cold'. A little later, when Haller protests at having to listen to Handel's music so badly distorted by the wireless set, Mozart again responds with laughter. This time it is 'cold, ghostly, noiseless'. Both descriptions bring to mind the final line of the poem 'The Immortals', mentioned earlier, which reads: 'Cool and star-bright, our laughter knows no end.'

Goethe and Mozart are portrayed as belonging to the ranks of these 'Immortals'. Both are seen as outstanding human beings who, to use the cosmological imagery of the Steppenwolf Tract, have escaped the gravitational pull of the 'bourgeois' world by making a daring leap into the icy realms of starry outer space. This pattern of imagery, especially the three elements of vast, empty space, icy coldness and the stars, recurs frequently in the novel in connection with Hesse's vision of the 'Immortals' as rare individuals who have achieved the ideal goal of becoming fully human. Precisely the same pattern, as it happens, recurs in connection with the 'Übermensch' or 'Superhuman Individual' in Friedrich Nietzsche's *Thus Spake Zarathustra*, a work that had a profound impact on Hesse when he first read it as a twenty-year-old. What is more, two skills the prophet Zarathustra regards as essential to the so-called 'higher human beings', those aspiring to the condition of 'Übermensch', are dancing and laughter. Here, then, we have a clear philosophical source for two key elements in Harry Haller's education. Indeed, to judge from what the Tract says about his being 'blessed with sufficient genius to venture along the road to becoming fully human', Haller may be regarded as a 'higher human being' in this

Nietzschean sense. However, as he himself acknowledges at the very end of the novel, his education is far from complete. He still has to learn to play life's game better, still needs to learn to laugh.

Socio-political aspects of the novel

Steppenwolf may primarily be concerned to chart the educational development of a single character who is a self-portrait of the author. By introducing long-dead figures such as Goethe and Mozart into a twentieth-century setting and locating much of the final action in a 'Magic Theatre' it can also be seen to venture into surreal realms. Yet for all this, as has been indicated before, a strong case can be made for the novel as a realistic portrayal of the social and political conditions of its time and in a particular place. Though the novel's city scenes are based on Basel and Zurich, Hesse very much has an eye to the Weimar Republic of his native Germany when evoking the atmosphere of the 1920s. This is especially evident in the portrayal of the professor Haller visits one evening. On the one hand a highly sophisticated academic, an expert on Eastern mythologies, he is on the other hand 'blind to the fact that, all around him, preparations are being made for the next war; he considers Jews and Communists to be detestable; he is a good, unthinking, contented child'. This description would fit many, if not a majority, of those holding professorial chairs at German universities during the period. Militarism, anti-republican feeling, hostility to democracy and anti-Semitism were rife in academic circles, including the student body. Such reactionary attitudes were fostered in part by the right-wing press, especially the very high proportion of newspapers owned by the nationalistic media magnate Alfred Hugenberg. The professor reads just such a paper, delighting in the way its editor pillories pacifists and cosmopolitans like Haller. Later we learn that Hermione has come across an article denouncing Haller in much the same terms in another paper. When he points out to her that two thirds of his compatriots read publications of this kind, stirring up their hatred and inciting them to seek revenge for Germany's defeat in the war, he is clearly a spokesman for Hesse's own insight into the power of a propaganda machine that is helping to make a second war inevitable. None of those in positions of power – the generals, the industrial magnates, the politicians – are, Haller argues, prepared to acknowledge their share of guilt in the slaughter of the last war, a criticism again voiced by Hesse himself in essays of the time.

Interestingly, however, Hesse's criticism is not just confined to these familiar targets that most historians now agree played a significant part in the failure of the Weimar Republic. He also points more speculatively to the negative influence of German intellectuals over the years: philosophers, artists and writers like himself. 'We German intellectuals, all of us, were not at home in reality, were alien and hostile to it, and that is why we have played such a lamentable role in the real world of our country, in its history, its politics and its public opinion,' is the indictment pronounced by Haller after an evening spent listening to a concert of early music. If his own passion for music triggers such thoughts it is because he views his whole relationship to it as 'unwholesome'. Music is associated in his mind with things other-worldly, purely aesthetic and also irrational. Indulgence in it comes at the expense of reason, the Logos, the word, which ought to be the preferred 'instrument' of intellectuals. This argument may strike readers as vague and speculative, but Hesse is not alone in propounding it. Thomas Mann had already set up a similar opposition between music and words in *The Magic Mountain* and he was later to expand on this theme when exploring the roots of Nazism in his novel *Dr Faustus* and his 1945 essay 'Germany and the Germans'. In a more general way Thomas Mann's elder brother, Heinrich, had prepared the ground for such arguments in a number of essays written before and during the First World War in which he castigated German intellectuals and writers for their relative indifference to socio-political developments, especially compared to their French counterparts such as Voltaire or Zola.

Harry Haller's criticism of German intellectuals for being 'alien and hostile' to reality can, ironically, be seen to apply in no small measure to himself, particularly where the reality of the modern world is concerned. In the first few pages of his notebooks we find him railing against modern life with its mass entertainments as something essentially shallow, characterized by mindless consumption. When he later visits a cinema to kill time he is horrified to see the sacred stories of the Bible reproduced on a commercialized epic scale before an audience that is gratefully consuming not only the film but also the sandwiches it has brought along with it.* He abhors jazz, thinking that something similar must have been played under the last Roman emperors since it is 'the music of an age in decline'. In all these respects Haller seems to share the cultural pessimism expressed by many intellectuals at the time, most notably by Oswald Spengler in his popular *Decline of the West*. At one point, when attending the funeral of a complete stranger, Haller reflects that the whole world of culture as he knows it is like a vast cemetery in which the names of Jesus Christ, Socrates, Mozart, Haydn, Dante and Goethe are now barely legible on the graves. The God of the modern age, in Haller's eyes, is technology, something he is also hostile to, witness his enthusiastic participation in the wholesale destruction of cars in one sequence from the Magic Theatre and his aversion to early wireless sets, whether

* Though not named, the film, to judge from Hesse's description, must be Cecil B. DeMille's 1923 silent epic, *The Ten Commandments*.

constructed by his landlady's nephew as a hobby or by Mozart in order to tune in to a broadcast of Handel's music. Haller's hostility to some of these features of modern life, such as the dominance of the motor car or the mindless consumption, may well explain the novel's lasting appeal in times of greater ecological awareness. It was certainly, as indicated before, shared by the 'drop-outs' of the hippie generation in America in the 1960s, for many of whom *Steppenwolf* became a cult book.* Ultimately, however, the novel offers no blanket endorsement of Haller's cultural pessimism, since Mozart, in the Magic Theatre, insists that he must learn to listen to 'life's damned radio music' without allowing the dross it contains to destroy the true spirit of it.

Structure and style

In a letter of 1927 Hesse complained that no critic had appreciated the innovative form of *Steppenwolf*. It was not, as many thought, a fragmentary work, but had a clearly proportioned structure like a sonata or a fugue. He later made a similar claim about the novel's musical structure, arguing that it was rigorously composed in sonata form around the Tract as an intermezzo. Were this the case, it would be a highly appropriate form for a novel in which music plays a considerable thematic role. However, despite some ingenious attempts by academic critics to substantiate it, the analogy is not altogether convincing. Subtle shaping along musical lines would, in any case, appear to conflict with Hesse's own statement, quoted above, that he had long since abandoned all 'aesthetic ambition'.

Steppenwolf does have an unusual structure, but it is perhaps

* The novel's cult status also owed a great deal to the drug scene of the time, especially after Timothy Leary recommended it as 'the master-guide to the psychedelic experience and its applications'.

more helpful to see this as determined by considerations of perspective. The novel begins with a seemingly objective view of Haller in the form of a reflective memoir by the unnamed landlady's nephew who styles himself as the editor of the notebooks left behind by the lodger. We then enter the subjective world of Haller via a first instalment of his notebooks, ominously headed 'For mad people only', suggesting that our perspective on events will be totally different from that of the eminently commonsensical 'bourgeois' editor. A switch to a third narrative perspective occurs when Haller records the contents of the Steppenwolf Tract that has mysteriously come into his possession. This, in his own estimation, is 'highly objective, the work of someone uninvolved, picturing me from the outside and from above'. For the remainder of the novel – much the longest section – Hesse reverts to the subjective vision of Haller's notebooks, though that vision is progressively modified, to an extent under the influence of the Tract, partly also as Haller learns from his encounters with Hermione and Pablo to view himself in radically different ways. The most striking change of perspective comes in the long Magic Theatre sequence at the end. Here all semblance of reasoned objectivity is left behind, as is suggested by the words 'PAY AT THE DOOR WITH YOUR MIND' that Haller reads on the announcement of the evening's entertainment.

Hesse's use of multiple narrators certainly makes *Steppenwolf* a more complex text in the modernist manner than any of his previous works. There is also evidence of his striving to achieve contrasts in tone and register within the novel's different sections. Whether he is entirely successful in this is, however, debatable. The language of the nephew in the first section is, it is true, generally simpler than that of Haller when we first encounter him in the notebooks, where the sentences are far longer and more intricate. Yet even the supposedly non-intellectual nephew is familiar with aspects of Nietzsche's thought and proves capable of analysing Haller in ways that don't differ markedly from what is later argued in the Tract. The Tract itself is a curious mixture stylistically. It begins like a fairy tale with 'Once upon a time', reads for a while like the cheap 'self-help' manual it appears to be, but then, despite its occasionally playful, mocking tone, it develops into something more akin to a sociological and psychological treatise with generalized comments on the bourgeoisie, suicide, and the complex psychological make-up of human beings. In other words, it is ultimately much more like the 'study' Hesse initially intended to call it than a cheap pamphlet obtained from a street vendor. The Tract is variously couched in the 'I' and the 'we' form, but exactly who the author or authors of the document are remains a mystery. There are suggestions that the perspective is that of the 'Immortals' and that they are the owners of a number of Magic Theatres like the one that Haller will eventually visit. Yet the sometimes ponderous and pompous style of the piece is very different from that of the inscriptions on that theatre's doors, which is more appropriate to the kind of crude 'peep show', as Pablo calls it. And at no point do the Tract's authors mock Haller for his own pomposities as scathingly as Mozart does in that theatre's last scene.

In short, it seems that Hesse has not entirely solved the stylistic problems arising from the structure he has chosen to adopt in the novel. Nor is that structure as radically modernist as is claimed by critics such as Thomas Mann, who regarded *Steppenwolf* as comparable with innovatory works of the same period, such as Joyce's *Ulysses* or Gide's *Faux-monnayeurs*. The novel's strength lies rather in its honest depiction of a personal neurosis, which, as the 'editor' points out in the preface, is also the neurosis of a whole generation. As such, it has succeeded in appealing to several subsequent generations too.

PENGUIN MODERN CLASSICS

SIDDHARTHA
HERMANN HESSE

Siddhartha, a handsome Brahmin's son, is clever and well loved, yet increasingly dissatisfied with the life that is expected of him. Setting out on a spiritual journey to discover a higher state of being, his quest leads him through the temptations of luxury and wealth, the pleasures of sensual love, and the sinister threat of death-dealing snakes, until, eventually, he comes to a river. There a ferryman guides him towards his destiny, and to the ultimate meaning of existence. Inspired by Hermann Hesse's profound regard for Indian transcendental philosophy and written in prose of graceful simplicity, *Siddhartha* is one of the most influential spiritual works of the twentieth century.

With a new Introduction by the bestselling author Paulo Coelho

'A subtle distillation of wisdom, stylistic grace and symmetry of form'
Sunday Times

PENGUIN MODERN CLASSICS

THE AGE OF REASON
JEAN-PAUL SARTRE

'For my money ... the greatest novel of the post-war period' Philip Kerr

Set in the volatile Paris summer of 1938, *The Age of Reason* follows two days in the life of Mathieu Delarue, a philosophy teacher, and his circle in the cafés and bars of Montparnasse. Mathieu Delarue has so far managed to contain sex and personal freedom in conveniently separate compartments. But now he is in trouble, urgently trying to raise 4,000 francs to procure a safe abortion for his mistress, Marcelle. Beyond all this, filtering an uneasy light on his predicament, rises the distant thread of the coming of the Second World War.

The Age of Reason is the first volume in Sartre's *Roads to Freedom* trilogy.

Translated by Eric Sutton
With an Introduction by David Caute

PENGUIN MODERN CLASSICS

THE PLAGUE
ALBERT CAMUS

'Camus's great novel rings truer than ever; a fireball in the night of complacency'
Tony Judt

The townspeople of Oran are in the grip of a deadly plague, which condemns its victims to a swift and horrifying death. Fear, isolation and claustrophobia follow as they are forced into quarantine, each responding in their own way to the lethal bacillus: some resign themselves to fate, some seek blame and a few, like Dr Rieux, resist the terror.

An immediate triumph when it was published in 1947, Camus' novel is in part an allegory for France's suffering under the Nazi occupation, and also a story of bravery and determination against the precariousness of human existence.

'An impressive new translation ... of this matchless fable of fear, courage and cowardice' *Independent*

Translated by Robin Buss
With an Introduction by Tony Judt

WINNER OF THE NOBEL PRIZE FOR LITERATURE

Contemporary ... Provocative ... Outrageous ...
Prophetic ... Groundbreaking ... Funny ... Disturbing ...
Different ... Moving ... Revolutionary ... Inspiring ...
Subversive ... Life-changing ...

What makes a modern classic?

At Penguin Classics our mission has always been to make the best books ever written available to everyone. And that also means constantly redefining and refreshing exactly what makes a 'classic'. That's where Modern Classics come in. Since 1961 they have been an organic, ever-growing and ever-evolving list of books from the last hundred (or so) years that we believe will continue to be read over and over again.

They could be books that have inspired political dissent, such as *Animal Farm*. Some, like *Lolita* or *A Clockwork Orange*, may have caused shock and outrage. Many have led to great films, from *In Cold Blood* to *One Flew Over the Cuckoo's Nest*. They have broken down barriers – whether social, sexual, or, in the case of *Ulysses*, the boundaries of language itself. And they might – like *Goldfinger* or *Scoop* – just be pure classic escapism. Whatever the reason, Penguin Modern Classics continue to inspire, entertain and enlighten millions of readers everywhere.

'No publisher has had more influence on reading habits than Penguin'
Independent

'Penguins provided a crash course in world literature'
Guardian

The best books ever written

PENGUIN 🐧 CLASSICS

SINCE 1946

Find out more at www.penguinclassics.com